THE
# DARLING DAHLIAS
AND THE
# VOODOO LILY

# THE
# DARLING DAHLIAS
## AND THE
# VOODOO LILY

*Susan Wittig Albert*

PERSEVERO PRESS

PUBLISHER'S CATALOGING-IN-PUBLICATION DATA

Names: Albert, Susan Wittig, author.
Title: The Darling Dahlias and the voodoo lily / Susan Wittig Albert.
Series: Darling Dahlias
Description: Bertram, TX: Persevero Press, 2020
Identifiers: ISBN 978-1-952558-11-5 (Hardcover) | 978-1-952558-12-2
(pbk.) | 978-1-952558-13-9 (ebook)
Subjects: LCSH Women gardeners--Fiction. | Gardening--Societies,
etc.--Fiction. | Bakeries--Fiction. | Nineteen thirties--Fiction. | Murder--
Investigation--Fiction. | Alabama--Fiction. | Historical fiction. | Mystery
fiction. | BISAC FICTION / Mystery & Detective / General | FICTION /
Mystery & Detective / Women Sleuths | FICTION / Mystery & Detective /
Historical | FICTION / Mystery & Detective / Cozy
Classification: LCC PS3551.L2637 D396 2020 | DDC 813.54--dc23

*For those who
aren't afraid of a little voodoo magic.
(You know who you are.)*

May 1935
The Darling Dahlias Clubhouse and Gardens
302 Camellia Street
Darling, Alabama

Dear Reader,

It's been a while between books, and we apologize. But there have been so many goings-on in Darling recently that it's been hard for us to sit down and collect our scattered thoughts. Ophelia Snow says it's like writing a letter home to your folks after you've been to a big city and there's so much to tell that you hardly know where to start—or how much you ought to leave out (in case some of it hurts your mother's ears).

But Mrs. Albert tells us that you've been asking for another book, so we intend to do our best. We hope she's got plenty of time to spend at her typewriter because this time, we're giving her plenty to write about. If some of it is a little hard to believe . . . well, all we can say is, that's voodoo for you.

It hasn't exactly been business as usual in our little Darling. For one thing, we have got ourselves a radio station! Its call sign is WDAR, and it is the brainchild of Earlynne Biddle's boy Benny and the Musgroves' oldest, Tommy Lee. WDAR is on the air several hours every day now, which has some folks so excited they can hardly sit still. Earlynne and Mildred Kilgore are broadcasting from their new bakery. Beulah Trivette tells everybody about "Darling Comings and Goings," and Clyde Barlow reads the weather and the daily markets from his usual table at the Diner. We're sorry to say that Charlie Dickens, editor of the Darling Dispatch, *is grumbling about the competition for advertising, but we figure he'll get over it.*

*And anyway, Mr. Dickens has plenty else on his plate. He has hired Baby Mann to sweep up, a young man to run his big press, and a new reporter to replace Ophelia Snow, who has now got herself an exciting new job with the Feds. (No, not Mr. Chester P. Kinnard and his revenuers, but the FWP, which is part of the WPA, which is the successor to the FERA, which is about as far as we can go with that.) We'll have to let Mr. Dickens explain how he manages to keep all his boys busy—and keep one of them (or himself!) from being arrested for counterfeiting.*

*If you read our Christmas book (*The Darling Dahlias and the Poinsettia Puzzle*), you'll remember that one of our Darling children was in danger of being kidnapped and taken off to Hollywood to become another Shirley Temple. That little plot was foiled but another is afoot. There's much more to be told on the subject of Hollywood temptations, but that's where the Voodoo Lily comes in and we don't want to spoil the story, so we'll change the subject.*

*Speaking of which, if you're one of our regular readers (thank you!), you'll remember that Mrs. Albert always asks us which plant she should put on the cover of her book. This time, we voted to use the voodoo lily, because of its place in our magic garden, and because . . . well, you'll see. According to our Darling librarian, Miss Rogers, the proper Latin name for this unusual plant is* Amorphophallus konjac, *although she could only blush and giggle when we asked her what* Amorphophallus *means. (We understood when Mrs. Albert told us to look at the last seven letters.)*

*However, the vote was not unanimous. For some of us, the voodoo lily's bloom smells a lot like poor old Mr. Wilkins, who had been dead for three days when the milkman found him. But we thought it was appropriate because of Violet Sims and Big Lil the conjure queen, which will become clear by the time you get to chapter 10. If you're interested in voodoo and too shy to pay a visit* to Big Lil, drop in and have a talk with Aunt Hetty Little, who isn't shy at all, especially when it comes to conjuring and conjure folk and rootwork and such.

If you're not one of our regular readers, you might ought to know that our garden club is named for Dahlia Blackstone, who gave us our beautiful little clubhouse and vegetable and flower gardens. With so many Darling folk still down on their luck, our big vegetable garden may seem more important than a few pretty flowers, especially when folks are looking at a bowl of stewed okra with onions and fatback, or boiled new potatoes with butter and parsley, or black-eyed peas with sausage and cornbread.

But while a vegetable garden feeds the body, pretty flowers (voodoo lily excluded) are a balm for the spirit. Aunt Hetty likes to remind us of the words of that famous horticulturist Luther Burbank, which she has done up in cross stitch for a sofa pillow: "Flowers are sunshine, food, and medicine to the soul." During this Great Depression, even a few rays of sunshine go a long way to brighten a person's day.

Well, that does it for now. As always, thank you for reading. We hope you'll enjoy this story so much that you'll forgive us for not getting around to it sooner. We'll try to do better next time.

Sincerely,
The Darling Dahlias

# THE DARLING DAHLIAS
# CLUB ROSTER

*Spring, 1935*

**Fannie Champaign**, noted milliner and proprietor of Champaign's Darling Chapeaux. Married to Charlie Dickens, editor, publisher, and owner of the Darling *Dispatch*.

**Voleen Johnson**, matron with a garden interest in tropical and exotic flowers (like the voodoo lily). Widow of the late George E. Pickett Johnson, the former president of the Darling Savings and Trust Bank.

**Mildred Kilgore**, co-owner (with Earlynne Biddle) of The Flour Shop. Married to Roger Kilgore of Kilgore Motors. They live in a big house near the ninth green of the Cypress Country Club, where Mildred grows camellias.

**Aunt Hetty Little**, senior member of the club and Darling matriarch. Student of voodoo and occasional practitioner of natural magic, Aunt Hetty is a "regular Miss Marple" who knows far too many Darling secrets.

**Lucy Murphy**, supervises the kitchen at the CCC Camp outside of town and grows vegetables and fruit on a small market farm on the Jericho Road. Married to Ralph Murphy, who works on the railroad.

**Raylene Riggs**, Myra May Mosswell's mother. Cooks at the Darling Diner, manages the garden behind it, and lives at the Marigold Motor Court. Raylene tries not to make a big issue of her clairvoyant abilities.

**Dorothy Rogers**, Darling's librarian. Knows the Latin name of every plant in the Dahlias' garden and insists that everyone else does, too. Longtime resident of Magnolia Manor.

**Beulah Trivette**, owner of Beulah's Beauty Bower, where all the Dahlias go to get beautiful. Artistically talented, Beulah loves cabbage roses and other exuberant flowers.

**Alice Ann Walker**, secretary to Mr. Duffy at the Darling Savings and Trust Bank. Alice Ann grows iris and daylilies. Her disabled husband, Arnold, tends the family vegetable garden.

# THE
# DARLING DAHLIAS
## AND THE
# VOODOO LILY

# CHAPTER ONE

# THE VOODOO LILY BLOOMS

*Sunday, May 19, 1935*

*Darling Dahlias Clubhouse and Garden*

"I vote for lopping it off," Verna Tidwell said. "And throwing it away. *Far* away." She spread the last of the cucumber-butter mix on a slice of Wonder Bread, topped it with a second slice, and cut off the crusts with a flourish.

"I agree one hundred percent," Ophelia Snow said emphatically. "If you stand too close, the smell just about knocks you over. Plus, the name of that plant gives me the willies." She looked at Verna's sandwich stack. "Do you need another loaf of bread, Verna?"

"Yes, please." Verna brandished her knife. "I could go out there right now and take care of it. One quick slice is all it would take."

"I wouldn't be too quick to lop off that lily, girls," Aunt Hetty Little cautioned. She pointed through the Dahlias' kitchen window and into the garden, where a couple of dozen people dressed in their Sunday best (suits, ties, and hats for the men; pretty spring dresses with gloves and hats for the ladies) were standing around, holding plates of finger sandwiches and chatting. "Voleen Johnson is the one who planted it. It's persnickety about blooming, you know, and she's right proud of it. Cut it down, and she's likely to pitch a hissy."

Verna gave a sardonic sniff. But Ophelia knew from personal experience that Voleen Johnson was not to be trifled with. The widow of Mr. George E. Pickett Johnson (the former president of the local bank) and current president of the Darling Ladies Guild as well as a Dahlia, Voleen considered herself one of the town's major opinion leaders. She probably was.

Aunt Hetty paused, lowering her voice. "Plus, there's all those old stories about that plant."

Ophelia handed Verna a loaf of bread. "Old stories?"

"Cut down the blossom and a death will follow," Aunt Hetty said. "That's why it's called the voodoo lily. And one reason it's planted in our magic garden."

"Rubbish," Verna huffed. "Cut the thing down and we'll all breathe a lot easier."

"You've been warned," Aunt Hetty said. She added Verna's cucumber triangles to the sandwich plate she was assembling. As chair of the refreshment committee for today's event, she was in charge. "Ophelia, do you have any more of that curried egg salad? We could use a few more of those squares you were making."

"I do," Ophelia said, opening the container of egg salad she'd brought from home. The eggs were laid by the half-dozen hens that lived in a coop behind the Snow garage, along with their rooster, Buster. Business was slow as molasses at the Farm Supply these days, which meant that Opie wasn't always able to put beef or pork on the supper table. But thanks to the chickens, they rarely ran out of eggs. And thanks to the lusty Buster, they weren't likely to run out of chickens.

"And Verna," Aunt Hetty added, "a half-dozen more of the tuna salad ought to just about do it. Tuna was cheap this week," she added. "I got those two cans of Del Monte for twenty cents each. The Meadow Grove cream cheese went up to twenty-five cents a pound. But that big bunch of celery Alice Ann is working on was only six cents, I'm glad to say."

As vice president, Ophelia knew that the Dahlias didn't keep much money in their treasury, just enough to pay taxes and do repairs on their Camellia Street clubhouse. So when they served refreshments at one of their club events—like the talk Aunt Hetty had given that afternoon about the plants in their new magic garden—they tried to make every penny count. When it came to celery sticks, six cents a bunch went a long way.

But the habit of pinching pennies wasn't new to any of the Dahlias, or the citizens of Darling or the entire population of the United States, for that matter. The economy had taken a nosedive when the Wall Street bubble burst, back in 1929. This catastrophe had kicked off a long and dreary Depression, putting people out of work, interrupting personal plans, and forcing everybody to trim their spending to the bone.

But now that Franklin Roosevelt had been in office for two years and several of his much-ballyhooed New Deal schemes had kicked into action, things seemed to be looking up. At least, that's what Ophelia was hoping. What she read about the New Deal sounded good—especially this new job of hers, with the Federal Writers' Project. But as Jed always said, it wasn't smart to bank on help from Washington. They might not get it. If the economy took another nosedive, they'd be in even worse trouble. And then what? The farm supply business was barely hanging on now.

Working on the other side of the kitchen table, Alice Ann Walker looked up from the four-inch celery sticks she had just cut. "If you ask me, it would be a real pity to chop that lily down just because it smells a little." She wiped her fingers on her apron and began stuffing the celery with cream cheese mixed with bacon crumbles, chopped pecans from the tree at the edge of the garden, and a few drops of Tabasco sauce. "The blossom is gorgeous," she added. "And exotic. We've never seen anything like it around here."

"There's a reason for that," Verna retorted. "I don't care how gorgeous it is, nobody wants a flower that smells like a three-day-old corpse. If Voleen likes it, she can keep it. In her greenhouse. With the door shut."

Ophelia agreed with Verna about the smell, but she had to admit that Voleen's lily, which came from tropical Africa, was truly exotic. It produced a single spectacular blossom, shaped like a giant calla lily, at the top of a three-foot stalk. The enormous ruffled petals—a shiny, deep burgundy color—surrounded a mottled green-and-purple flower spike over two feet tall and fatter than a fat cattail. From a distance, it didn't look quite real. Up close . . . well, you didn't want to be up close. In Ophelia's personal opinion, it was worse than being downwind from an outhouse. But of course, you had two legs. Nobody was forcing you to stand downwind.

"The voodoo lily smells like roadkill for a reason, you know." Ophelia dumped a pint basket of washed strawberries into a bowl and began picking off the stems. "She wants to attract flies to come and pollinate her."

Verna rolled her eyes and made a scoffing noise. A person with a sharp-as-nails brain and a deeply suspicious nature (personality traits that had earned her the job of Cypress County clerk and treasurer), she would never agree that plants were thinking, feeling creatures with their own personalities. Like all the Dahlias, Verna loved plants. But to her literal way of thinking, a plant was a plant, not a distant cousin from a different branch of the family.

"Everybody seems to be having a good time," Alice Ann said, filling another strip of celery. "They must not mind the smell too much."

Alice Ann was a small woman with mousy brown hair, a soft mouth, and an amiable expression. She always seemed uncomfortable when folks got crosswise of one another, so she would do what she could to smooth things out. It was a habit that sometimes encouraged others to get the wrong idea and decide that "sweet little Alice Ann" would always go along to get along. But Ophelia knew better. Alice Ann had perfected her own subterranean way of getting things done, all the while appearing to do nothing at all.

Verna looked up. "The wind must have shifted," she said. "See?"

She went to the window and pointed toward the refreshment table. A little while before, club members and their guests had crowded around it. Now, it was deserted.

"I don't think anybody wants to rub elbows with that lily," she added with a chuckle. "They don't want that smell on their Sunday clothes."

Just as Verna made that remark, Liz Lacy (the Dahlias' president), Mr. Benton Moseley (Liz's guest) and Mildred Kilgore and her husband Roger picked up the table by its corners and—carefully, so as not to spill anything—moved it to the other side of the garden, under the Lady Banks rose. Lady Banks was in full bloom, her sprays of glorious golden flowers like arcs of pure sunshine. In a moment, she was bestowing her sweet, spicy scent upon the people who had followed the table and were making a beeline for the cookies.

Ophelia left her strawberries and went to the window beside Verna. "Oh, there's Miss Tallulah," she said. "She's wearing the cartwheel hat Fannie made for her."

Fannie Champaign, the proprietor of Champaign's Darling Chapeaux, had recently achieved some quite remarkable recognition for her fanciful millinery. Lilly Daché, a well-known French milliner who had happened to see Fannie's work in

Atlanta, had commissioned her to make several hats a week for the Daché shops in New York and Hollywood.

"Miss Tallulah?" Verna peered through the window. "I don't see her. Where?"

Ophelia pointed. "Beside the peony. She's talking to Mrs. Whitworth. I ran into her yesterday at Musgrove's. She's just back from Chicago."

A Darling legend, the stately, white-haired Miss Tallulah LaBelle wore a wine-colored dress that must have been chic during Teddy Roosevelt's administration and a wide-brimmed hat swathed in yards of fine tulle and decorated with white silk rosebuds, a red ostrich floss, and loops of gold velvet ribbons. Cartwheel hats had been popular in the years before the Great War but were banished in favor of cloches. Miss Tallulah had been heard to say that those head-hugging felt helmets made women look like British bobbies.

Aunt Hetty came to the window. "Tallulah is looking right sprightly for her age."

Ophelia smiled. Aunt Hetty and Miss Tallulah were exactly the *same* age, which was several years past eighty. Not that you'd notice, though, was the general opinion. Both were as spry as many Darling ladies half their age.

Alice Ann took off her apron. "*I* would dearly love to take a trip to Chicago. Or to the Pacific Exposition, out in San Diego." She sighed regretfully. "But that's out for us."

Ophelia put a sympathetic arm around her friend's shoulders. "Out for us, too, Alice Ann. The past couple of years have been hard on the feed business."

But things had been harder for the Walkers, Ophelia knew. Alice Ann still talked about the trip that she and her husband Arnold had made back in 1926, when they drove their Packard to Atlanta to visit the zoo. The next year, Arnold lost his leg when he fell off a caboose and the railroad let him go. Now, he made a little money selling the wooden garden ornaments he whittled and honey from the beehives he tended behind the barn. While he was keeping an eye on the three orphaned grandchildren they had taken in the year before, Alice Ann worked as Mr. Duffy's secretary at the Savings and Trust, earning twelve dollars a week. Most of it went for Arnold's doctor bills, rent on their ramshackle farmhouse, and school clothes for the children. And just recently, the Walkers' old Packard had given up the ghost and Alice Ann had to rely on Buford Tuttle, a neighbor, for a ride to and from town.

"The LaBelles have always had the money to come and go pretty much as they please," Aunt Hetty observed. "Reckon Tallulah can buy a hundred hats if she feels like it."

For decades, the LaBelles had been the acknowledged aristocrats of Cypress County. Miss Tallulah was the sole surviving LaBelle, still living on the family plantation, over a thousand acres of rich bottomland along the Alabama River. The old lady had pulled the family fortune out of the stock market just before the Crash. Ophelia had heard it whispered that she acted on the advice of Big Lil Boudreaux, aka the Voodoo Lily. Cypress County boasted at least a half-dozen conjure queens, but Big Lil was the most respected. She was known to have a special understanding when it came to matters of money and business success—and a special insight into the future, although whether she would share that with you was another matter entirely. Big Lil was her own woman.

But the whispers about Miss Tallulah's wise move hadn't come from Big Lil, who was well known to be the soul of discretion. Other conjure queens might have exercised bragging rights, but not Lil, who had never once let on that Miss Tallulah had consulted her. Of course, Miss Tallulah wasn't saying, one way or the other. But it was undeniably true that the old lady had moved her money out of the market in the nick of time and was in better financial shape than anybody else in the county. She'd even had enough money to rescue the Darling Savings and Trust when Mr. George E. Pickett Johnson, the bank president, had unexpectedly cashed in all his earthly checks and gone to meet his Maker.

"I was surprised to hear that Tallulah put some money into the new radio station," Aunt Hetty remarked.

"I believe Mr. Duffy had something to do with that," Verna replied. "She was glad to help." Upon Mr. Johnson's departure, Alvin Duffy had become president of the Savings and Trust and did business with Miss Tallulah on a regular basis. He was also Verna's steady boyfriend, so Ophelia thought she must know what she was talking about.

"Well, let's hope WDAR succeeds," Ophelia said, going back to her strawberries. "If it does, it could be really big for Darling. Just imagine—we have the only radio station between Mobile and Montgomery!"

If you asked a Darlingian to name their most treasured possession, you could bet it would be a *radio*. Ophelia and Jed had bought their first Silvertone battery-operated model from the Sears Roebuck catalogue several years before the Crash. Now, the four national networks—CBS, Red and Blue on NBC, and the new MBC—kept the Snows entertained every night. They gathered in the parlor to listen: Jed with his account books, Opie with her knitting, the two Snow teenagers with their homework.

And first thing tomorrow, Darling would have its own brand-new station: WDAR, at 550 on the dial. What's more, the inaugural program—*The Flour Hour*, scheduled bright and early at nine a.m.—would be broadcast remote from The Flour Shop, the bakery that Mildred Kilgore and Earlynne Biddle had opened on the courthouse square just before Christmas. You could bet that every Dahlia would be tuned in, listening eagerly to hear what Mildred and Earlynne had cooked up for their first show. If the new station was a success, it could be one of the most important events that had ever happened in their little town—right up there with the arrival of the telegraph and the Louisville & Nashville Railroad spur, both of which connected Darling with the big, wide world beyond the horizons of the little town.

"Time for me to go," Alice Ann announced, hanging her apron on a hook by the door. "The Tuttles are giving me a ride home. I'll just wait for them out front."

"Let me get you a few sandwiches for Arnold and the kids." Ophelia took the wax paper out of the cupboard. "Will we see you at the quilting session tomorrow night?" The Dahlias were making an appliqued flower quilt to enter in the Ladies Guild's annual competition, and the club members were getting together once a week to work on it.

"I'm not sure." Alice Ann smiled a little. "I don't have a car, so unless somebody . . ." She left the hint hanging in the air like a tempting red apple.

If her mother had been listening, Ophelia thought, she would have said that Alice Ann was mealy mouthed. She never came straight out and asked for what she needed; she always beat around the bush. That was one reason some people didn't like her very much. The other was that she had once been suspected of embezzling from bank customers' accounts. She'd been cleared, but whiffs of suspicion, like yesterday's stale perfume, still clung to her.

Verna picked up Alice Ann's unspoken hint. "I'll be glad to come and get you," she offered. She loved to zip around the countryside in her sporty red LaSalle convertible.

"That would be swell, Verna," Alice Ann said brightly. She pinned on her hat, picked up her pocketbook, and took the sandwiches Ophelia handed her. "See you on Thursday night."

Poor Alice Ann, Ophelia thought, going back to her strawberries. Life couldn't be very much fun, with a disabled husband and no extra money for a few special treats. Not to mention those three grandchildren and a boring job at the bank. Ophelia admired her for the courage she showed in what had to be a challenging situation.

When Alice Ann had gone, Aunt Hetty said, "I guess everybody's heard that the Walkers have to find a new place."

"I hadn't," Ophelia said, surprised. "Why in the world?"

"Because their landlord didn't pay the property taxes on that place Alice Ann and her husband are renting," Verna said. "Len Bixler bought it for back taxes. Mr. Tombull told me they mean to tear the house down."

"Oh, poor, *poor* Alice Ann," Ophelia exclaimed. Len Bixler owned a gravel business and Amos Tombull (chairman of the board of county commissioners and therefore Verna's boss) was his partner. They were probably going to start digging gravel out of the creek right next to Alice Ann's house. "And she didn't say a word about it!"

Aunt Hetty made a face. "That's Alice Ann for you. She keeps it all to herself and never lets on a word about what's bothering her—which must be plenty, these days. It won't be easy for her and Arnold to find a place they can afford."

"I'm sure she'll find a way," Verna said. "Alice Ann is smarter than people give her credit for."

Ophelia was still thinking about this when the back screen door opened and Liz Lacy came in, carrying an empty pitcher. "We've run out of tea," she announced. "Is there any more?"

"Plenty," Aunt Hetty said, and went to the refrigerator for another pitcher.

Verna looked up from the tuna salad sandwiches she was making. "Thanks for moving that table, Liz. We were threatening to behead Voleen's lily when you took matters into your own hands, so to speak."

"We didn't have any choice," Liz said. "We had to move it. After that plant got stepped on and smashed, the smell was making people gag."

"Got *stepped* on?" Aunt Hetty whirled around. "Somebody stepped on the voodoo lily?"

"Who?" Verna asked.

"Charlie Dickens," Liz said. "At least, that's who we think it was. He wouldn't 'fess up. I wonder if he didn't do it on purpose."

Ophelia saw the stricken look on Aunt Hetty's face. "Oh, come on, now, Aunt Hetty," she said, patting her on the shoulder. "You don't really believe that old superstition, do you?"

"Of course she doesn't," Verna put in.

"You bet I do," Aunt Hetty said grimly. "You mark my words, Verna."

"What superstition?" Liz asked. Aunt Hetty told her, and she nodded. "Well, if Voleen knew for sure it was Charlie who smashed her plant, death would have followed on the spot. She was definitely *not* pleased."

"I can just imagine," Ophelia said. Ophelia thought that Liz was looking prettier than ever these days, in her light blue Letty Lynton style dress with its fanciful ruffled sleeves and a wide white organdy collar. Her golden-brown hair was parted in the middle and pinned back on either side with blue barrettes, her gray eyes were sparkling, and her cheeks were pink. Was she excited about her book that was coming out in another couple of months? It was a historical novel about the War Between the States, called *Inherit the Flames*. Ophelia had read the manuscript and liked it very much, especially for its tough-minded, down-to-earth, unromantic view of women—white and colored—and their plantation lives.

Or maybe Lizzy had a romantic interest. Ophelia was dying to know, but while the two of them were the best of friends, they had both been so busy lately that they'd had to skip their usual lunchtime get-togethers.

Liz smiled at Ophelia. "Opie, I've been wanting to tell you that I am just so happy that you signed onto the Federal Writers' Project. With your reporting experience, you're perfect for the coordinator's job." She gave Ophelia a quick hug. "And just think—you'll be helping to write the new Alabama state guidebook!"

"It's going to be fun," Ophelia said, returning the hug. "I can't tell you how grateful I am to you for recommending me to Mr. Nichols."

Ryan Nichols, the regional director of the Writers' Project, had originally offered the coordinator's position to Liz. When she decided to stay on as Mr. Moseley's legal assistant, she recommended Ophelia, who had jumped at the chance. For several years, Opie had been working two jobs, one at the Darling *Dispatch* and the other in Captain Campbell's office at the Civilian Conservation Corps camp south of town. When the captain offered her full-time work and a nice raise, she had left the newspaper—reluctantly, because she loved being a reporter.

But six weeks later, Captain Campbell was reassigned to Washington and the new commandant didn't like the idea of working with a civilian, especially a female. Ophelia couldn't go back to the *Dispatch* because editor Charlie Dickens had already found a new reporter to take her place. And she *had* to work, even though his wife's ability to bring home a paycheck put Jed's nose out of joint. He hated to be confronted with the fact that Snow's Farm Supply barely produced enough income to pay the mortgage, much less buy groceries or shoes for the kids or any little thing for the house.

So the job as local coordinator of the Federal Writers' Project couldn't have come along at a better time. The FWP was managed under the Works Progress Administration, the New Deal's answer to America's colossal unemployment problem. But the WPA put people—mostly men—to work constructing roads, parks, and public buildings. The Federal Writers' Project, on the other hand, promised employment for historians, teachers, writers, and librarians, many of whom were women. Instead of picking up a shovel or a hammer, they would pick up a pencil and go to work creating guidebooks for all forty-eight states or documenting the social histories of local people. It was even rumored that, in the South, the Writers' Project planned something called a "slave narrative collection." If that was true, it would be a first for Alabama, where slavery was part of a dark past that most people weren't eager to talk about. Collecting stories wouldn't be easy. But if that was part of her job, Ophelia was determined to do it as well as she could.

"I'm sure you'll like Mr. Nichols," Liz said. "He has a lot of good ideas."

Verna had been listening. "That's not his only attraction," she said, with a sly smile at Liz, who flushed and looked quickly away. "When are you starting, Ophelia?"

Briefly, Opie wondered what that was about. Was there something going on between Liz and Mr. Nichols? But she always tried to curb her nosiness when it came to her friends' personal lives, so she didn't allow herself to ask.

"This week," she replied. "Mr. Nichols is coming to Darling on Friday. I'm ready to get to work."

She was looking forward to getting started on the new guidebook and all the other projects. It would be fun to organize her part of the project and get people involved in the actual writing. But to tell the truth, she was *really* looking forward to the paycheck. She owed Mrs. Hancock at the grocery store and Jeb owed Jake Pritchard at the Standard Oil station and the property tax was overdue in Verna's office. The sooner she could get to work, the sooner the bills would get paid.

The screen door opened and everybody looked up.

"Any more sandwiches?" It was Bessie Bloodworth, coming into the kitchen with an empty silver tray. "Since the table got moved, they've been going at it like they're killing snakes. They've about got us cleaned out."

A plainspoken woman and a spinster, Bessie was short and stocky, with thick, dark brows and neatly curled silver-gray hair. She owned Magnolia Manor, a boarding house for genteel older ladies, next door to the Dahlias' clubhouse. Bessie was Darling's resident historian and the author of an intriguing little book called *A Few Skeletons in Our Closets: A Peek into Darling's History.* What Bessie Bloodworth didn't know about the town wasn't worth knowing. Ophelia was glad that she had agreed to be a part of the team that was working on local history for the Writers' Project—although the most interesting things that Bessie knew were unprintable.

"These stuffed celery sticks are finished," Aunt Hetty said, transferring them to Bessie's tray. "And it looks like Opie's strawberries are ready. Verna, what about those tuna salad sandwiches?"

"Here you go," Verna said, moving a dozen sliced sandwiches to Bessie's tray.

"And here's a dozen deviled eggs I found in the fridge," Ophelia said. "I think Beulah brought them." She grinned. "I guess when this is gone, folks will just have to stop eating."

When the tray was filled, Bessie picked it up. "This should be enough. Thank you, girls." Over her shoulder, she added, "When you're done in here, come out and join the party. Everybody's talking about the magic garden, and some people have more questions about the plants."

Aunt Hetty took off her apron. "Think I will go out," she

said, patting her hair in place. "I always like to talk about those magical plants. Verna, there's another pitcher of tea in the fridge. Ophelia, you could bring—"

But the screen door had opened again and a short, stout colored lady burst in, wearing a black uniform and a white apron. Ophelia recognized Roseanne Stewart, from next door at the Manor. She and Bessie worked together as a team, managing the cooking and cleaning and laundry. "Don't know what I'd do without Roseanne," Bessie always said. "She's never let me down."

Now, Roseanne's wide dark eyes fastened immediately on Bessie. A little out of breath, she said, "Miz Bessie, I's sorry to interrupt. But you got to come on home. Right *now*."

"I promised to help with the cleanup here, Roseanne," Bessie said, smiling. "I'll come when we're done—probably no more than an hour. Whatever it is can keep until then."

"It cain't keep." Roseanne fastened a hand firmly on Bessie's arm. "It's Miz Randall."

"Not *again*." Bessie rolled her eyes. "Emma Jane will be the death of me."

"Emma Jane?" Verna asked. "Don't believe I know her."

Aunt Hetty snorted a laugh. "You haven't met Emma Jane yet, Verna? You are in for a treat. She is one cantankerous old lady."

"Emma Jane is our newest Magnolia resident," Bessie explained diplomatically. "She's been with us for a number of weeks, but she still hasn't settled in. There have been several unfortunate little episodes."

"You mean," Aunt Hetty elaborated, "that Emma Jane is pitching double-barreled hissy fits."

Ophelia knew that, hard as Bessie tried, she didn't always have an easy time with her boarders. As a rule, ladies came to live at the Manor because they had lost husbands or children or money or homes and could no longer manage on their own.

Bessie did her best to ease the transition to their new lives in what she liked to call their "happy little family." But some did not take the change in their circumstances gracefully. It sounded like Emma Jane was one of them.

Roseanne was shaking her head mournfully. "Well, there won't be no tempers no more," she said. "Leastways, not far as Miz Randall is concerned."

"She's changed her ways?" Bessie inquired archly. "Somehow, I doubt that."

"Oh, she's *changed*, all right." Roseanne drew herself up. "Miz Randall, she's dead."

"Dead!" Bessie exclaimed.

"Dead?" Opie asked.

Hands on her hips, Aunt Hetty turned to Verna.

"What did I tell you?" she demanded. "It's that voodoo lily. *That's* what it is."

# CHAPTER TWO

## THE FLOUR HOUR

*Monday, May 20, 1935*

"ARE WE READY?" MILDRED KILGORE ASKED NERVOUSLY. SHE sat down at the card table in the corner and cleared her throat, hoping her voice wasn't going to quaver too much.

"Just about," said Earlynne Biddle's boy. Benny was tall and gangly and still carried the traces of teenage acne, but he seemed to know what he was doing. He adjusted his headset and pushed the microphone toward Mildred, smiling reassuringly. "Tommy Lee will introduce you from the station, Mrs. Kilgore. And I'll be right here in case you have any trouble."

"Don't be nervous, Mildred," Earlynne admonished from behind the bakery counter. She had put on a clean white apron to wait on any customers who might come in while Mildred was doing their show. "Just be your own sweet self, and everybody will love you."

"I'm not nervous," Mildred snapped. "I just want to do a good job, is all."

Well, of *course* she wanted to do a good job. Today was the first day of broadcasting for Darling's very own WDAR, and everybody in town would have their Philcos and RCA Victors and Zeniths tuned to 550 on the dial. They would all be listening to *The Flour Hour*, originating right here in Mildred and

Earlynne's bakery, The Flour Shop, on the courthouse square in downtown Darling.

This extraordinary event was the brainchild of a pair of bright teenage boys, Benny Biddle and his best friend, Tommy Lee Musgrove. Several years before, they had gotten their hands on a US government publication that told how to build a crystal radio receiver. Tommy Lee was a whiz when it came to deciphering a technical manual and Benny could wield a mean screwdriver. Between the two of them, they had built themselves not just one crystal set but several, learning as they went.

Unfortunately, since Benny built his radios in the Biddle basement and Tommy Lee built his in the Musgrove attic, neither pair of parents knew a whole lot about what their boys were up to until the kids announced one day that they had learned as much as they cared to learn about receivers. Now, they had a more ambitious project. They intended to buy a used fifty-watt transmitter from a radio station in Ohio, apply for a call sign from the new Federal Communications Commission, and go into the broadcasting business.

The two sets of parents were understandably startled— wouldn't you be? But to their credit, the Biddles and the Musgroves refrained from crying "Have you boys lost your *minds?*" Instead, they went straight to the obvious next question: "And just how do you think you're going to pay for this?"

But these enterprising young fellows had already come up with a plan. They would pay for the equipment (and maybe even earn a small salary) by selling advertising spots. This wasn't a novel idea. Back in 1922, a music store in Seattle had begun advertising phonograph records on station KFC, while in Massachusetts, a car dealer was hawking his automobiles on station WGI. By 1930, nine out of ten radio stations were selling advertising, and dozens of network shows—*The Palmolive Hour*, for instance, *The A&P Gypsies*, *Lux Radio Theater*, and *The Maxwell House Showboat*—were underwritten by major corporations.

Little Darling wasn't home to any big soap or grocery or coffee companies. But Benny and Tommy Lee already had a leg up when it came to potential advertisers. Benny's father, Hank Biddle, managed the Coca-Cola bottling plant outside of town. Benny's mother was half-owner of The Flour Shop, the town bakery. And Tommy Lee's father, Marvin, owned Musgrove's Hardware. The bottling plant, the bakery, and the hardware store could be counted on to buy a few ad spots. As well, there was Hancock's Grocery, the Darling Diner, Mann's Mercantile, Dunlap's Five and Dime, the Palace Theater (two movies a week!), and the Old Alabama Hotel, which ran dinner specials on weekends. Surely these businesses would be glad to buy some airtime on WDAR.

But the equipment had to be bought and paid for first. So Benny and Tommy Lee drew up their business plan and took it to the Darling Savings and Trust, where they presented it to Mr. Duffy. It turned out that he, too, was a radio booster and understood that even a small station could make a big contribution to the Darling economy. While he wasn't comfortable about forking over the full amount that the boys were asking for, Mr. Duffy knew somebody who might be willing to help. He introduced them to Miss Tallulah LaBelle. Prompted by Benny's sweet, shy smile and Tommy Lee's smooth presentation, she had generously opened her pocketbook. The boys' big show was on the road.

It took a while to get the equipment. When it arrived, Tommy Lee installed it in an empty garage the boys rented from Mr. Barton, who couldn't make the payments on his 1928 DeSoto and had to sell it. The garage had a dirt floor, but it was wired for electricity and the roof only leaked a little. Benny painted the call letters, WDAR, on a board and hung it over the door, and they were in the broadcasting business.

That is, they were in business after they climbed the Darling water tower (what a scary adventure that was!) and installed their T-wire antenna. They hoped that the tower would provide enough height to give WDAR's signal a range of maybe eight or ten miles—far enough to reach Miss Tallulah's RCA Victor, anyway. Exactly how far and under what conditions was only a guess until they were actually broadcasting and their listeners called in to report that they could hear a program out on the Jericho Road or two miles past the cotton gin.

And even then, the reception would depend on the weather. All radios were prone to static and the mysterious "skip," which meant that sometimes you couldn't get a peep out of Mobile's WALA (We Are Loyal Alabamians) while WLS in Chicago (World's Largest Store, owned by Sears Roebuck) or even KOL—all the way out in Seattle!—came in just fine.

Throughout the early 1930s, daytime network broadcasting was mostly aimed at the "little woman," who listened as she went about her sweeping, dusting, bed-making, laundry, ironing, and countless other household chores. To reach her, the networks aired fifteen-minute musical segments, diet and exercise programs, and advice from child-rearing experts.

But homemakers' hands-down network favorites were the dramatic shows mostly underwritten by soap companies and quickly nicknamed "soap operas." The list was usually topped by programs like *Betty and Bob*, *Ma Perkins*, and *Backstage Wife*, which was sponsored by Dr. Lyon's Tooth Powder. It opened with a man's resonant announcement: "We present once again, *Backstage Wife*, the story of Mary Noble, a little Iowa girl who married one of America's most handsome actors, Larry Noble, matinee idol of a million other women." Listeners went around for the rest of the day singing the program's theme song, "Stay as Sweet as You Are" and dreaming of all the wonderful ways *they* would change if they were only lucky enough to marry Larry Noble and live the life of a backstage wife.

Smaller, non-network stations like WDAR had to find other ways to reach their audience. They featured hometown musical talent, readings by members of the ladies' clubs, performances by school children, and—their listeners' favorites—the "radio homemakers." These were local women who often broadcast from their homes instead of the studio. They might include a few tunes by a local musician or an interview with a guest. But mostly their programs were filled with local news and neighborhood gossip, recipes, homemaking tips, and gardening advice.

Iowa housewives, for instance, tuned in to KMA and Leanna Driftmier's *Kitchen-Klatter*, which was mostly cooking and household hints. They also loved Edythe Stirlen, who broadcast direct from her "little white house on Sixth Avenue," accompanied by her singing canary and a friend's wheezy accordion. Edythe shared recipes, read snips from the local newspaper, and told children's stories.

The truth was, though, that it didn't much matter what Leanna and Edythe actually said—it was their companionship that counted. The radio homemaker was a friend who dropped in every day for an hour or two. When she left, her listeners were already looking forward to her next visit.

This was the idea that Benny Biddle, youthful radio impresario, had shared with his mother, Earlynne Biddle, and her bakery partner, Mildred Kilgore. A few months before, the two Dahlias had opened The Flour Shop next door to Fannie Champaign's Darling Chapeaux. After a bit of a rough start, they got the hang of things and within a few weeks, they were selling Earlynne's delicious, delectable scones, tarts, cinnamon rolls, and French pastries. Bread was still a challenge, but even though they couldn't beat the price of Mrs. Hancock's nine-cent Wonder Bread, they could be counted on to produce a decent eleven-cent loaf—most of the time. Earlynne hated to bake bread, though. Left to her own devices, she'd spend the day making cupcakes. Or beignets. Or croissants.*

And now Mildred and Earlynne were about to become the stars of their very own radio broadcast, with Mildred doing the program one week, and Earlynne the next. In fact, they were going to have the satisfaction of being the only "radio homemakers" ever to broadcast from their very own bakery, courtesy of the telephone wire that would carry their voices the two blocks to Mr. Barton's garage and then all the way up to the antenna on top of the water tower. It was a thrilling event.

So Mildred took a deep breath as Benny held out his ear-phones and she heard Tommy Lee saying, in a deep, grown-up voice, "And now, ladies and gentlemen, WDAR is proud to present *The Flour Hour*, sponsored by your very own Flour Shop, on the west side of the Darling square. With no more ado, I give you . . . Mrs. Mildred Kilgore!"

And then Benny dropped his hand to indicate that she was on the air, and Mildred was saying, brightly, "Good morning, Darling friends, I'm Mildred Kilgore and isn't it just the love-liest day ever, right here in our lovely little town? The spring sun is shining, the blue skies are smiling, and your friend and neighborhood baker Earlynne Biddle is waving at you from behind the counter of our little bakeshop. Say good morning to the folks, Earlynne."

And Earlynne piped up in a squeaky little voice, "Good morning, everybody! Glad you could be with us for our first broadcast. We are so excited!"

Mildred put a sunny smile into her voice. "Earlynne and

---

* *The Darling Dahlias and the Poinsettia Puzzle* tells the story of The Flour Shop's first few challenging days.

I wish we could send our yummy bakery smells through the airwaves and right into your kitchen. She has just brought in a tray of mouthwatering fresh-baked pastries and my, oh my, they do smell delicious." She took a deep sniff to illustrate. "If you were here, we would sit down with a cup of hot tea and a flaky croissant or a buttery scone and have a nice little visit.

"But we want to start the morning with two announcements for you, so grab a pencil and get ready to make notes. Elizabeth Lacy says that the Dahlias will be working on their appliqued quilt tonight, at their clubhouse at 302 Camellia Street. Be sure to bring the piece you're working on—and your thimble." She took a breath. "Millicent Merkel asked us to tell you that the Girls Make Glee Club will meet on Tuesday evening in the basement of the Methodist Church for some mother-and-daughter barbershopping. So drag your daughter away from *Kate Smith Sings* on the radio and do some real live singing yourselves."

She nodded at Benny, who picked up his ukulele and played a few bars of "Shuffle Off to Buffalo" to indicate that the announcements were over. He was still playing when the shop bell tinkled and the door opened.

"Aren't we lucky?" Mildred cooed into her microphone. "We've just finished our announcements and here comes our very first guest, Mrs. Beulah Trivette, proprietor of Beulah's Beauty Bower and one of the most popular ladies in our little town. Everybody wants to go to the Bower to get beautiful—and to hear the very latest news, of course. So here's our Beulah, and oh, how I wish you could *see* her! She is so pretty in a bright yellow sundress with a big lace collar that looks handmade, with that blond hair of hers just expertly curled. If we're really nice to her, I'm sure she'll tell us all the Darling news." Mildred gave a little giggle. "The news that's fit to hear, that is. After all, this is *radio*. Good morning, Beulah!"

The choice of Beulah as their opening guest had not been

an easy one. Mildred and Earlynne had been friends since they were girls, but it was rare for them to agree on anything. It was no surprise that they couldn't agree on their all-important first guest.

"We need somebody who knows who's gone visiting or got their appendix out or won a prize for the best chocolate cake," Mildred said. "Somebody with her finger on the pulse of Darling."

"Sounds like Leona Ruth Adcock," Earlynne said. "She knows more about Darling than anybody."

Mildred rolled her eyes. "That may be true, but if you ask Leona Ruth, you'd better grab a broom. She will start spilling *dirt*." Mrs. Adcock, a thin, angular woman with a nose like a ferret, was a notorious gossip who could be trusted to pass along every dirty little secret she knew. "And you can't trust Leona Ruth any farther than you can throw her, you know," Mildred added. "She gets things all twisted."

Anyway, Mildred had a better idea. "How about Charlie Dickens? After all, he's the newspaper editor. If anybody knows news, it's Charlie. And he checks things out. If he prints something, it's *true*."

Earlynne frowned. "I thought of Charlie, too. In fact, I've already mentioned this idea to him. He said no. He won't be on the radio. He's not happy about WDAR, apparently."

"Not happy?" Mildred asked, surprised. "Whyever not?"

"Because of the competition," Earlynne said. "He says radio will be the death of newspapers all over the country. He thinks WDAR will kill the *Dispatch*. And he might be right. Why would people go to the trouble of reading when they can just listen?"

Mildred pulled her brows together. "There might be something to that."

"What would you think of Beulah Trivette?" Earlynne asked.

"She can tell us the news she hears from her clients at the Beauty Bower. And she's on Mrs. McCurdle's party line, which stretches clear out to the end of Dauphin Street."

Mildred had to admit that Beulah's location was a definite advantage when it came to news, since there were eight households on the Dauphin Street party line. If each one reached one (the way the revival preacher said they were supposed to do, to throw their sinful neighbors a lifeline to heaven), that made sixteen households on Beulah's side of town collecting and sharing news. Sixteen at the very least, actually, because when it came to news, each one was likely to reach three or four, so you were really collecting news from over fifty households.

Mildred hated on principle to agree with Earlynne, but this was an exception. "That's a good idea, Earlynne," she said. So it was settled.

And here, walking in the front door of The Flour Shop, was their society reporter herself, the blond, beautiful Beulah Trivette. She wore a bright smile, a pair of deep dimples, and a yellow print dress that seemed to glow with the morning's sunshine. Beulah was an optimist and a great believer in the power of beauty. She preferred *good* news, and unlike Leona Ruth, she was likely to share only the news that put everybody in the very best light.

Mildred motioned to Beulah to pull up a folding chair and sit down while she finished her commercial for the Palace Theater, Darling's one and only cinema. All this week, it would be showing *It Happened One Night*, last year's box-office smash starring Hollywood heartthrobs Clark Gable and Claudette Colbert. She added that the Palace was open at seven every evening but Wednesday (which was prayer meeting night), and that the two p.m. matinee on Saturday would include a Looney Tunes featurette starring Porky Pig, especially for the kids.

"Matinee admission is still only fifteen cents," she added, "or a dime for your under-twelves. And Mr. Greer says to tell you that if you mention *The Flour Hour*, he will personally hand you one free bag of buttered popcorn." She gave a hearty laugh. "As my grandma would say, you can't beat that with a stick, can you?"

And with that, Mildred introduced Beulah. "So you've just dropped in from the Beauty Bower," she prompted. "What are the ladies talking about while they're getting shampooed and set these days?"

Beulah took out her list. "Oh, my, just lots of things," she confided happily, settling into her chair and acting as natural as if she were at her very own hair-cutting station. "There's a new baby in the Singer family—Sally Sue Singer, who is just about the prettiest little thing you'd ever hope to see. Mrs. Singer says Sally Sue weighs seven pounds and twelve ounces and is a sweet little pig at her bottle."

That was just for starters. Over the next few minutes, Beulah lovingly covered all the important what's-what and who's-who in Darling, such as Miss Tallulah LaBelle's visit to Chicago, where she saw Benny Goodman and his orchestra playing on the new revolving bandstand at the Congress Hotel. And Pauline DuBerry's birthday, which she celebrated by sharing her cake with all her guests at the Marigold Motor Court. And so on.

When she got to the end of her list, Beulah's voice dropped. "I wish all the news was happy news, but of course it never is. Mr. Parrish's Red Wattle hog got out of the barn again early this morning. If you happen to see Ruby—that's her name— please put a rope on her and leave a message with the Exchange switchboard. Somebody will run next door and let Mr. Parrish know. He's doing some roof repairs at Musgrove Hardware."

She took a breath and let it out in a sigh. "Oh, and Bessie Bloodworth tells us that Emma Jane Randall, who recently moved into Magnolia Manor, passed away unexpectedly yesterday. Mrs. Randall moved to Darling from Birmingham to be near her brother George Clemens and her niece Zelda. She quickly made friends with all the other Magnolia ladies. She will be greatly missed."

Mildred raised her eyebrows. You could trust Beulah to put a pretty face on uncomfortable facts, which was probably natural, since she was a beautician. In this case, though, Mildred knew better. She had met Emma Jane the week before when she stopped at the Manor to discuss some garden club business with Bessie. It was her clear impression that the old lady had *not* made friends with the other Magnolias. In fact, Bessie had told her privately that Emma Jane was the most quarrelsome boarder ever. She had taken Mrs. Sedalius' place at the dining table and refused to give it up, and she insisted on listening to Fred Allen's *Town Hall Tonight*, which the other ladies hated. They were about to revolt.

"I'd tell the old lady to move out, but she's got nowhere else to go," Bessie had said. "Her brother and her niece won't have a thing to do with her. The only person who comes to visit is her second cousin, Alice Ann Walker."

Mrs. Randall's passing *must* have been unexpected, Mildred thought. She had seemed as healthy as a horse. But they were on the air. So Mildred only said, in a sympathetic tone, "I know we're all very sorry to hear about Mrs. Randall, Beulah. And if any of our listeners see Ruby, they should call the Exchange right away, so Mr. Parrish can come and get her." She put a bright smile in her voice and went on.

"And now it's time for a few friendly words from another one of our wonderful sponsors, the Darling Diner, where Myra May Mosswell, Raylene Riggs, and Euphoria Hoyt have already got the whole day's mouthwatering quota of pies baked and cooling on the counter, waiting just for you—yes, that's *you*, personally, friends. Myra May says they're having a special today, only ten cents a slice or seventy-five cents for the entire pie. And they've got all *three* of your sweet-tooth favorites! Tart lemon topped with a mile-high meringue. Euphoria's down-home apple spiced with cinnamon and nutmeg. And a rich, creamy double-chocolate pie with Raylene's famous Karo syrup meringue. The early bird gets the worm, you know. Get your pie before somebody else does!"

She gave a little chuckle to show that she'd just made a joke. "And now, Benny Biddle is going to play my favorite song, 'Tiptoe Through the Tulips.' Let's hear it, Benny!"

# CHAPTER THREE

# THE EARLY BIRD GETS THE PIE

"I'm a bit surprised to hear about Bessie's boarder dying, Mama." Myra May Mosswell wiped the glass and put it back up on the shelf. The Diner's breakfast crowd had left and Myra May and her mother, Raylene Riggs, were listening to *The Flour Hour* on WDAR while they started getting ready for the lunch bunch.

"I was at the Manor last week," Myra May went on. "The old lady seemed pretty spry. Ornery, too. Bessie said that the other Magnolia ladies didn't like her one little bit. In fact, Miss Rogers caught her cheating at bridge. I doubt she'll be missed."

"Shush," Raylene Riggs said, and turned up the Philco on the shelf behind the Diner's service counter. "Mildred is doing our radio ad. I want to hear it."

Myra May hung up her towel and she and Raylene listened in appreciative silence as Mildred told everybody about their pies, reading from the script they had given her and ad-libbing a bit here and there. When she was finished, Raylene chuckled.

"The early bird gets the worm? I wonder if Mildred said that to be funny."

Benny Biddle swung into "Tiptoe Through the Tulips" on his ukulele, and Myra May turned down the volume. "Well, that was an expensive announcement," she said. "We paid a whole fifty cents for that little bit of a mention. Money down the drain, likely."

Myra May was tall and strong, with short brown hair, a firm mouth, and a determined jaw. Her shrewdness and good common sense had helped to make the Diner a going concern since the day she and her friend Violet Sims had bought it from old Mrs. Hooper. But she had a tendency to look on the dark side of things and sometimes needed a little nudge to help her brighten up.

"I'm sure that our little investment will pay off, Myra May," Raylene said with a smile. "In fact, I have the feeling that today's going to be a very good day for pies. That's why Euphoria and I came in early. We've baked four already, plus two lemon meringue especially for Mr. Sherman. There's four in the oven now, and Euphoria is working on four more."

"Fourteen pies?" Myra May squawked. "What on earth possessed you, Mama? Why, even on a good day, we can't sell more than three or four. We will never in this world sell fourteen pies in one day! And what's this about Mr. Sherman?"

At that moment, a tall, broad-shouldered man in a blue work shirt and twill trousers opened the Diner's screen door and strode up to the counter. "Good morning, ladies," he said. "I happened to be driving past when I heard about the pies on the radio. Thought I'd stop and pick up a couple for the boys."

Ozzie Sherman owned the Pine Mill Creek sawmill and drove a Chevrolet with a Motorola radio, one of only two or three car radios in town. This had already prompted several protesting letters to the editor in the *Dispatch* from Darlingians who feared that a radio would cause wrecks by distracting drivers' attention when they fiddled with the knobs.

"Lemon meringue, if you haven't sold out," Mr. Sherman added. "Still seventy-five cents for a pie?"

Myra May was surprised. Ozzie Sherman was not known for his generosity to his workers. "Mama, do we have—"

"Yes, we do, dear," Raylene said sweetly, and smiled at Mr. Sherman. She wasn't at all surprised. She had seen it coming, for in addition to being a gifted cook who managed the kitchen with a deft hand and a creative imagination, Raylene had another gift. A tall, striking woman with a few gray streaks in her auburn hair, she knew what was going to be wanted—not always, but often enough to take it out of the realm of chance. Sometimes (like this morning) she even knew who and when, as well as where and why.

So she was ready when Ozzie Sherman showed up for the two lemon meringue pies she had baked especially for him. She didn't advertise her gift, but she didn't make any secret of it, either, so folks who knew her usually accepted it as just part of who she was.

And anyway, most native Darlingians had their mystical side. Like Mrs. Meeks, who had planted a bottle tree (mostly blue Phillips' Milk of Magnesia bottles) in front of her boarding house on Railroad Street, to catch any evil spirits that might be hanging around the door. Or like old Caleb Thorpe at the post office, who refused to let anybody take his picture because he was afraid the camera would steal his soul. And like Eugenia Wilson, who swept her house from front to back so she could sweep anything bad right out the back door.

Like lots of other folks, white and colored, who regularly visited their favorite conjure queen to ask for her help with this or that little problem they were facing. They would pay her two or three bits for a mojo bag full of charms and jujus and do their best to do what she told them, lighting colored candles in the four corners of their bedroom and sprinkling powders and saying the words she had written down for them on a scrap of paper.

And even people who didn't consult a conjure queen had their own beliefs. Ophelia Snow always showed you out of her house by the same door you entered, to make sure you'd come back again. Bessie Bloodworth wouldn't let you put a hat on a bed because it was sure to invite an intruder—not a nice fellow, either. And when you went to visit Aunt Hetty Little, you'd see a mirror beside her front door, hung there so the devil could see his reflection before he went into the house. Ask her why, and she will tell you that the devil will be so appalled when he sees his real face that he will forget all about going in and raising Cain. He'll run off as fast as he can and never come back.

Of course, you could call this plain old silly superstition, and some of it is. In the South, it goes by different names: granny magic or voodoo, according to white folks. Hoodoo, to use the colored word. But most Darling folks feel that there is more to it than mere superstition. Raylene's ability to see into the future came as no surprise to those who believe that they live in a world of invisible spirits who move things from here to there and make things happen in ways people don't (and don't want to) understand. Why should they doubt such things, when children are taught about Santa Claus and the Tooth Fairy and every preacher in town spends hours on Sunday talking about the Holy Ghost?

So Mr. Sherman went off with his pies. Raylene returned to the kitchen, and Myra May was left alone, wrapping the silverware for the lunch bunch. After a few minutes, she looked up to see her friend and partner Violet Sims come down the stairs from their second-floor flat, wave a friendly hand, and go into the Telephone Exchange in the Diner's back room. Skipping along beside Violet was her little niece, Cupcake, dressed in the orange cotton shirt and yellow pants Raylene had made for her and the pretty red Mary Janes her friend Liz Lacy had bought for her.

Cupcake was four-and-a-half, with dimpled cheeks, dancing blue eyes, and strawberry blond hair that had lost its baby curls but would turn into fat bananas when it was twisted overnight in tight little rag knots. And with those bouncy curls, Cupcake was the spitting image of the movie star, Shirley Temple, and just as talented, too. She knew all the words to "On the Good Ship Lollipop" and "Animal Crackers in My Soup" and Shirley's other songs. She seemed to have the magical ability to make people smile and feel better about things in general.

"As long as our country has Shirley, we will be all right," President Roosevelt had said when he saw *Bright Eyes*, the little girl's latest movie. And Darling folk felt exactly the same way about Cupcake. As long as their town had her to cheer them up, they could survive just about anything. "What a charmer," people said admiringly. "She should have a career in Hollywood!" Which of course thrilled Violet right down to the tips of her toes. She was an ardent movie fan herself—she adored Clark Gable and Myrna Loy in *Manhattan Melodrama*, which she had seen five times—so she always brightened when anybody said that Cupcake should be in the movies.

"Oh, do you *think* so?" she would ask breathlessly. "Myra May and I agree, of course." (Which was not exactly true, and Violet knew it.)

Unfortunately, Cupcake's cuteness and Shirley-style talent had invited a serious threat. The previous fall, Violet had enrolled Cupcake in Nona Jean Hopworth's popular kiddy dancing class, over in Monroeville. Nona Jean, a former Ziegfeld Follies dancer, had spotted the little girl's natural talent and featured her in the class recital, where she put on an amazing performance for such a little tyke.

But the recital had attracted the attention of Cupcake's father, a vaudeville song-and-dance-man who, when his wife Pansy died, had been more than happy to let her sister—Violet

Sims—make off with her newborn niece. Utterly captivated with his daughter's performance of Shirley Temple's show-stopping routine from *Stand Up and Cheer*, he decided he would take her to Hollywood, where he was convinced that they could find stardom as a father-daughter dance team.

Fortunately for Darling, this scheme had been foiled by Liz Lacy and the Dahlias, and when it was all over, there had been a very happy outcome. Mr. Moseley had helped Violet and Myra May file for Cupcake's adoption, which Judge McHenry had granted forthwith. She was *their* little girl now, according to the law, and her two mamas should be very happy and contented.*

But they weren't, for different reasons.

Until recently, Violet—a pretty, petite young woman with soft brown hair and a sweet and loving personality—had been supremely content with the Darling life she and Myra May shared at the Diner and the Exchange; the pretty flat upstairs where they made a home together; their flourishing vegetable garden behind the garage; and of course, their dear little Cupcake, the source of so much shared joy. While times were hard and they had to pinch pennies, they were *together*, which made every day a new bouquet of its own particular pleasures.

But the possibility of Cupcake's stardom seemed to have seduced Violet, corroding her contentment. It began when Verna Tidwell had mentioned that Shirley Temple's new movie contract was worth a thousand dollars a week for the little girl plus two hundred and fifty for her mother, with a fifteen-thousand-dollar bonus for every movie the child completed.

"A thousand a week!" Violet had said to Myra May when she heard this. "And a bonus to boot? Just think what that kind of money would mean for Cupcake's future, Myra May. Why, it would buy college and clothes and cars and . . . and everything!

---

\*    You can read this story in *The Darling Dahlias and the Poinsettia Puzzle*.

We wouldn't have to stay here in Darling. We could live in California, right next to the ocean. We could go to Paris or to New York or London. We could go anywhere and do anything." She clasped her hands prayerfully. "Just think of it," she whispered. "Our future would be *secure!*"

Of course, the years since 1929 had been enormously difficult for everyone. Jobs were scarce, money was hard to come by, and people had to count every penny twice. It was probably safe to say that every American would give almost anything for a little financial security. But Violet had a special reason for dreaming of a more affluent life. She had grown up in a dirt-poor family in Northern Florida, one of six girls who were lucky if they got as far as the eighth grade before they married one of the young men who herded cattle on their cracker ponies through the pines and swampy scrublands. If they married well, they might one day have a cow and some goats and chickens and a little cracker house with a veranda out front and a garden out back. If they didn't, they could always stay home and help with the cooking and washing and babies. There was work enough for everybody and everybody worked.

But Violet had stars in her eyes even then. As soon as she could, she escaped, first to Pensacola and then to Memphis. Her sister Pansy followed her, and for a time, the two of them—quick learners, with good figures and a girl-next-door prettiness—danced in a chorus line at the Orpheum, one of the biggest vaudeville theaters in that part of the country. They had money and nice clothes and attracted the admiring attentions of plenty of men.

But Violet often felt as though she were feeling her way through a maze of blind alleys, with no clear vision of the future, no clear way to see the path ahead of her. One day, she decided it was time to go—go where, she couldn't say. Just *go*, she thought.

So she packed her suitcase and got on a Greyhound bus heading south. A few days later, tired of riding, she got off the bus in Darling, found a job waiting tables at the Old Alabama Hotel, and met Myra May Mosswell. They were friends from the moment they laid eyes on one another, and then business partners. Now they were the parents of a beautiful little girl.

And Violet had stars in her eyes again.

For her part, Myra May listened to all the talk about Hollywood and New York and Paris with a stomach-churning despair, for it had never occurred to her that Violet might want to have a life that different than the life they had now, together. Myra May had lived in Darling most of her life, and she knew she would never be happy anywhere else. Until now, she had been sure that Violet felt the same way.

But lately, Violet had become obsessed with the idea of getting Cupcake into the movies. She read all the movie magazines—*Picture Play* and *Movie Classic* and *Silver Screen*—that Mr. Lima carried at Lima's Drugs. She went to the movies (and dragged Myra May with her) every Saturday night and sometimes on Friday night, too. She kept scheming for ways to pay for the bus tickets to Hollywood and the clothes they'd need and the money for room and board until Cupcake got her first contract. Could they borrow it? How about inviting their customers to buy shares in Cupcake, the way a group might finance a filly in the Alabama Stakes? Or maybe they could sell a piece of the Diner—to Tallulah LaBelle, for instance, who had plenty of money. They could buy it back with the bonus from their first movie contract.

Myra May thought she understood her friend's desires. After all, Violet had grown up in an impoverished family with few opportunities and even fewer hopes. To her, Hollywood must seem a magical world, like the world in those wonderful Oz books, where the wildest, most improbable dreams come true, even for folks from the wrong side of the tracks.

So at first, she had tried to respond encouragingly, even while she secretly hoped that Violet's wild enthusiasm would burn itself out. When it didn't, she tried logic, pointing out the flaws and very real dangers in her partner's plans. Naturally, this didn't please Violet, who had pouted, stamped her pretty foot, and protested that Myra May just didn't want their little Cupcake to succeed.

And then things took a turn for the very worst. The night before, Violet had shown Myra May a clipping from the *Nashville Banner* headlined "Wanted! Nashville's Own Shirley Temple!" She intended to take Cupcake to Nashville to enter her in the Shirley look-alike competition—that very Friday night!

"And just look at the prize!" she had cried excitedly, thrusting the clipping under Myra May's nose. "A two-week, all-expenses-paid trip to Hollywood, with meetings scheduled with movie producers and casting directors and dance coaches and singing teachers. Isn't it just the swellest opportunity? Cupcake will win—I know she will. And then it's on to Hollywood! She'll be as famous as Shirley! And Mickey Rooney and Dickie Moore and Jackie Cooper—all those other child stars!"

Myra May felt her stomach knot. If Cupcake competed in that contest, she was very likely to win. And if Violet and Cupcake went to Hollywood, they might never come back. This chilling thought made her turn icy cold, inside and out.

Still she tried to make herself sound calm and reasonable. "What kind of lives do these Hollywood kids have, Violet? They may be this year's blue-plate special because they rake in money for the studios, and maybe they earn some for themselves. But what kind of hours do they have to keep? What happens when they get too old for the roles the studio wants them to play?

What about school and friends and family? What about just being a *kid*?"

But Violet wasn't listening. "I simply do not understand how you can be so selfish," she cried angrily. "Especially when everybody says that our little girl has so much talent! All she needs is a chance to prove what she's made of. And a chance is what I am determined to give her!"

That was last night. This morning at breakfast, Myra May had been glad to see that Violet seemed calmer and even a little happier, as if she had resolved something in herself. Now, she was smiling sweetly as she disappeared into the Exchange.

And then the customers started coming in and Myra May had to turn her attention to them—with some surprise, since it was becoming clear that radio advertising was paying off, at least where pies were concerned.

After Ozzie Sherman had taken his two lemon meringue pies and left came Mr. Musgrove from the hardware store. He wanted a piece of apple pie for himself (with a scoop of vanilla ice cream on top) and one for Mr. Parrish, who was working on the hardware store roof and was ready to take a break.

Then it was Mr. Dunlap, who had walked over from the Five and Dime. "Heard on the radio that Raylene was bakin' chocolate pies with that good Karo meringue this morning," he said briskly. "Sounded so tasty I thought I'd have me a slice. The missus said bring her one, too." He beamed, because he was recently married (to Liz Lacy's mother) and was still new enough at the job to want to brag about it.

When Mr. Dunlap had gone back to the Five and Dime, plump, cheerful Mrs. Hart came across the street from the Peerless Laundry to ask if Myra May would trade her a lemon meringue pie for a basket of washed and ironed laundry. Myra May did a quick calculation, decided that it was a fair enough trade, and said to go ahead and take the pie now and she'd send the clothes over later.

Mrs. Hart had just left when the stranger came in. Myra May had gotten used to calling him that because he hadn't volunteered his name. Since the middle of last week, he'd dropped in several times. He had always taken the back corner table, where he watched the crowd with an alert attention. Somebody said he was staying at the Old Alabama Hotel, which meant that he must be on an expense account, because those hotel rooms cost a dollar-fifty a night. Somebody said he was in town on L&N business, but Myra May thought he looked sharper than your usual railroad man. He wore a tailored suit with wide lapels, a fresh white shirt with a striped tie, shiny patent-leather shoes, and a snap-brim fedora, which he hung on the back of his chair. He had red hair combed back from an off-center part, the way James Cagney wore it in *Public Enemy*, and he had Cagney's sneer, as well. Myra May shivered, remembering the startling scene where Mr. Cagney had shoved half a grapefruit into his girlfriend's face. She had read in one of Violet's movie magazines that the scene had become so famous that when he ate at a restaurant, other diners would order a grapefruit for him.

A full coffee mug in hand, Myra May approached the table. "Good morning, stranger." She put the coffee in front of him. "What'll it be? Apple, lemon, or double-chocolate?"

"Apple what?" he snarled. "What're you talking about, lady?" He picked up his mug and Myra May saw that he was missing a finger.

"Never mind," she said, stepping back. She wrinkled her nose. What *was* that smell? Burma-Shave? "What can I get for you today?"

"Two eggs over easy, ham and gravy, toast." He unfolded a copy of the *Montgomery Advertiser*. "Oh, and half a grapefruit."

He opened the paper to the sports page and buried himself in a story headed "Dizzy Dean Hurls Cards to 6-1 Win over Bucs." But Buddy Norris, who came in a few minutes later, *was* looking for pie.

The khaki shirt and pants he wore were what passed for the Cypress County sheriff's uniform, and a nickel-plated star was pinned to his shirt pocket flap. With blue eyes, brown hair, and a nicely cleft chin, Buddy was a dead ringer for Charles Lindbergh, who had piloted the *Spirit of St. Louis* all the way from Long Island to Paris, France. Like Lucky Lindy, Buddy looked like he was about fifteen, maybe sixteen, which led some folks to say that he was too young for the job of sheriff. And like Lucky Lindy, he usually managed to keep a poker face, although his unconcerned expression was somewhat contradicted by the trace of a jagged scar across his cheek, testimony to a knife fight he'd broken up at the Red Dog juke joint over in Maysville when he was still a deputy.

Buddy had become sheriff when his predecessor, Roy Burns, met a rattlesnake when he was fishing alone at the bottom of Horsetail Gorge.

On a Sunday morning, some were quick to point out.

When he should've been in church.

It was no accident, people whispered, that Sheriff Burns' end came in the shape of a serpent.

Buddy had not been a shoo-in. His opponent in the special election that followed Roy Burns' departure from this earth was Jake Pritchard, who owned the only Darling gas station—the Standard Oil station, on the Monroeville highway—and was a well-known bon vivant and man-about-town. But a couple of weeks before the election, Jake had made the mistake of raising the price of gas from ten to fifteen cents a gallon. Some folks felt that if he got elected, it might go to his head and he'd raise it another five or ten cents. So enough of them had voted for Buddy to swing the election.

It was a proud day when Judge McHenry pinned Roy's tin star on his shirt, shook his hand, and said, "You've inherited a mighty big pair of boots to fill, son." Buddy, who wasn't sure when he'd be able to think of himself as a *real* sheriff, had agreed.

Buddy had also inherited Roy's gun, although he wasn't wearing it today. Actually, he had once told Myra May in confidence that, if it was left up to him, he wouldn't wear the damned thing, ever. If he wasn't armed, he reckoned he wouldn't be as likely to get shot. Anyway, most of the crimes around Darling were perpetrated by the moonshiners, and they were federal agent Chester P. Kinnard's problem. On top of that, Deputy Wayne Springer was known to be a crack shot. If any shooting had to be done, Buddy said, it was better if it was Chester P. or Wayne doing it.

"Mornin', Myra May,' Buddy said, sitting down at the counter. When she brought him the usual cold bottle of orange Nehi soda, he twisted off the metal cap and took a thirsty swig, his Adam's apple bobbing. He wiped his mouth with his sleeve.

"I'm looking for a piece of that chocolate pie I heard about on the radio. Got any left?"

"Oh, you bet, Sheriff." In a moment, Myra May was back with the pie and a fork. "Anything else?"

She was finally getting used to calling him sheriff. Myra May was older, but Buddy had lived just down the street when they were growing up. His mother had died years before, so it had always been just Buddy and his dad, trying to take care of each other. She still remembered the skinny little kid pulling a red Radio Flyer wagon piled high with watermelons or sweet corn or kindling Buddy had split and was peddling door-to-door. He had grown quite a bit since then, she thought. He wasn't a skinny little kid. He had broad shoulders and real muscles, if you liked that sort of thing.

"Got a question for you, Myra May," Buddy said as he attacked his pie. He lowered his voice. "That fancy new switchboard of yours—is there any way you can find out who called somebody?"

Myra May tilted her head. They'd had the new switchboard for a couple of months now, but it was the first time anybody had asked her *that*.

"Well, sure, if you mean while the people are still talking. It was easier on the old switchboard. You could just look and see where the call was coming from and where it was going. It's harder with the new board because there's more than one line to a jack. But it can be done."

"No, I mean after." The sheriff chewed thoughtfully. "Later. Like now."

Myra May leaned both elbows on the counter. Buddy had never been a man of many words. She hazarded, "So you're saying that somebody called you and didn't give their name and now you want to know who it was?"

"Right." The sheriff looked pleased. "Got the call in the office this morning, early, round about seven-thirty or so. Any idea who it was?"

Myra May frowned. It was still possible for the girls on the switchboard to know that Josephine Dankworth had spent twenty minutes talking to her mother on the other side of town, or that Joe Jenkins was calling Snow's Farm Supply to order a bag of laying pellets for his white Leghorns. But there was usually enough traffic that they didn't have time to listen in. What's more, they weren't *supposed* to, according to Myra May's rules. And her rules were strictly imposed. She had recently fired Sally Plum—one of her afterschool operators—for listening in on a conversation between her boyfriend and her best friend.

At that moment, Violet came down the stairs with a wicker basket of laundry perched on her hip—the basket for which Myra May had traded that lemon meringue pie. She was trailed by Cupcake.

"We're going across the street to the laundry," she said to Myra May. She smiled at Buddy. "How are you this morning, Sheriff?"

"Rarin' to go," he said cheerfully. To Cupcake, who was hiding behind Violet, he said, "How's my pretty little girl this morning? You gonna sing a song for me?"

Cupcake nodded shyly. "Should I sing 'Lollipop'?"

"Let's do that later, honey." Myra May straightened. "The sheriff's asking a question, Violet. You were on the switchboard this morning. Did you happen to notice who it was called his office about seven-thirty?"

"Seven-thirty?" Violet thought, frowning. "Sorry. It was just Opal and me, and we had our hands full. The only one I remember was Miss LaBelle calling Doctor Roberts. She can never be bothered to give us the number and always just says, 'Doc Roberts, please. Tell him it's Miss Tallulah calling.' I don't recall the others."

The sheriff eyed Violet appreciatively as she left, flouncing her hips in the way that always made Myra May wish she wouldn't. In the back corner, the stranger was eyeing her too, over the top of his newspaper. Myra May clenched her jaw.

"Too bad about that call," Buddy said, turning back to Myra May. "Your girls oughtta listen in more often. I sure would give a lot to know who it was."

Myra May picked up a damp cloth and swiped hard at the linoleum counter, thinking that Violet liked to do that just to show she could. "What was the call about?" she asked, mostly to be saying something.

The sheriff considered. "Rather not say," he replied after a moment. "But could you ask Opal if she remembers? If you could find out who it was, I'd sure appreciate it."

"I'll see what I can do," Myra May said, turning to the pass-through shelf. She picked up the stranger's order—eggs, ham and gravy, toast, and grapefruit—and carried it to his table. He laid his paper aside and grunted a thank-you, looking up as the screen door opened and Charlie Dickens came in with the new *Dispatch* reporter, Wilber Casey, and Doc Roberts, who happened to be Charlie's brother-in-law.

The doctor said "See ya" to Charlie and headed for the counter where the sheriff was sitting. Charlie and Wilber took their usual table by the window, and Myra May poured their coffee.

"Chocolate pie for me," Charlie said. "You, Wilber?"

"I'll have the lemon meringue," Wilber said. In his early twenties, slight and thin-shouldered, he had gingery hair and round, wire-rimmed glasses. He smiled at Myra May. "You got my attention with your commercial on WDAR this morning, Miz Mosswell."

"A commercial?" Myra May asked, interested. "Is that what radio advertising is called? I wasn't sure it would work, but Mama seemed to think it would." She liked Wilber. He was a nice young boy. And Charlie's wife Fannie had said that he was taking a big load off Charlie's shoulders.

"That's what it's called," Wilber said. "Worked for me. Got me to thinking how good it was going to taste."

Charlie looked grim. "Radio comes in one ear and goes out the other and doesn't linger in between. Want business, buy an ad in the newspaper. It stays right there in front of you, and you can come back to it over and over. When everybody's done with it, you can tack it up on the outhouse wall." He nodded toward the stranger in the back corner, buried in his newspaper. "See that? New man in town, reading the *Dispatch*."

"It's the *Montgomery Advertiser*," Myra May said.

"Doesn't matter," Charlie replied stoutly. "It's a newspaper. Anyway, he's a drifter."

"Radio is friendlier," Wilber said, leaning forward. "It's the sound of the human voice. Radio can—"

"Radio *can't*," Charlie said firmly. "And what's more—"

"I'll get your pie." Myra May said.

When she got back behind the counter a few minutes later, Doc Roberts was sitting beside the sheriff. He was wearing his usual blue suit, the elbows and seat rubbed shiny, one button missing from his vest and a coffee stain on his tie. He could use a haircut, too. His wife, Edna Fay (Charlie Dickens' sister), did what she could to keep him tidy. But it was pretty much a losing cause.

"Mornin', sweetheart," the doc said to Myra May. "Got any more of Euphoria's apple pie? Miz Kilgore made it sound so good on the radio that I thought I'd better come in and get me some before it was all gone."

"Coming right up," Myra May said, pouring his coffee. When she got back with the pie, the doctor and the sheriff had their heads together, their voices low and guarded.

" . . . murder," the sheriff was saying. "So that's why I was askin'."

*Murder?* Myra May thought, startled. She put the slice of apple pie down in front of the doctor, added a fork, and stepped away—but not far enough to be out of earshot.

"Sure beats me," the doctor said. "She'd been vomiting, but the other Magnolia ladies said they didn't think it was any too serious. Somebody'd given her a chocolate cake and she ate almost all of it, apparently. I figured it was a stroke." He pulled the pie toward him. "Frankly, poison didn't occur to me."

"You ever done that test?" the sheriff asked.

"Not me myself." The doctor picked up his fork and attacked his pie. "But Doc Martin over in Monroeville did it last year.

He had to autopsy a kid who got into a can of insecticide in his granddad's poison cupboard. The procedure is called Stas-Otto, after a couple of foreign guys." He raised his voice. "Damned good pie, Myra May. You tell Euphoria I said so."

Myra May nodded. She had found a cloth and was polishing the coffee urn. "How does it work?" the sheriff asked. "The procedure, I mean."

The doctor forked up his pie. "Way I understand it, what you're testing is digested in alcohol and tartaric acid, the fatty and resinous matters are precipitated with water, the fluid is turned alkaline, and the alkaloids are extracted. With chloroform." He grinned around a mouthful of pie. "Simple enough for the village idiot, wouldn't you say, Sheriff?"

"Hang on a minute," the sheriff said, taking out his notebook and a pencil. "I gotta write that down." After a minute, he frowned. "Say, how do you spell chloroform? K-l-o-r-o—"

As the doctor spelled it, Myra May went on polishing, her ears tuned to the conversation. Whatever they were talking about, it sounded dreadful. Murder? Poison? In Darling? What in the world was going on?

The sheriff closed his notebook. "They don't pay me enough to understand this stuff." He rolled his eyes. "How soon can you get the results of this test you're talkin' about?"

The doctor finished his pie. "Noonan's got the body. I'll tell him to put it back in the hearse and drive it over to Monroeville this morning. If Doc Martin can get to work on it right away, we might have something by this time tomorrow."

"That'd be good," the sheriff said, looking pleased. "I'll stop at Moseley's office and tell him what we've got in the works. Need to see Judge McHenry and get a search warrant before I head over to the Manor."

The doctor nodded. "If you see any of that chocolate cake laying around, nab it. I'll tell Doc Martin to test it, too."

Myra May kept on polishing the coffee urn. Lionel Noonan owned Darling's funeral parlor and Mr. Moseley was the county attorney and Judge McHenry was a crusty old man who liked his eggs over easy with three strips of bacon so crisp it crumbled and knew everything that was going on in Darling.

But what was this test they were going to do? Whose body were they talking about? And then, all of a sudden, Myra May understood. It was the woman she'd heard about on Mildred's radio show. The new boarder at Magnolia Manor, the one that Miss Rogers had caught cheating at bridge. Poison in a chocolate cake, it sounded like. Myra May shuddered, thinking that maybe she should tell Euphoria to substitute her carrot cake for the chocolate they'd been planning for the lunch and supper menus. When word got around, chocolate cake might not be so popular for a while.

"And I'll give Noonan his marching orders," the doctor added. He lifted his fork and raised his voice. "Myra May, honey, I'll take another piece of that apple pie, if you don't mind putting it on a plate that I can take back to the office for Edna Fay. She heard Mildred telling everybody in town how good it was. Said she wanted some, too."

Thinking that the fifty cents they'd spent on radio advertising was definitely going to pay off in pies, Myra May turned to go into the kitchen. If she had looked up, she might have seen the stranger at the back table, watching Charlie Dickens and Wilber Casey with a look of dark suspicion on his narrow face.

But she didn't.

And neither did Charlie.

# CHAPTER FOUR

# LIZZY MAKES NOTES

ELIZABETH LACY FINISHED TYPING THE LAST PARAGRAPH OF the brief and pulled it out of her typewriter. Mr. Moseley would need it later in the week for the hearing before Judge McHenry. He was representing Clovis Richards in a lawsuit against Phineas Holland. Mr. Richards had wrecked his nearly new 1933 Chevrolet when he struck and killed Phineas Holland's heifer, which had gotten out of her fence and was lounging in the middle of Piney Ridge Road. Mr. Holland (represented by Harold Parsons), was countersuing Mr. Richards, arguing that the cow—a nearly-white Charolais—was visible for at least fifty yards, and that if Mr. Richards hadn't spent the previous three hours at the Cotton Gin Roadhouse, he should have been able to see her in time to stop.

Lizzy stacked the pages of the brief and slipped them into the usual green folder, then reached into her bottom desk drawer for the feather duster. She carried both into Mr. Moseley's office, where she put the folder on his desk. He'd be arriving any minute now, so she opened the wooden blinds and began applying the feather duster to the slats, appreciating the spring sunshine that flooded in through the tall, narrow window.

The Moseley Law Office was located upstairs over the office

of the Darling *Dispatch*, offering an excellent view of the Cypress County courthouse on the other side of the street. Built in 1905 of brick and boasting a decorous white dome and clock tower, it was surrounded by a neatly clipped lawn of green grass, several large tulip trees (*Liriodendron tulipifera*, according to Miss Rogers), and wooden benches where the old veterans liked to sit and exchange recollections of the battles in the War for Southern Independence. The Dahlias had taken on the task of planting and maintaining the flower beds around the courthouse, and in a few weeks, they would be bright with summer annuals—marigolds, zinnias, cosmos, petunias, and the like. The years since the Crash of '29 had been long and hard, and the club knew that a few pretty blossoms went a long way toward brightening Darling's dismal days.

And times were still hard in Darling, even though a few folks didn't act like it. Bailey Beauchamp, for example, whose 1929 lemon yellow Cadillac Phaeton was just coming into Lizzy's view. The canvas top was folded back so she could see that it was driven by Mr. Beauchamp's uniformed colored man, Lightning McFall. Mr. Beauchamp himself, wearing a white summer suit and a Panama straw hat, was puffing on a Cuban cigar in the back seat, the picture of old Southern privilege and completely out of step (at least as Lizzy saw it) with the modern world.

Or there was Tallulah LaBelle, who had enough money to behave as if there was no such thing as a Depression—not here in Darling, anyway. But she might be at least partly right. She and some others had visited up North and seen something of life in the big cities, where it was very hard. In Chicago, for instance, where people didn't know one another well enough to ask for help and had to line up at the Salvation Army for a bowl of soup and a few crackers and hope that the Red Cross shelter would have a quiet corner where they could catch a few winks.

"We'd rather be right here in Darling than anywhere else,"

these folks were likely to say when they got back home. "Especially when things are bad. Down here, we've got friends and family. Up there in Yankee land, people are on their own." Which was true, because the Darling churches and clubs made it a point to help everybody who needed a hand, colored and white alike.

And while Lizzy's ideas about law and justice had certainly changed in the years she had worked in Mr. Moseley's office, the courthouse still seemed to stand for a lot of what was good about Darling. Now, as she dusted the blinds, she thought of the case that Mr. Moseley would be arguing before Judge McHenry—not a very important case, really, just Clovis Richards' Chevrolet automobile against Phineas Holland's Charolais heifer. But even a little case could be heard in that courthouse, and every person had the right to expect justice. The thought was comforting.

She turned from the window, caught a glimpse of dust on the framed print of blindfolded Justice that hung beside Mr. Moseley's desk, and wielded her duster. Of course, when she first went to work at Moseley and Moseley, she had been young and quite naïve about important things. She had believed all the comforting words she'd heard about the rule of law and the American way and all that.

But the more she had seen of the law in action, the more she understood that sometimes justice didn't work the way you thought it should, or even the way it was supposed to. That blindfold in the picture, for instance, now puzzled her. Maybe people still thought Justice was blind, but Lizzy's experience prompted a different image. Now, she had seen so many otherwise inexplicable judgments from the bench and the jury box that she had to imagine that Justice must be peeking under that blindfold to see whether the person about to be whacked with that sword was female or male, colored or white. Justice's decision often seemed arbitrary, and some of its rules were so arcane and complicated that nobody could understand them. Lizzy couldn't begin to guess whether Judge McHenry would rule for the car or the cow, and Mr. Moseley probably couldn't, either. Sometimes justice took you by surprise.

Lizzy whisked her duster quickly over the bookcases, then went back into the outer office, where she switched on the radio on the shelf behind her desk. She had intended to listen to the morning broadcast of *The Flour Hour*, but Mildred's animated conversation had distracted her from her typing, and she had turned it off. Now, she tuned in again just as her friend Beulah—a guest on the show—was reporting on Emma Jane Randall's death, which Lizzy had heard about just before the party ended yesterday afternoon.

But there hadn't been many details yesterday, and Beulah's report told her something she didn't know. The woman who had died, Mrs. Randall, turned out to be the sister of one of Lizzy's near neighbors, George Clemens, a man she had known since she was a girl. She had also learned that Mr. Clemens' daughter, Zelda, was back in Darling. Lizzy made a mental note to call on her way home from work and offer her condolences.

On the radio, Mildred finished telling everybody about pies and Benny Biddle began playing "Tiptoe Through the Tulips." She turned the volume up, smiling as she remembered that Nick Lucas had sung that song in *Gold Diggers of Broadway*, a Technicolor musical that she and Mr. Moseley had enjoyed a few months before. She began humming it along with Benny as she set about the morning's dusting chore—except that it wasn't really a chore. She loved the serene, old-fashioned room, with its high pressed-tin ceiling; its large Oriental rug, worn almost bare in patches; and the bookcases, filled with ranks of leather-bound books and reassuring in their solid upright-ness. She even appreciated the stern, gilt-framed portraits of the three senior Moseleys, now deceased: Mr. Moseley's great-grandfather, his grandfather, and his father, all with distinctive gray beards.

The fourth Moseley was somewhat of a renegade, for Mr. Benton Moseley refused (among other things) to sit for his portrait. "All bad traditions have to come to an end sometime," he said, whenever he was asked. "I am thrusting a stake through the heart of this one right now. Anybody wants to know what I look like, they can by God take a gander at my face."

Mr. Moseley might have had the portraits removed, of course, which would have put an end to the questions. But he left them on the wall as a reminder, he said, "that the sins of the fathers are forever with us, especially in the woefully misbegotten South."

Which Lizzy supposed she understood, but wasn't quite sure and didn't like to ask, especially when he added, beneath his breath, "The inequities of the fathers, to the third and fourth generations."

Lizzy knew that Mr. Moseley was quoting from Exodus chapter twenty. But he was a friend of William Faulkner, who was from neighboring Mississippi and had recommended that Lizzy read *The Sound and the Fury*—definitely about the sins of the fathers. When she finished, she'd told Mr. Moseley that she had liked it, sort of, but she wished that Mr. Faulkner could tell a story without so many zigzags back and forth in time.

Mr. Moseley had been mightily amused. "I think he prefers that you work out the chronology for yourself," he'd said. "That way, you'll understand it better."

Mr. Moseley. That was what she had to call him here in the office, so that's how she thought of him now, as she wielded her feather duster over the tops of the Moseley library, which included a much-thumbed *Black's Law Dictionary*, Thomas Owen's *A History of Alabama*, and five calf-bound volumes of

*Blackstone's Commentaries.* This set of *Blackstone's* was so rare that, in the event of a fire, Lizzy had been instructed to snatch all five of them and take them with her when she ran down the stairs.

But a few months before, she and Mr. Moseley had started seeing one another outside of the office, where she was trying to get used to calling him Bent. This unexpected turn of events had begun at Christmas, when they'd shared what began as a playful under-the-mistletoe kiss and turned into something that, as Mr. Moseley put it, "rattled the rafters." He had followed this with the startling admission that he had been thinking of kissing her for a very long time—something he hadn't realized until he saw her with Ryan Nichols, the man from the Federal Writers' Project.

Lizzy had laughed at this admission, although the kiss had rattled her, too. But her laugh hid the wrenching recognition that she had not, after all, entirely suppressed her adolescent longings for Mr. Moseley. When she had come to work for him right out of high school, she had been possessed by a crush the size of the state of Alabama. For years, she had yearned for him every waking moment and dreamed about him every night.

But finally, with determination and practice, she had managed to substitute the practical realities of the situation for her silly romantic fantasies. Mr. Moseley appreciated her work but he had no personal interest in her. Moreover, he was married. And after he and his wife were divorced and Adabelle returned to Birmingham, he had become quite the ladies' man, getting involved with first one and then another well-connected socialite in Montgomery, the state capital, where he also had an office. Sometimes he dated just one, sometimes there was a gaggle—and all very beautiful, according to Darling gossip.

Because she was really quite a sensible person, Lizzy understood that facing facts was the only way she could continue to work for Mr. Moseley. There would never be anything between them except for their professional relationship. Whatever her personal feelings, she was proud of having kept them private until she could congratulate herself on the fact that they had vanished at last, for good and for all. And if they hadn't really disappeared but just slipped into hiding, she couldn't have admitted it. That would have meant admitting that she had managed only to hide them—from herself. It wasn't something a sensible person would like to admit.

But Lizzy understood that she had to have a life. She had been going out with Grady Alexander, a very nice young man who held a responsible job as the Cypress County agricultural agent and had earned her mother's enthusiastic approval. She might have married him, too, if he hadn't gotten Sandra Mann in trouble and had to marry *her*. But Sandra hadn't lived to enjoy her new son and her husband. Now a father and a widower, Grady was anxious to renew their relationship.

"We can start over again," he'd told Lizzy, not long ago. "And it'll be better this time. We can have a family of our own—give little Grady a sister and a brother, and more if you like. Please, Liz. Nothing has changed between us. I love you. I *need* you."

She felt sure he did, under the circumstances. She had heard that his little boy had been sick, and she was sure that Grady Junior needed a mother as much as Grady Senior needed a wife.

But she didn't need a husband or a child, at least, not in the same way. And need wasn't the same thing as love, was it? Need—which had something about it of obligation, of necessity, of duty, even—need complicated love, especially when all the need (or most of it, anyway) was on one side. How could she and Grady turn back the clock and become the free and unobligated people they once had been? What was done was done, wasn't it? Surely it was. They had become different people. She had, anyway. Grady had, too, whether he recognized it or not.

And there were new people in her life. There was Bent Moseley, for one—not really new, but yet he was. Or their relationship was. Or it might be, if . . .

If she could finish that sentence, which was proving to be much more difficult than she had thought.

And there was Ryan Nichols, the regional director of the Federal Writers' Project. The more she saw of Ryan, the more powerfully attractive she found him, in a way that was undeniably and astonishingly physical. Lizzy had never been a prude when it came to sex, but she hadn't given in to Grady because she hadn't wanted him to think she was ready to marry him. Which is exactly what he *would* have thought if she had said *yes* on one of those steamy nights when they were parked on the hill overlooking the country club.

Lizzy hadn't given in to Ryan, either, on the two or three occasions when things had gotten steamy with him and some part of her kept crying *don't stop please don't stop*. But that was because Ryan seemed to set his own limits and stop himself when the situation threatened (or promised) to get out of hand. This made it easier for her but was a little harder to deal with. She was grateful when he pulled back, but at the same time, she couldn't help feeling . . . well, regretful. And wondering. Didn't he *want* to?

Of course, even in these modern days, good girls (and Lizzy thought of herself as mostly good, most of the time) weren't supposed to want sex outside of marriage—and even in marriage, unless you wanted children. But Lizzy didn't think it was wrong, at least not morally wrong, in spite of the preacher's stern Sunday-morning warnings that God was watching what everyone was doing. She was of the opinion that God being God, he had bigger fish to fry, especially when what his children were doing gave them pleasure and didn't hurt anybody else. (If it did, that was another matter entirely, and she shouldn't do it.)

So, in Lizzy's mind, that intriguing option was still open. She went out with Ryan when he came to Darling, and she was looking forward to seeing him on Friday, when he was in town to meet with Ophelia. She was also seeing Mr. Moseley—Bent—once a month or so, when *he* was in town. And Grady was . . . well, Grady was here. And Grady was persistent. Which she supposed might have its own attractions. And here *she* was, betwixt and between. On the one hand, there was Ryan's almost irresistible physical magnetism. On the other, there were her complicated romantic yearnings for Mr. Moseley—for Bent—stirred and sweetened by their Christmas kiss and ripened a bit by age and maturity. And Grady, in spite of everything. Talk about a quandary!

Luckily (or not, depending on how you looked at it), there had been plenty of time to reflect on the situation. Ryan's responsibilities for the Writers' Project kept him traveling around the South, on a regular circuit from Washington to Atlanta to New Orleans. He had only been in town a couple of times since Christmas. The Alabama Legislature had been in session for the past three months, which meant that Bent had spent most of his time with clients in Montgomery, where his practice had more to do with legislative politics and less with dead cows. Instead of going to work for the Writers' Project, she had decided to stay on part-time with Mr. Moseley because (she told herself) it gave her more time to work on her next book, a sequel to *Inherit the Flames*, which would be published very soon. When she told Ryan what she meant to do, he had said he understood and asked her to recommend someone. Lizzy was glad when Ophelia agreed to take the position. She would do a first-rate job.

The bell over the office door dinged and Liz turned to see Sheriff Norris. "Good mornin', Liz," he said, hanging his brown cap on the peg by the door.

Lizzy smiled. She and Buddy Norris had been friends for a long time, and she wasn't surprised when he became sheriff. When he was a kid, he'd been enterprising and ambitious, always looking for a way to stand out from the crowd. He hadn't been interested in school, but he was smart. Lizzy remembered that he had ordered a how-to book on scientific crime detection from the Institute of Applied Sciences in Chicago and taught himself how to take fingerprints, identify firearms, and make crime scene photographs—skills he had put to use when Sheriff Burns hired him on as a temporary deputy.

"I'm sorry, Buddy, but Mr. Moseley isn't—" she began, but stopped when Mr. Moseley followed the sheriff in, a dark expression on his face.

"Good morning, Liz," he said, all business. "Sheriff, my office. Liz, we'll have coffee, please. And bring your notebook."

Several minutes later, she had served both men their coffee and taken her usual unobtrusive chair in the corner. Buddy Norris was seated on one side of the desk and Bent—Mr. Moseley—on the other, his suit jacket off, revealing red suspenders that matched his red tie. Really, Lizzy thought—it was no wonder that she had fallen for the man when she first came to work in the office. Back then, he'd been a lean and good-looking twenty-something with a ready smile, a glint in his eye, and an incisive wit. Now in his forties and heavier, his brown hair graying at the temples, he might not smile as often but was even more attractive—and he knew it.

He was politically shrewd, too, with a reputation for knowing how to deal with the power brokers who ran the state's business. He himself had already served ("survived," as he put it) two terms in the state legislature in Montgomery, which was why there were so many autographed photographs of politicians on the walls of his office: Alabama governors Bibb Graves and Benjamin Miller; the Kingfish, Huey P. Long, US senator from Louisiana; W. E. B. Du Bois, one of the founders of the NAACP; Harry Hopkins, head of the WPA; even President Roosevelt. In fact, there were several pictures of Mr. Moseley and FDR, taken both at the White House and at the Warm Springs Little White House. One of the photos even included Mrs. Roosevelt and her friend, journalist Lorena Hickok, both of whom Lizzy longed to meet.

Back home in Darling, Mr. Moseley currently held the office of Cypress County attorney, which was rotated among the town's three lawyers. That was probably why Buddy Norris was here this morning, Lizzy thought. He frequently came in to discuss a case he was investigating or a legal matter he needed help with.

Buddy was in the middle of a sentence when Lizzy came in, so she opened her notebook and quickly began taking short-hand notes in her private version of the Gregg she'd learned in high school.

"—wouldn't say who it was," he was saying. "Fact is, I couldn't tell if it was a man or a woman. Gruff, it was, and muffled, like somebody talking with a sock over the mouthpiece. Calling local—not long distance, I mean. Said that Emma Jane Randall was murdered. Nicotine poison. Said it was in some chocolate cake she ate."

Startled, Lizzy sucked in her breath. The death she had heard about at the party yesterday—it was *murder?*

"Hang on." Mr. Moseley peered over the tops of his dark-rimmed reading glasses. "Randall. That's the lady I heard about on WDAR this morning? The one who lived at Magnolia Manor?"

"Yessir, that's her. Emma Jane Randall, age eighty-eight. After the caller hung up, I right away telephoned Bessie Blood-worth and asked her to tell me what happened. She said the housekeeper found Emma Jane dead in her room yesterday afternoon, while everybody was over at the Dahlias' garden party. Doc Roberts had a look and said she'd likely died of a stroke. The family sent Lionel Noonan to take the body to the funeral parlor early this morning."

"The family?" Mr. Moseley asked. "They're here in Darling?"

"Sorry." Buddy turned down his mouth. "I didn't think to ask."

Lizzy raised her voice. "I heard on the radio this morning that George Clemens is Emma Jane's brother. He lives on my block. I thought I'd stop on my way home today to give him my condolences."

"George Clemens. Didn't we . . ." Mr. Moseley looked questioningly at Lizzy.

"You helped him settle a dispute two years ago," she reminded him. "With Bevis Parkinson."

"Oh, right," Mr. Moseley said. "The irate old guy who got in an argument with a neighbor over the property lines." He gave a rueful chuckle. "Took a baseball bat to Parkinson's windows, as I recall. Lucky he didn't take the bat to Parkinson's head."

Buddy pulled out a small notebook and leafed through the pages. "According to Miz Bloodworth, Miz Randall came here from Birmingham. She was getting infirm and planned to live with her brother in Darling." He paused. "That didn't work out, seems like, so she moved to the Manor. Bessie says she didn't settle in very well, though," he added. "She didn't get along with the other ladies."

"Bad temper ran in the family, maybe." Mr. Moseley leaned back in his chair. "Did your anonymous caller say where the cake came from?"

Buddy paused. "Said it was sent by the woman who's fixin' to inherit. The person was real positive about that."

A *woman* was going to inherit? Liz frowned. What woman? Wasn't it more likely that George Clemens would get his sister's property? Of course, this anonymous caller might be a prankster who was just trying to stir up trouble. Or—

"So the caller is telling us to look for a killer whose weapon is nicotine." Mr. Moseley said. "And implies that she did it to speed up her inheritance. Is that how you understand it, Sheriff?"

"Yessir." Buddy nodded. "That's pretty much how I got it figured."

"But the caller didn't tell you the name of the alleged poisoner?"

"No, sir. When I started to ask, the connection went dead."

"How about the chocolate cake? Any confirmation?"

Buddy nodded again. "I asked Bessie Bloodworth if she'd noticed any food in Miz Randall's room. She said her ladies weren't supposed to have food upstairs, 'cause of mice and cockroaches. But when she went to look, she found what was left of a chocolate cake in a box under the bed. I told her to lock up the room and I'd be over directly to have a look." He held up a piece of paper. "I've got a warrant ready to go to Judge McHenry. Figured I'd better make it official, so I can get the cake tested. I'll give that room a real good look-see, too."

"You figured right." Mr. Moseley rubbed his jaw. "You know anything about nicotine poisoning, Sheriff?"

Buddy shifted in his chair. "Not just a whole lot. Doc Roberts does, though. He phoned up Doc Martin over in Monroeville and got him to agree to do an autopsy and some sort of chemical test." He looked at his notebook again. "It's called the Stas-Otto procedure, after a couple of foreign guys who thought it up. Doc Roberts says it'll tell us for sure whether it's nicotine or not. He's arranging with Lionel Noonan to take Miz Randall's body over to Monroeville this morning. I'll send that cake, too, if I find it. Doc Martin says that if everybody gets on the job right away, we might could get the results tomorrow. Wednesday at the latest."

Mr. Moseley scowled. "Sure wish we knew who made that anonymous call."

"Right. Well, I talked to Myra May at the Diner just a little bit ago and asked her if the girls on the switchboard maybe happened to know who the caller was. Violet said they was so busy this morning that it wasn't likely anybody took notice, but Myra May is going to ask."

"The alleged poisoner is a woman who's 'fixin' to inherit.' That's what the caller said?" When Buddy nodded, Mr. Moseley pointed his finger at Lizzy.

"Liz, I want you to call the other attorneys here in Darling and find out whether any of them has drawn up a will for this lady—Mrs. Randall. If we're lucky, it'll be somebody here, rather than Birmingham. They won't want to say, but you tell them you're inquiring with regard to a possible criminal matter. If you get a yes, arrange to take a look at the document—see who's the legatee and what kind of estate we're talking about. If it's not George Clemens, who is it? In case the test comes back positive for nicotine, we'll need that information."

"Yes, Mr. Moseley," Lizzy murmured, making notes.

He swiveled back to Buddy. "When you go to the Manor, find out how that cake showed up. Did somebody drop it off? If so, who was it? If it came in the mail, see if you can find the packing. Oh, and maybe the lady kept a copy of her will. Look around. See if you can locate it."

"Yessir," Buddy said.

"That's it, folks." Mr. Moseley stood up. "Liz, where's the brief on that dead cow?"

Lizzy closed her notebook. "In the green folder."

"Thank you." He smiled at her, a smile that made her silly heart tremble. "What would I do without you?"

# CHAPTER FIVE

# THE NEXT BIG STORY

DOWNSTAIRS, BELOW THE OFFICES OF MOSELEY AND MOSELEY, Charlie Dickens was regarding his typewriter with a black look. It was Monday morning. He should be pounding out a story for the next edition of the *Dispatch*, but he was suffering from writer's block.

Well, not that, exactly. More like writer's reluctance.

The problem wasn't the lack of national news, of course. There was certainly plenty of that, and he wouldn't have to rewrite it. It would arrive in the form of preprinted pages—news, photographs, as well as comics and business, sports, and women's columns. It came by subscription from the Western Newspaper Union, a syndicate that provided the latest news from the Associated Press and the United Press wire services to small-town newspapers all across the country.

The bundles of ready-print would arrive from Mobile on the Thursday afternoon Greyhound bus. The old Babcock flatbed cylinder press would run half the night, printing the four local pages and folding them with the four pages of ready-print. The stacks of freshly printed newspapers would go to the paper boys—all three of them—who would stuff their Darling route bags for delivery after school on Friday. Charlie himself would fill the newspaper racks around the square for Friday night movie goers and Saturday shoppers. And Wild Bill Oakley, the mail carrier, would load the rest into his flivver early on Saturday morning for the RFD-route subscribers. Subscribers could relax on Sunday with their newspapers.

There hadn't been much good news lately, though. In the front-page stories of last week's edition, Adolf Hitler was reported to be conscripting all able-bodied German men over the age of nineteen for his Wehrmacht, while France and the Soviet Union were promising to defend the other should either become the victim of Hitler's unprovoked aggression. (Charlie had been a young infantryman in the War to End All Wars and knew without a doubt that they were heading for another one. All this talk about peace was nothing but hooey. He gave it five years.)

On the lighter side, last week's ready-print had included a full page of photos of the Dion Quints, all the way up there in Toronto. They were almost a year old now, living in their own private enclave, officially Wards of the Crown. Certainly cute enough, but where were Mom and Dad? It looked to Charlie (always the skeptic) like the Ontario government intended to profit from making them a significant tourist attraction.

In the national news, there had been a finger-pointing story in the continuing saga of the loss of the USS *Macom*, the helium-filled airship dubbed a "flying aircraft carrier" that had crashed into the Pacific off the coast of California in February—amazing that more people hadn't been lost, Charlie thought. There was also a follow-up piece on the electrocution of Richard Hauptmann, who had been convicted for the kidnapping and murder of twenty-month-old Little Lindy, the firstborn of Charles and Anne Lindbergh. The whole country had been hanging on this story, and the national papers were reluctant to let it go.

There was also a story about FDR's Social Security Act, which the Senate had been chewing on for months now. On the table: old-age pensions, unemployment insurance, health insurance for people who couldn't afford to buy their own, and financial aid for the disabled and widows with children. Charlie was generally in favor of it, but there was no telling what the damned thing would look like when the 74th Congress got through horse-trading.

And even if by some miracle it passed and FDR signed it, the Supreme Court—nine old men who had never been any too friendly toward the New Deal—was likely to swat it down as unconstitutional. If they didn't, you'd have to go to the post office and fill out an application form, after which you would get a national identity card with your very own nine-digit identification number, yours for life. Socialism, that's what it was, in Charlie's considered opinion. He was suspicious of anything that was doled out by the hand of Big Government. But how the hell else were you going to take care of old folks and people who could not find a job no matter how hard they looked? Social Security might be socialism, but he was prepared to live with it.

And on that same subject, there had also been a story about unemployment, which had retreated from its 1933 high of an appalling 25 percent to just over 20 percent—an improvement but still a helluva long way from its 1929 low of 3 percent, when pretty much every man who wanted a job had one and sometimes two. It was all well and good to listen to the happy talk coming out of the administration and pretend that the government's temporary Band-Aids were permanently curing the patient. But Charlie knew the grim truth: the Depression was still raging in full fury across the land and would be for a long time to come. The best they could hope for was the war that he knew was coming down the pike. When it got here, every man jack would be lined up and handed a gun. Wouldn't be any trouble with employment then.

And there a grim weather story, too. The Plains had been socked by another gargantuan dust storm that had rolled across eastern New Mexico, Colorado, and western Oklahoma, blanketing houses and animals and people with a suffocating layer of silt. It was said that the black cloud had blown all the way to Washington, where it dirtied the pages of the Social Security Act the Congress was arguing over.

On the local scene last week, though, the news had been a little brighter. The Vanity Fair factory was hiring another ten girls, the Coca-Cola bottling plant had hired three more men, and L&N had added a new train on Wednesdays. The Methodists rejoiced in a mighty week-long revival out at the county fairgrounds, the preacher reporting that some two dozen sinners had been saved from eternal damnation, praise the Lord. On the secular side, the Darling Academy's theater program had everybody laughing with a production of *The Vinegar Tree*. And in sports, Lester Ames took first place in the Darling Horseshoe tournament, Jerry Ray Holt caught a twelve-pound largemouth bass on a cricket and an eight-pound line at the reservoir, and Hiram Sherman bagged a turkey gobbler over on Poor Man's Ridge. It weighed twenty-six pounds.

Which brought Charlie face-to-face with his typewriter and the next big story. The launch of WDAR should headline the local page, but Charlie didn't feel like writing it. In fact, he thought it would be a very *bad* idea if he did write it, because he didn't trust himself to treat the subject objectively. He wasn't surprised that everybody was excited about their shiny new hometown radio station, which promised to beam the bright light of the future right into their living rooms—or so they thought. Free news and entertainment, a chance for local folks to perform, a way to get the word out about Darling meetings and church picnics and births and deaths and the like. And yes, to sell pies. But that was the province of the *Dispatch*, damn it. Not WDAR.

Sell pies! Charlie grunted sourly. His father must be turning over in his grave. Randolph Dickens had edited, owned, and published the *Dispatch* for four decades, back when the newspaper was the voice of *all* the news, not coming in second after some local on-the-fly radio station run by a pair of kids still wet behind the ears. All they had to do was string up some wire, rig up a microphone, push a few buttons, and turn a few dials and they were in business, while the *Dispatch* required skilled people putting in long days of hard work just to keep the damned thing afloat.

And the *Dispatch* wouldn't even be afloat if it weren't for Charlie. He had taken it over when the old man died of lung cancer the year after the Crash—not because he wanted to (he did *not*), but because the Depression had wiped out all his other options and handed him a mess that he had to make the best of. A wanderer by nature, Charlie had left Darling when he was young, soldiered in France, hoofed it through Europe and the Balkans, then worked as an itinerant reporter for the *Cleveland Plain Dealer*, the *Baltimore Sun*, and the *Fort Worth Star-Telegram*. His life as a nomadic journalist had not only left him with an itchy foot but also with a jaded and entirely un-Darlingian view of the world. If he could, Charlie would have sold the *Dispatch* for a dollar or two, stuck the money in his pocket, and hopped the first freight out of town.

Of course, all that had changed when Fannie Champaign came to town and stole his bitter heart, calloused by too many disappointments in love and work. Now, he was happy to publish the little newspaper and wait for better times. But he didn't have to work on every damned story that crossed his desk.

He raised his voice. "Wilber, get over here. I've got a job for you."

"Give me a few minutes, Mr. Dickens," Wilber called from the Linotype machine. "I'd like to finish this column."

Charlie picked up his pencil and began making notes for the boy's assignment. Wilber Casey had been a lucky find, a *very* lucky find. When Ophelia told Charlie she was quitting the *Dispatch*, Charlie had taken a deep dive into the Slough of Despond. Ophelia had a nose for stories, she could spell like a dictionary, and she could *write*. What's more, she could type sixty words a minute, operate that damned balky old Linotype, and sell ads like a carnival barker. Where in the bloody hell would he find anybody to replace her?

The answer, oddly enough, was sitting in the warden's office at the Jericho State Prison Farm, where Charlie had met Wilber Casey, the warden's assistant. Witness to enough felonies to lock up Warden Grover Burford for the rest of his life, Wilber was an honest young man who was troubled by what he knew and more than willing to share it with law enforcement. His information had resulted in a raid on the industrial-size moonshine operation the warden had been building. Once it was in full production, the still's six tanks would have held nearly five thousand gallons of sour mash, enough to boost bootleg whiskey to the top of the prison farm's long list of cash crops—lumber, corn, sorghum, cotton, cattle, pigs, chickens, and prisoner labor—and make Warden Burford a wealthy man.

Acting on Wilber's tip, Agent Kinnard had smashed the still and arrested the warden. Charlie had helped Wilber write the story that eventually ran in newspapers all across the South. The boy had always wanted to be a reporter when he grew up, and he was deeply grateful to Charlie for giving him his chance. Wilber Casey was now a cub reporter for the *Dispatch*. What's more, he had taken to the Linotype like a duck to water, and he had even begun learning the old jobbing press.

Osgood Fairchild had been another lucky find, although Charlie couldn't take any special credit for the discovery. Osgood had shambled into the Dispatch office one rainy winter afternoon and declared that he wanted to be a printer. He was just out of his teens, tall and ungainly, with a head of shaggy black hair, arms too long for his shirtsleeves, and legs too long for his britches. He had a shy smile and a slow speech that was thick with down-home *y'alls* and *cain'ts* and *might coulds* and *fixin' tos*. He came from a very small town—Pinetucky, far out in the Alabama boonies—where (he said) he'd been lucky enough to have a teacher who had fired in him a reverence and a heartfelt passion for the printed word.

Since he couldn't afford the education to be a writer, Osgood said, he yearned to become a printer. He'd had some experience on another small-town newspaper, and he knew how to run the big Babcock and the smaller Kelsey jobbing press. Salary? All he needed was some spending money and enough to pay Mrs. Meeks for a bed and meals over at her boarding house on Railroad Street. Fifteen dollars a week would do it.

Charlie figured he'd gotten himself a great bargain, cheap— and he figured right, as it turned out. Osgood had surprised him with his ability to quickly absorb and remember instructions and with his devotion to the job. He already knew the basics: how to lock the Linotype columns into the forms and set them in place on the Babcock. How to ink the rollers, load the paper, and run the home print—pages two and seven, four and five—on the blank sides of the ready-print pages: one and eight, three and six. How to feed the folded papers into the mailing machine so that each one came out with the name and address of a subscriber printed at the top—all 543 of them.

It didn't take more than a couple of weeks for Osgood to

show that he could manage the temperamental old Babcock and handle even the most complicated repairs when it broke down, as it regularly did. It wasn't long before Charlie—realizing that he was on to a very good thing—was entrusting the boy with the Thursday night press run. So instead of spending every Thursday night with the Babcock thundering in his ears and under his feet, Charlie could turn the print run over to Osgood and go home to his affectionate Fannie. On Friday morning, he could come in, rested and cheerful, to stacks of freshly printed newspapers, ready for the paper boys, the boxes around the square, and Wild Bill Oakley and his flivver—all thanks to Osgood.

And even more remarkably, Osgood was an expert when it came to the Kelsey jobbing press, which was old enough to have printed handbills calling for volunteers for the Confederate Army. In fact, he could handle the diabolical machine far more competently than Charlie, although that probably wasn't saying much, since Charlie had detested that blasted letterpress since the day he first laid eyes on it. The jobs were usually small runs with finicky setups that required frequent adjustments—handbills, auction notices, announcements, flyers, hotel menus, and the colorful Darling Dollars that had substituted for actual money when the bank closed a while back and the town ran out of real money. The Kelsey required the touch of an artist, almost, and Osgood seemed to have it.

Plus, he was a good teacher. Both Wilber and Baby Mann, the other young employee, professed an interest in the Kelsey, but Charlie didn't have the time—or the patience—to teach them. Osgood, on the other hand, seemed to enjoy the role of instructor. Before long, even Baby could produce a simple job on the Kelsey, which tickled him no end.

Baby Mann's real name was Purley. He was a big strapping twenty-one-year-old boy who ran errands and swept and cleaned and put things back on the shelves where they belonged. Everybody called him Baby, on account of his baby-fine silvery hair and his guileless expression. Baby might be on the slow side when it came to adding and subtracting and he'd never gotten much farther in his reader than *See Spot run*. But now he carried his Bible and could be found painstakingly spelling out verses aloud to himself and anybody who would listen. Which was a story all of its own and one in which churchgoing Darling took a great deal of pride.

And well they might, for Baby Mann was a Prodigal Son who had gone and gotten himself born again. It wasn't just his reading skills that had improved, either. For several years, Baby had worked for his cousin, Mickey LeDoux, who was the undisputed moonshine king of Cypress County. But when Baby got saved and the scales fell from his eyes, he realized that what he had been doing out there at Mickey's still hadn't exactly been the Lord's work. Possessed by the Spirit, he felt he owed it to Jesus to stop the flow of Demon Drink at its source. So it was that one fateful day, Baby ratted out the location of Mickey's still to revenue agent Chester P. Kinnard.

Agent Kinnard wasted no time. In the bloody raid that followed, Mickey's kid brother Rider was shot and killed by one of Kinnard's men. The raiders took their axes to the still, which in Charlie's informed opinion had produced the best moonshine he had ever been privileged to drink. Mickey himself was nabbed, tried, convicted, and sent away to the state penitentiary, where he was now serving out his sentence.*

Of course, as far as the temperance folk in Darling were concerned, Agent Kinnard had done a blessed night's work. It was certainly too bad about Rider, but collateral damage was to be expected, wasn't it? If you dance with the devil, you can't

---

* You can read about the raid in *The Darling Dahlias and the Silver Dollar Bush*.

complain when your eyebrows get scorched. And if you weren't a teetotaler and wanted your moonshine, you didn't have to go without. You could get it from Bodeen Pyle, whose tiger juice might not be as smoothly potent as Mickey's but was certainly an acceptable substitute.

And Baby? Oh, he got himself a nice reward (real government-green legal tender, not those fake Darling Dollars). He was invited to tell his born-again story during Testimony Time at the Baptists' Wednesday night prayer meetings, he was front and center when the all-church revival came to town, and he was the star of the semiannual baptizing on Cedar Creek. Plus, he got work around town—restocking at Dunlap's Five and Dime, repair work and gardening at the Diner, cleanup at the newspaper office, even ushering at the Palace Theater, which only paid ten cents an hour but came with free movies and the popcorn that was left over when Mr. Greer cleaned out the popcorn machine after the last show.

But Baby's betrayal of his cousin and the ensuing murder of Rider had caused an awful rift in the family. Over the weeks and months since the raid, the rift had turned into a corrosive feud, with the stubborn tribe of Manns on one side and the outlaw LeDoux clan on the other. While there hadn't been any bloodshed yet, there was plenty threatened. What's more, none of Baby's old friends would have anything to do with him, now that he "had revealed his true spots as a stool pigeon," in the picturesque phrase of one of the boys at Pete's Pool Parlor.

In fact, most folks in town said that the only good thing about it was that Baby got baptized and Mickey—who was probably the hot-headedest LeDoux of them all—was still cooling his heels in Wetumpka Prison. When he got out, he would be mad as hell and looking to wreak his revenge on Baby, who had got Rider murdered and Mickey sent to prison. When he got out, it would be Katy bar the door, for sure.

If any of this affected Baby, he didn't let on. Around town, he wore his usual cherubic smile and said his *amens* and *praise the Lords* and *hallelujahs* more enthusiastically than ever. At church (the First Baptist, over on Peachtree Street), he sang in the choir, with a sweet, high tenor that folks said made them think of angels. At the newspaper, he was painstakingly careful in his work and painfully honest in his doings, since he aimed to use every minute of his life to celebrate being saved.

With all this in mind, it is therefore quite understandable that Charlie Dickens, editor and publisher of the *Dispatch*, was congratulating himself on having assembled a first-class staff: Wilber to handle reporting, advertising, and the Linotype; Osgood to sweet-talk the Babcock and the Kelsey; and Baby to sweep up and put away.

Charlie gave his typewriter a more charitable look. Instead of sitting here, suffering from writer's block over that radio story he did *not* want to write, he could turn it over to that eager young cub reporter. Wilber would handle it with gusto and a very real pleasure, while Charlie put his mind on the next big story.

He didn't know what that might be. There hadn't been much going on in Darling since the holidays, when there was all that ruckus out at the prison farm. But with such a good, dependable staff, Charlie felt he could afford to relax and take it easy for a while, content in the knowledge that the newspaper was in very good hands. Why, he and Fannie might even get in his old green Pontiac and drive over to Warm Springs, Georgia, where Fannie's son—

"Okay, I'm ready, Mr. Dickens." Carrying his notebook, Wilber pulled up a chair and sat down, an earnest expression on his fresh young face. "What did you have in mind?"

Charlie swung his feet onto his desk, leaned back in his chair, and clasped his hands behind his head. "Well, I'll tell you, son.

I was intending to write the WDAR story myself, since it's such a big one. It isn't every day of the week that a small town in the South gets its very own radio station. Puts Darling on the map, so to speak. But I've decided to turn it over to you, instead. What do you say, kid? Want to take a crack at it?"

"Do I want to take a crack at it?" Wilber's eyes were alight and his grin was so wide it threatened to split his face. "Do I want—gee willikers, Mr. Dickens, that is swell! That is the *berries*. I can't even begin to tell you—"

"That's right, you can't," Charlie said. "Now, let me give you a few pointers to start you off right. You can begin by going over to Ollie Barton's garage, where the boys have set up their studio. You can interview—"

The bell over the front door clinked and Charlie looked up to see a man come in and stride purposefully to the counter. The man's narrow, high-cheekboned face was strikingly pale, as if he hadn't seen the sun in months, and his hair was clipped so close you could see his scalp.

Charlie stared. The fellow looked ten years older. He had lost maybe forty pounds and his wrinkled blue work shirt hung loose on his gaunt frame, but there was no mistaking him. It was Mickey LeDoux.

With a sudden jolting foreboding, Charlie abandoned his instructions to Wilber, swung his feet onto the floor, and stepped apprehensively to the counter.

"Mornin', Dickens," the man said, in a raspy, uninflected voice, so low it was almost a whisper. His once-cheerful face was hard and expressionless and his eyes were flat and dead. A raw, red scar angled across his jaw. "Reckon you remember me."

"Remember you?" Charlie felt the skin prickle across his shoulders. The two of them had shared many a good story and a late-night drink. But this hard-eyed man—

He cleared his throat. "Oh, you bet I remember you. Welcome home, Mickey."

"Home?" Mickey grunted sourly. "Well, maybe that's how you see it. Don't feel like home to me."

Charlie managed a smile. "Actually, I wasn't expecting you for . . . oh, a couple of months or more. They turn you loose early?"

"Yeah. Good behavior was what they said." Mickey glanced over Charlie's shoulder. "I hear that my cousin has been workin' here at the newspaper while I been in jail. Baby around anywhere? I need to see him. I got something for him."

The prickle became goosebumps and Charlie's stomach muscles knotted. He sneaked a quick glance across the counter. No holster, no sign of a gun in the belt. A derringer in a boot, maybe? Or a knife up a sleeve? A knife in Baby's gut would be just as effective as a bullet, and a whole lot more personal.

Charlie swallowed. "Not here," he said. "He doesn't come in until late afternoon. You might check down the street at the Diner. I hear he's been doing some painting in Myra May's back room. You know, the Exchange."

"I'll have a look," Mickey said. He leaned closer, his voice even lower. "If I don't find him before he gets here, you can tell him from me that I'm lookin' for him. We'uns have us a little something to talk about." He stepped back. His mouth was a thin, hard line. His eyes were flint. "You got that, Dickens? You'll tell him?"

"I got it," Charlie said, and shivered. "I'll tell him."

Oh, he got it, all right.

The next big story had just walked in the door.

# CHAPTER SIX

# SHERIFF NORRIS INVESTIGATES

Bessie Bloodworth had grown up in Magnolia Manor, although of course it hadn't been called that when she was a girl. After a tragic love affair early in her life, she had remained at home, keeping house for her father, as girls were expected to do. When he died, the place came to her, and since she needed to earn some money, she decided to turn it into a boarding house.

That's how the old Bloodworth family home became Magnolia Manor. Bessie put up fresh wallpaper in the living and dining rooms, dusted the upstairs bedrooms, and hired Roseanne Stewart to cook and help with the cleaning. Her first advertisement in the Darling *Dispatch* read "Opportunity for older unmarried and widowed ladies of refinement to occupy spacious bedrooms at Magnolia Manor."

She knew it was a good opportunity, too, for the alternatives were altogether unsuitable. Over on West Plum, for example, Mrs. Brewster ran her Home for Young Ladies by very strict rules that more mature ladies would not appreciate. Mrs. Meeks catered to single men who worked on the railroad or at Sherman's sawmill. Visitors were welcome at the Marigold Motor Court on the Mobile highway and at the Old Alabama Hotel on the courthouse square. But the Marigold rented by the night to motorists (a noisy lot, and who knew what they were getting up to in those rooms). The hotel—which offered daily linen changes and snowy white tablecloths in the dining room—was too expensive for most local folk. Within a week, all the Manor bedrooms were spoken for. Bessie was in business.

Unfortunately, Magnolia Manor was not what you'd call a major money-making affair, since most of Bessie's renters were not well fixed. Miss Rogers earned a few dollars a week as Darling's librarian. Leticia Wiggens had a widow's pension from her husband's service in the War Between the States—not much, but at least it was regular. Mrs. Sedalius' son, a prominent Mobile doctor, sent Bessie checks for his mother's room and board, but only after he was reminded twice or three times. Maxine Bechtel owned two rent houses in neighboring Monroeville, but that wasn't regular, either. Recently, one of Maxine's renters had paid her with a bushel of potatoes, the other with a promise. They were still eating mashed potatoes and home fries with Roseanne's good redeye gravy. The promise, everybody agreed, wasn't worth a hill of beans.

If everybody could be just a little patient, however, things might change. Bessie had read in the *Dispatch* that President Roosevelt's secretary of labor, Frances Perkins (a woman, naturally—who else cared two hoots about folks who labored?) was proposing something called "social security" that would provide a pension for every older person in the whole, entire country.

Bessie hadn't been an admirer of FDR when he was first elected. She had voted for him only because she was fed up with Hoover's do-nothing happy talk, and FDR surely couldn't be any worse. She hadn't been in favor of everybody turning in their gold, either. Or of Repeal, which every Darling preacher railed against as the work of the devil. But she was a big fan of Huey P. Long, who had an idea for something like this social security thing. She hoped Congress would get up on its hind feet and pass the bill, the sooner the better.

Today was Monday, and Bessie went into the kitchen where she and Roseanne had just finished putting the breakfast dishes away. Roseanne was cutting up a fat hen for supper. The Magnolia ladies loved her stewed chicken and drop dumplings, which were always fluffy and delicious, especially when they were smothered in chicken gravy.

"That was the sheriff on the phone," Bessie said. "He's coming over in a few minutes. He wants to take a look at Emma Jane's room."

Roseanne cocked her head. "Whyfo' he wants to do that?"

"Beats me," Bessie said, irritated at this interruption in her morning. "Something to do with her death, I guess, although I can't imagine what. Mr. Noonan has already put poor Emma Jane in the hearse and driven her to the funeral parlor." She straightened her shoulders. "After the sheriff leaves, I'm going to the newspaper office. I want to be sure to get the ad for the room into the Friday paper. If you've got a grocery list, Mrs. Hancock can fill it while I'm at the *Dispatch*." Hancock's Groceries was next door to the newspaper.

"There's ten pounds of flour and ten of sugar on that list," Roseanne said, "along with two heads of cabbage and five pounds of apples. You tell Miz Hancock to get Old Zeke to deliver it in his wagon. You don't need to be totin' a heavy load, at your age."

Bessie smiled. She and Roseanne were very nearly the same age. But Roseanne liked to pretend that Bessie was older, and it didn't cost anything to play along, especially since Old Zeke needed the work and she needed his help.

"I'll do it," she said. "Anything else?"

"Yeah." Roseanne sliced a leg off the chicken carcass and tossed it into the big cast iron pot. "Sally-Lou and me'll be takin' Miz Violet out to Big Lil's tonight. Want I should ask Lil for something for you?"

Roseanne always asked Bessie this question when she was planning a visit to the Voodoo Lily, who lived all alone in a weathered shack in Briar Swamp. Well, not *all* alone, exactly, for Big Lil had a black cat with nine toes on each front foot, a three-legged dog, a flock of raucous guineas, and two very large Mulefoot hogs that ran free in the woods all day and slept on the front porch at night. Nobody knew whether these companions were actual animals or spirits dressed up in the form of animals and assigned to guard a woman who lived in a part of Briar Swamp that was considered to be . . . well, magical. Darling folk understood this when they went into the swamp late in the evening, during the threshold hour between bright daylight and pure dark. In that bewitched time, they were apt to feel that nature's ancient alchemy animated every single creature, from the rocks and twigs to the turtles and fish and birds, lending them a special kind of natural magic.

Big Lil herself was certainly magical, although she was less mystical and more pragmatic. Lil liked to see things *done*. People who consulted with her generally reported a striking success, telling their friends and relations that the Voodoo Lily had conjured this or that for them, from good luck in a new business to bad luck for a neighbor who was stealing ripe ears of corn from the garden. This reputation for practical achievement made Big Lil the most respected—and the busiest—of all the conjure women of Cypress County.

But what most folks didn't know (and never fully realized) was that there was a catch. Big Lil's voodoo magic didn't always work the way you expected, for she was the kind of conjure woman who would see that you got what you wanted only if she believed that you were asking for a good thing—good for you and for the other people involved in what you were asking for.

If everything you had in mind was square and right and good, her conjure magic was sure to work. You'd go home satisfied and get more and more satisfied as time went on, knowing that you asked for the right thing, the thing that was fit and proper. But if you were asking for something you shouldn't have or didn't know how to use, or something you could use to hurt somebody who didn't deserve to be hurt, Big Lil's conjure had a magical way of . . . well, running out of magic, like a top that was running out of spin. You wouldn't know it, though. You'd go home congratulating yourself that you'd got Big Lil on your side—that she was helping you get exactly what you asked for—when her intentions were completely otherwise.

So even if you followed her instructions to the letter and put colored candles in the corners of your room and burned the right herbs and anointed your mojo with oil and said the magic words she gave you, you would eventually figure out that things weren't going the way you expected them to go. It might take weeks or months for the light to dawn, and during that time you might or might not have understood that you were asking for the wrong sort of thing, with the wrong dreams and hopes tied to it. You might even have understood that this was the very lesson the Voodoo Lily had in mind for you. So, after all, you got what you needed even when you didn't know what that was.

Of course, if you were still determined on having or doing that unfitting thing, whatever it was, you always had the option of looking up another conjure queen, somebody who didn't care how her mojo was used. And some stubborn folks probably did just that.

Roseanne had been one of Big Lil's regular customers for as long as Bessie had known her. She made it a practice to go once a month, usually on the night of the full moon, when the swamp's natural magic was strongest. Lil charged a quarter for every visit, the same amount you would pay (as she liked to point out) for a ticket to the picture show at the Palace. But she was happiest when you took her a gift, along with your quarter. Roseanne always gave her something out of the garden—roasting ears in season, or tomatoes or a couple of Mason jars of canned peaches.

Roseanne wasn't the only one of Bessie's friends and neighbors who relied on Big Lil for help. Mrs. Carter, across the street, saw her every so often, hoping to cure her husband's gambling habit. (Lil stopped charging her after the third visit.) Mr. Musgrove, from the hardware store, swore by her cream for bad backs. Among the Dahlias, Aunt Hetty Little always visited on the solstices and the equinoxes, when Big Lil hosted a special feast on trestle tables beside the bayou to celebrate the turning of the year's wheel. Roseanne usually went with one of her colored kin, either Sally-Lou or DessaRae. Bessie couldn't remember her taking a white person before.

Frowning, Bessie said, "Why are you taking Violet Sims out to Big Lil's? I'm just . . . well, wondering if that's such a good idea." Violet was a little excitable. Very nice, of course, a hard worker at the Diner and the Telephone Exchange, and a good mother to her adopted child, little Cupcake. But highstrung and maybe a bit impulsive. "What does Myra May think about that?"

"Now, Miz Bessie." Roseanne sliced off a thigh. "You know better'n to ask that. What's between Big Lil an' the one askin' has got to be a secret, or the conjure won't work. When Miz Violet said she had a reason for goin' and asked me would Big Lil help her out, I asked Lil and Lil said yes. All I gotta do is get her there. I don't figger on bein' responsible for anything else."

There was a moment's silence as Roseanne picked up her knife and sliced off the other chicken leg. "I was thinkin', though, that I might could ask for some purification for Miz Emma

Jane's bedroom. That lady was so devilishly perverse in life, her spirit might jes' insist on lingerin' around here for longer than it should." She tossed the leg into the pot. "I could see about gettin' us some goofer dust."

It was a commonly held hoodoo belief that the spirits of the dead could visit their former homes at midnight on any night they chose. But they had to be back in the cemetery at two o'clock sharp or they would be shut out by the watchman and forced to wander until the next midnight. "Goofer dust" was dirt from the cemetery, mixed with different herbs, depending on which conjure queen you got it from. It was said to send the spirit back to his—or in this case *her*—grave as expeditiously as possible.

"That's not a bad idea," Bessie agreed. "A little goofer dust certainly couldn't hurt."

"Couldn't hurt" was what she usually said in a situation like this. And when it came to something that might hinder Emma Jane's spirit wandering unfettered around the house at midnight, Bessie was definitely all for it. That lady had caused more than enough trouble in life; there was no telling what kind of trouble she might get up to now that she was dead—especially if Bessie was successful in finding another boarder to move into her room. It would be just like Emma Jane to object.

And while Bessie herself had never visited Big Lil, she had lived long enough and seen enough strange things come to pass that she didn't discount the conjure queen's abilities—or, for that matter, the whole mysterious business of conjure. As in many things, she had an open mind on the subject.

The doorbell rang and Bessie went to answer it. It was, as she hoped, Sheriff Norris.

"Glad to see you, Sheriff," she said. "Come on in. And I do hope you're going to tell me what in the world is going on."

"Glad to," he said. "When I've got it figured out."

Bessie had known Buddy Norris since she was a young woman and he was their neighborhood paper boy, slinging the *Dispatch* into the azaleas far more often than onto the front porch. He might be a grown man now and wearing a shiny tin star pinned to his shirtfront. But to Bessie, he was still Buddy the paper boy. She had a lot of trouble imagining that somebody who couldn't hit the porch with a newspaper could actually catch a crook.

Which might be why she had been so provoked when he telephoned her just as she was enjoying her coffee this morning, telling her to go look around and see if there was any food in Emma Jane's room. And when Bessie had reported that she had found the remains of a chocolate cake under the bed, he had told her to leave it there and lock the door.

At first, Bessie had scoffed at the idea of food, because every resident of the Manor knew perfectly well that under no circumstance was she allowed to have food in her room. All the ladies were expected to observe this most basic of rules or the whole house would be overrun by battalions of mice and cockroaches. But Emma Jane never saw a rule she couldn't break, so Bessie hadn't been too surprised when she went upstairs and discovered the remains of a chocolate cake in a box under the deathbed.

Of course, Emma Jane Randall was not the first person to die at Magnolia Manor. Several of Bessie's residents had already ended their lives there, dying peaceably of old age. But, aside from the sadness and grief that Bessie and the other ladies felt at the loss of a friend, dealing with the death itself was not a difficult matter.

In most cases, all she had to do was call Doc Roberts (if he wasn't there already), notify the dead lady's nearest and dearest (if they weren't there too—sometimes the bedroom had gotten a bit crowded), and arrange for Lionel Noonan to take the deceased to the funeral parlor. The next day, she and Roseanne would roll up their sleeves and change the bed, clean out the closet and the bureau drawers, and give the floor a good sweeping. Then she could place a "Magnolia Manor room available" ad in the *Dispatch* and wait for the telephone to ring—although now that WDAR was on the air, she was wondering if radio might work even better. Maybe she could arrange with Mildred to advertise it on *The Flour Hour*.

But here was the sheriff, and he was waiting.

"The room's upstairs," she said. "This way."

The sheriff took off his cap and followed her to the stairs. "I hope your ladies weren't too terribly upset by what happened yesterday," he said.

Bessie frowned. The Magnolia ladies were a close group that took comfort in each other, more like sisters than friends. They understood each other's frailties and sympathized with each other's infirmities. They were of the same general age and—for the most part—had the same interests.

After supper, for instance, Mrs. Sedalius and Miss Rogers liked to play mahjong, Leticia Wiggens, Maxine Bechtel, and Roseanne pulled out their needlework, and all of them were avid readers who enjoyed talking about books or having a good political debate. They also had their radio favorites. On Sunday night, they liked to listen to *The Fleischmann's Yeast Hour*. On Saturday night, they enjoyed the *Grand Ol' Opry* and *Lum and Abner*, which featured two Arkansas hillbillies who were regularly fleeced by the crafty Squire Skimp. They listened and laughed and reminded themselves that the real folks who lived in Darling, Alabama, weren't all that different from the fictional folks who lived in Pine Ridge, Arkansas. People everywhere had pretty much the same answers to some of the very same problems, didn't they?

Unfortunately, Emma Jane had shown no interest in the

friendly sisterhood that listened to the radio or played cards or read books. She had a sharp tongue, loved to tattle, and enjoyed trading malicious gossip. In fact, Bessie and Roseanne privately agreed that Emma Jane was a born troublemaker who took a perverse delight in setting people against one another, stirring up bitter animosities and hurting fragile feelings.

Of course, everybody was shocked by Emma Jane's sudden and unexpected death, and nobody would dare to say that she was asking for it. But if they were honest, Bessie suspected that every single one of the Magnolia ladies would have to admit to a feeling of relief. At last, they could get back to the kind and comfortable friendliness that had been their easy way with one another for so long.

In the upstairs hallway, Bessie unlocked the door to Emma Jane's room, stepping aside so the sheriff could go in. "What are you looking for?" she asked.

"Cake," he said.

Bessie sighed. "Under the bed."

He got down on his hands and knees and pulled out a cardboard box. It contained one large slice of chocolate cake, frosted in glossy dark chocolate. "Was there a whole cake in here when this box arrived?" he asked, putting the open box on the bed. "Or just a few slices?"

"I'm afraid I wouldn't know," Bessie said. "I wasn't here when it came."

"I was," Roseanne said, coming into the room with a dust mop in her hand. "It was a great big chocolate cake—big enough for all the ladies, and the card even said it was for ever'body. But when Emma Jane saw whut it was, she clapped her hands an' said it was all hers, ever' crumb of it. Said she loved chocolate better than anything, and nobody was gettin' a bite of it but her." She tut-tutted critically. "No big surprise that lady had a stroke, if'n you ask me. That much chocolate is bound to be bad for a body."

Bessie frowned. "Why didn't you tell me about the cake, Roseanne? You know the ladies aren't supposed to have food in their rooms."

"Cuz the way Miz Emma Jane was talkin', she was gonna make that whole cake disappear before bedtime. Didn't figger to bother you about it."

The sheriff closed the box. "I wonder if you happen to know how the cake arrived—Roseanne, is it?"

"Yessir, Mr. Sheriff." Roseanne frowned. "Excuse me, but how come you askin' 'bout the cake?" She narrowed her eyes. "We ain't talkin' poison here, is we?"

"Poison?" Bessie shuddered. "Roseanne, you put that thought right straight out of your head, you hear? We are *not* talking—"

"I can't answer that question right now," the sheriff said. "But I might be able to figure it out a little faster if somebody will tell me how this box arrived."

Bessie pulled in her breath. "You can't *really* think Emma Jane was poisoned! I don't for a minute believe—"

"What about the box, Roseanne?" the sheriff asked.

"Came in Saturday's mail, while Miz Bessie was out shoppin'." Roseanne pointed her dust mop to a small wicker wastebasket beside the bureau. "Miz Emma Jane grabbed it an' ripped off the wrapping paper an' threw it into that there basket. The cake came with a card, but she threw that in the basket, too. Then she got her a knife an' a fork outa the kitchen an' commenced to stuffin' it down. Said she never could get enough chocolate an' she aimed to eat it all by her own se'f, fast as she could."

"Thank you." The sheriff retrieved some crumpled brown paper and a small white card from the basket. He held it up and read it aloud. "Says 'Dear Emma Jane, I hope you and all the Magnolia ladies enjoy this chocolate-coffee-chicory cake. Love from your cousin, Alice Ann.'"

Bessie was jolted. *From Alice Ann.* If the cake was poisoned— "Alice Ann." The sheriff looked from one to the other, an eyebrow cocked. "That would be Alice Ann Walker? Secretary to Mr. Duffy at the Savings and Trust?"

Bessie nodded slowly. "But I don't think . . ." She faltered, biting her lip. "That is, I honestly can't believe that Alice Ann . . ." Her voice trailed away. Whoever had sent the cake had meant it for *all* of them, not just Emma Jane. Emma Jane's greed had saved them—but it had killed *her.* On the other hand, maybe the cake baker had anticipated Emma Jane's greed and had known that she would insist on keeping it all for herself.

Roseanne tilted her head. "Miz Walker's got a real hard row to hoe, y'know," she said. "Husband who cain't work, three orphaned grandkids, and a house problem."

The sheriff regarded her thoughtfully. "A house problem?"

"The place the Walkers are renting was sold for back taxes," Bessie said.

"Mr. Bixler bought it," Roseanne said. "He intends on tearing the house down, so the Walkers gotta find someplace else to live."

"Tough spot." The sheriff glanced down at the card in his hand. "So Miz Walker and Miz Randall were cousins. They got along pretty well, did they?"

"Yes, they *did.*" Bessie was glad she could say something positive, so she emphasized it. "The last time Alice Ann was here, they sat outside with a pitcher of lemonade and had a pleasant conversation." She stepped to the window and pointed. "Right out there at the picnic table."

The sheriff cleared his throat. "Did Miz Randall ever tell you who was getting her money?"

"Her *money?*" Bessie turned, startled by the sheriff's question.

"I don't suppose she had any to speak of. But if she had anything, I expect it will go to her brother. George Clemens is his name, over on Jeff Davis Street. I called him last night to tell him his sister had died. He sent Mr. Noonan over to take the body to the funeral home early this morning."

"About money." Roseanne was shifting from one foot to the other. Finally, she said, "Well, I did happen to overhear . . ."

"Overhear?" Bessie said. She didn't like it when her ladies—

"Overhear what?" the sheriff prompted. "Come on, Roseanne. Spill the beans."

"Yessir. Well, the kitchen window looks out on that picnic table, y'see. The day the two of them was sittin' out there was a real nice day and the window was open. I was washin' dishes at the sink an' I overheard—"

"You listened in on their conversation," Bessie said reprovingly. "Roseanne, you know that's not—"

"I couldn't he'p it, now, could I?" Roseanne lifted her chin. "You know how that old lady was, Miz Bessie. She talked *loud*." She turned back to the sheriff. "I heard Miz Randall say she was cuttin' her brother out of her will 'cuz she was mad at him an' that girl of his. She said she was leavin' it all to Miz Walker."

"All of it?" Bessie asked weakly. She could see exactly where this was going.

"The whole kit-and-kaboodle."

"Interesting," the sheriff said thoughtfully. "Did it seem like Miz Walker already knew about this?"

Roseanne shook her head forcefully. "No, *sir*. It seemed like it was a great big surprise to her. She stammered around with this an' that an' fin'lly asked what about the brother. Said she didn't think it was a real good idea to skip Mr. Clemens in favor of somebody so far up the fam'ly tree. Out on a limb, like. He'd be upset. There'd be talk."

"And what did Miz Randall say to that?" the sheriff asked.

"That she didn't give a rip if there was talk." Roseanne flashed white teeth. "That it was none of nobody's gol-durned business who she left her property to, an' if Alice Ann couldn't find it in her heart to be grateful for the nice big house an' the money she was gettin', she might oughtta look around for somebody who'd show a little more 'preciation."

"The nice big house?" the sheriff repeated, turning it into a question. "What house?"

"If there is a house," Bessie allowed, "it must be in Birmingham. That's where she was living before she came to Darling."

Bessie wasn't sure about a house. There might be one, or it might have been only a fictional carrot that Emma Jane was dangling in front of Alice Ann's unsuspecting nose. But she *did* know that Emma Jane Randall had been a terrible bully—a bully in skirts, but a bully just the same—so she wasn't surprised to hear Roseanne's tale.

"Thank you, ladies." The sheriff put the card on top of the wrapping paper and the cake box. "Now, if you'll leave, I'll get to work."

"Work?" Bessie asked. "Aren't we finished?"

"You are." He brandished an official-looking document. "But I need to search this room. I have a warrant."

Bessie took it, saw Judge McHenry's signature, and handed it back. "Don't you go making a mess," she said, thinking of the way those azaleas had suffered.

"Yes, ma'am," the sheriff replied. "I'll try not to."

There was a twinkle in his eye, and she wondered if he was remembering the azaleas, too.

# CHAPTER SEVEN

# HOBART MOONEY
# INTRODUCES HIMSELF

IF YOU'RE LOOKING FOR THE SHERIFF'S OFFICE IN DARLING, you'll find it in the old Crumpler house behind Snow's Farm Supply, near the courthouse square. The four-room house belonged to Miss Josephine Crumpler and her cat until the bank foreclosed. Miss Crumpler moved to Nashville to live with her niece. The cat, an elderly, battle-scarred black tom with a firecracker temper, refused to be displaced from the home where he had spent eight of his nine lives. The bank, which had more foreclosed property than it could shake a stick at, gave the house and the cat to Cypress County. The county gave both to the sheriff and his deputy, Wayne Springer.

Sheriff Norris wasn't fond of the cat but he liked the house. It was right next door to the jail, which was upstairs on the second floor of Snow's Farm Supply. He and his deputy, Wayne Springer, could keep an eye on their prisoners, when they had any. The lockup was usually full on Sundays, when the town drunks were sleeping off their Saturday night indulgence.

Indoors, things had worked out pretty well, too. The sheriff put a desk and some shelves in what used to be Miss Crumpler's front bedroom, which is why it had pink and green honeysuckle wallpaper until the previous week, when he got around to painting the walls and ceiling with some light blue paint Marvin Musgrove sold him at half price. The former parlor had a big Warm Morning stove that kept the four rooms halfway warm in winter and a motley collection of straight-back chairs for people to sit in while they waited. The old dining room served as an office and workroom for Wayne.

As for the kitchen, Buddy told Wayne he could keep food in the icebox, cook on Mrs. Crumpler's old woodstove, and sleep on a cot in the pantry. Wayne liked this arrangement because it saved him the seven-fifty a week he would have to fork over to Mrs. Beedle to rent one of her upstairs rooms. Buddy liked it because Wayne was handy to answer the telephone at all hours and get up and go to the door if somebody pounded on it, looking for the sheriff in the middle of the night. The county commissioners liked it because they could tell the taxpayers that the Cypress County sheriff's office was professionally staffed around the clock. It made them look good.

Wayne Springer had been an unexpectedly good hire, and Buddy liked to think of him as his secret weapon. Springer was around thirty-five, dark-haired, rangy, lean and all muscle. He likely had some Cherokee blood—witness his high cheekbones and bronzed skin. He was an excellent stalker and could follow a trail through the woods every bit as well as Otis Teeger's pair of prize-winning bloodhounds. Buddy had hired Wayne away from Birmingham, where he'd had five years of law enforcement experience and earned a reputation for being able to hit anything he fired at with his .38 Special, even if it was moving fast. Buddy liked it that Wayne didn't treat him as his boss, which was good because Buddy didn't *feel* like his boss. Wayne was obviously a lawman through and through, while there were whole days when Buddy didn't feel like a real sheriff for even one minute.

The only troubling thing—and the thing Buddy still hadn't figured out—was why an experienced lawman like Wayne had been willing to give up the decent money he was earning in Birmingham to come to Darling and work for peanuts. Buddy had probed a time or two, but Wayne wasn't inclined to respond. And every time Buddy got to wondering about it, he made himself quit. Folks had a right to their secrets. He probably didn't want to know, anyway.

And if he was wanting to puzzle over something, he could puzzle over that piece of chocolate cake he had just dropped off at Doc Roberts' office, for Mr. Noonan to take to that doctor in Monroeville, along with Emma Jane Randall's corpse. *Nicotine poison?* What the hell was that? Something you made from cigarette butts? Something you could catch, like a cold, from cigarettes or chewing tobacco? Like every kid he knew, Buddy had stolen his dad's Luckies and smoked them when he was fifteen or sixteen. Was *he* likely to die from nicotine poisoning?

Back at the office, Buddy was glad to find the waiting room empty and everything quiet. He poured himself a mug of coffee from the pot that sat on the back of the kitchen range and carried it to the workroom, where Wayne was reading a copy of *True Detective*, his boots propped up on the table. The black tomcat—nobody knew what Mrs. Crumpler called him, but Buddy and Wayne called him the Beast—was sitting on the windowsill, flicking the tip of his tail in a malevolent way.

Wayne looked up from his magazine. "Josiah Parrish and me got a rope on Ruby just as after she got through the fence into Mrs. Adcock's garden."

"That's good," Buddy said. "Is this the second or third time?"

"Third. Mrs. Adcock heard about it on the radio and looked out her window and there was Ruby, big as life, with her snout under the wire. And on my way back here, Clarence Paley flagged me down. Said another naked yellow-haired lady climbed through his window last night and jumped into bed with him—a different one this time." He grinned. "Said she plumb wore him out."

Buddy nodded. This was Clarence's favorite fantasy, which he repeated a couple of times a year. "What did you do?"

"Told him I was real sorry I missed another chance. Wouldn't want to let an opportunity like that get past me again. So I looked around to see if I could find her."

"I guess you didn't," Buddy said. He'd looked, too, the first time Clarence called about the naked lady. It had been winter then, and Clarence was worried about her getting cold.

Wayne grunted. "Would I be sittin' here if I did?" The Beast jumped from the windowsill to the table and began to wash his paw.

Buddy put the empty cake box and the wrapping paper and note from Emma Jane Randall's room in front of Wayne. "What's nicotine poison?"

"Tobacco juice. Extracted, concentrated, used to kill bugs on plants. Poisonous as sin, or so it says on the label, which I reckon is true." He gave Buddy an inquiring look. "Don't you ever read the newspapers?"

"Well . . ." Buddy said. "Sometimes." He leaned against the doorframe, taking a sip of coffee and grimacing at the taste. He really ought to tell Wayne to stop making it so strong. It jolted him as hard as the time he shocked himself on the electric fan. "Not that often, I guess."

Truth be told, newspapers weren't his favorite things. If you had to read, westerns were better, especially if you could find one by Zane Grey or Max Brand. In his younger years, Buddy had dreamed of being a cowboy and still did, sometimes, when being sheriff of Darling began to seem like too hard a job. But he wasn't interested in being a cowboy who carried a gun and shot up the saloon on a Saturday night. He'd rather be the kind who had a guitar and rode out all alone on the open range, where the deer and the antelope played. The kind who always got the girl at the end, like that movie cowboy, Gene Autry.

Wayne put down his magazine and swung his feet onto the floor. "Well, maybe you read about that guy out in Napa Valley a couple of years ago. Killed himself by drinking the stuff they were using to spray the orange trees for bugs. Black Leaf Forty, it's called. Nicotine poison. He wasn't the first and he won't be the last, neither. Every now and then, some kid finds a can of it and drinks some. Pretty deadly stuff." He frowned. "How come you're asking?"

"Because," Buddy said, and told him about Emma Jane Randall. Then, since he remembered that Wayne had been out helping Josiah Parrish get a rope on Ruby when the anonymous telephone call came in, he told him about that and about his subsequent conversations with Myra May, Doc Roberts, and Mr. Moseley. And about the maybe-poisoned chocolate cake he had found when he searched the bedroom at the Manor— the cake that had been sent to Miz Randall with love by Alice Ann Walker, who (according to Roseanne) knew that she was going to inherit the old lady's property, which included a house in Birmingham.

Alice Ann Walker. Buddy repeated the name to himself. Now that he had time to think about it, hadn't there been some bad business at the bank a couple of years ago, involving Alice Ann Walker? He was pretty sure he remembered something.

A man of few words, Wayne got straight to the heart of the matter. "So you figure this Walker woman put bug poison in the old lady's cake because she knew she was due to inherit and hoped to hurry the money along a little?"

Buddy didn't much like the sound of that, but he had to agree. "It's possible. Of course, all we have is the housekeeper's word for it. Maybe Roseanne heard right and maybe she didn't."

He paused and added, half to himself. "Or maybe she lied and maybe she didn't." Come to think of it, Roseanne had popped up with that bit of information pretty quick-like, hadn't she? Maybe she—

"Huh," Wayne said skeptically. "You're thinking that maybe *she* did it? The housekeeper? Or maybe she was covering for Miz Bloodworth?"

Put like that, Buddy saw the hole in the logic. "It would've been a little hard for anybody to bake a cake in that house without somebody else noticing it. And anyway, it came in the mail." Buddy pointed at the wrapping on the table. "I thought it might be a good idea if you'd dust the paper and the box for fingerprints." Wayne knew how to do that. "Then I'll take the wrapping over to Mr. Thorpe at the post office and ask if he remembers who might've sent it."

Wayne bent over the wrapping paper. "Postmark says it was mailed from Monroeville."

"Oh." Buddy felt deflated. "Well, I can drive over there. I might need to talk to the doc, anyway."

"What about the will?" Wayne straightened. "Did you find one in the old lady's room?"

Buddy shook his head. "I ran a fine-toothed comb through that place. Nothing but letters and snapshots and stuff. No will."

The telephone rang and Wayne picked it up. "Sheriff's office," he said shortly. He listened a moment. "He's right here. Hold on." He handed the candlestick phone to Buddy. "Moseley's secretary. Asking for you." He sat back down and the Beast jumped from the table to his lap.

"Hey, Liz," Buddy said. He liked talking to Liz Lacy on the phone. She had a warm voice and was always pleasant. In fact, there was a time a few years ago when he would have asked her for a date if she hadn't been all tied up with Grady Alexander.

And then he'd met Bettina Higgens and they'd started seeing each other.

Liz usually got right down to the reason she was calling. That's what she did now.

"Hello, Sheriff," she said. "I'm phoning at the request of Mr. Moseley. Remember this morning when he told me to find out who Mrs. Randall named as her beneficiaries? Well, I phoned around and found out that Harold Parsons had drawn up a recent will for her, so I went over to his office to have a look." She cleared her throat. "The will names Alice Ann Walker as the beneficiary—and executor."

"Right," Buddy said.

There was a moment's silence. Then Liz said, "I was surprised to learn that, Buddy. Why aren't you?"

"Because Bessie Bloodworth's housekeeper overheard Miz Randall telling Miz Walker that she was going to inherit. Apparently, Miz Walker is some sort of cousin." He frowned, thinking about the overheard conversation. "Miz Randall said she intended on giving Miz Walker a house. Anything about that in the will?"

"The house is in Birmingham, where Mrs. Randall lived. Mr. Parsons thought it was a rather nice house in a good neighborhood. He didn't know the details, but he said that Mrs. Randall and her brother got into a disagreement—that's why Mrs. Randall went to live at the Manor. She originally intended to leave everything to her brother, but just two weeks ago, she made a new will, naming Alice Ann Walker. In addition to the house, there is some money on deposit at the Darling bank—several thousand dollars, Mr. Parsons thought."

*Several thousand dollars!* Buddy raised an eyebrow. That was a tidy little fortune. And it was in an account at the bank where Walker worked, so she would likely know exactly how much there was at any time she cared to have a look. Tempting, wasn't it?

"Miz Walker," he said thoughtfully. "You know her pretty well?"

Buddy already knew the answer to that, of course. Darling was a small town. Everybody who was anybody knew everything worth knowing about everybody else. And Liz Lacy had worked for Mr. Moseley for quite some time, which made her an important *anybody*. She knew most of the people in Darling.

"Alice Ann belongs to our garden club." Liz's tone was unusually guarded. "So yes, I know her. Quite well, I'd say."

"Garden club," Buddy said. It was obvious that Liz was a friend of Alice Ann Walker, which might make it difficult for her to be objective. She wasn't to blame for that, though, he reminded himself. It wouldn't be the first time somebody's feelings of friendship or affection or whatever got in the way of a more sober judgment. That was just human nature, pure and simple. But there was more.

"Garden club," he said again. "Do you think she might have a use for . . ." He paused and looked questioningly at Wayne, who mouthed something in response. "For Black Leaf Forty?"

"I suppose," Liz said. "I've used it on my roses once or twice. I'm sure that many other gardeners have used it, too." She paused. "Why are you asking?"

He didn't answer. "Word I heard was that the Walkers are about to get kicked out of their house, which has been sold in a tax sale and is likely to be torn down. You know about that?"

Liz hesitated. "Well, yes," she said reluctantly. "It's as you say. There's been a tax sale. The Walkers are looking for somewhere else to live."

"I also heard that Miz Randall accused Miz Walker of not being as grateful as she should for that house she'd be getting when the old lady kicked off. Miz Randall was upset about that. She threatened to give it all to somebody else."

"Alice Ann, *ungrateful*?" Liz exclaimed. "That doesn't sound like her at all. I'm sure she would have appreciated any help Mrs. Randall might be willing to offer." A defensive edge came into her voice. "I hope you're not thinking that she might have—"

"And back when Roy Burns was sheriff, wasn't there something about Alice Ann Walker and a chunk of money missing at the bank? Unless I misremember, her and her husband are always real hard up, even though she's got a decent job. Lost a leg on the railroad, didn't he? And now they've got some grandkids living with them?"*

"That's right." The defensive edge was clearer. "But if you'll recall, Sheriff Burns investigated and found that Alice Ann had absolutely nothing to do with that missing money. I'm sure that if there is any . . ." Liz paused and seemed to collect herself. She went on, in a steadier voice. "If there is a crime here, I'm certain you'll get to the bottom of it, Sheriff."

"I'll do what needs to be done," Buddy said in a reassuring tone that hid the ambivalence he felt. Liz could defend her friend all she liked, but that didn't change the facts, of which there were plenty. Incriminating facts, at that. Alice Ann Walker was the number one suspect in what was looking more and more like murder. A real sheriff wouldn't have a problem dealing with something like that.

There was a moment's silence, then Liz asked, "Have you learned anything more from the Exchange about who that anonymous caller might have been?"

"Nope. I need to give Myra May a call, soon as we hang up. You can tell Mr. Moseley that Wayne is dusting the box the cake came in for fingerprints. Same with the wrapping paper. I think the chances of finding prints may be pretty good. The box was mailed from the Monroeville post office. I figure on

---

* You'll find the story of the missing money and more in the first book in this series, *The Darling Dahlias and the Cucumber Tree*.

asking the postmaster over there if he has any recollection of who might have sent it." He paused. "Anything else?"

"Well, yes, there is." She sounded hesitant. "I'm not one to look for trouble before trouble comes around, but I wonder if you know . . ." Her voice trailed off uncertainly.

"Know what?"

He heard her take a breath. "Know that Mickey LeDoux is back in town."

"*What?*" Buddy's mouth felt suddenly dry. "But he's not due to get out of prison for a couple of months." To reassure himself, he threw a quick glance at the Snow's Farm Supply calendar on the wall. Yep, this was still May. "He doesn't get out until August, in fact," he added. "Happen to know that it's August twentieth."

But Buddy didn't just *happen* to know the date of Mickey's release. He knew it because he had been Sheriff Roy Burns' deputy when Chester P. Kinnard and his team of crack revenue agents busted Mickey's whiskey still out on Dead Cow Creek and shot and killed Mickey's little brother Rider, who was just fifteen, not even old enough to shave. Roy Burns had been in charge of the raid along with Kinnard, and Buddy had been just a deputy, but he still felt responsible. Everybody involved admitted that Rider's death was a bad thing to have happened and said they wished it hadn't. Mickey, however, had taken it personally and to heart. He had vowed up and down and sideways to avenge his kid brother's killing when he got out of prison, and Buddy had no doubt that he meant every word of what he said. That's why he knew the date. He was not looking forward to the twentieth of August.

"I'm afraid it *is* possible," Liz said quietly. "I happened to look out of the window a little while ago and saw him walking across the street toward the courthouse. It was definitely Mickey LeDoux, Buddy. I believe he had just come out of the

Dispatch office. You might ask Charlie Dickens if he's talked to him."

Buddy felt his stomach muscles knot up. "I'll do that, Liz. Thanks for filling me in. I 'preciate it."

"Just . . . be careful," she said. "You know how Mickey is."

"I know," Buddy said, and replaced the receiver.

"Mickey LeDoux?" Wayne asked.

"Sounds like it might be," Buddy said thinly. "Or might not."

"Sounds like trouble," Wayne said. He hadn't been around Darling when Rider LeDoux was killed, but when guys got together over at Pete's Pool Parlor or over a beer at the Cotton Gin Roadhouse, they talked about Mickey and his exploits and lamented the destruction of his still and the death of his little brother. He would've heard the whole sorry tale more than once.

"If it is him, it's an early release, most like." Buddy half turned away. He didn't want Wayne to see how bothered he was. But in this case, even a real sheriff was likely to be afraid—wasn't he?

"So what's the next step?" Wayne asked. "With LeDoux, I mean."

"No next step." Buddy avoided Wayne's glance. "No law against a man coming back to his old hometown, I reckon."

"But you know what he means to—"

"No, I don't," Buddy snapped. "I can't read the man's mind." Whatever it was that Mickey intended, he wouldn't know until it happened, and then he'd have to deal with it, one way or the other. His throat felt tight. "Let it go, Wayne. Okay?"

Wayne shrugged. "Whatever you say, boss. So—"

"And don't call me boss!"

"Whatever you say, Buddy." Wayne smiled. "So what about this other thing? This poisoning, if that's what we've got?"

"I'll see if Myra May has any news," Buddy replied, reaching for the phone again. "Then we'll just sit tight until we hear from that doc in Monroeville. Depending on what we find out, I'll have a little talk with Miz Walker. And I'll ask you to do some investigating. It'd be good to know just how bad off the Walkers are. Like, who do they owe and for what."

Wayne picked up his magazine and swung his boots onto the table again. "We're talkin' motive here, I reckon. Folks needin' money." Jostled out of a nap, the Beast jumped from his lap to the floor, glared at the both of them, and stalked out of the room, tail held high.

Buddy nodded, thinking of the difficulties confronting a woman who was the sole support of a disabled husband and grandchildren and who had to find another house to live in because they were losing theirs in a tax sale. With a sigh, he agreed.

"We're talkin' motive." He reached for the phone.

But Myra May had no information for him. "I couldn't reach Opal. Her mom says she drove over to Monroeville to the dentist. I'll try again later. But I gotta tell you, Sheriff, the girls are *not* supposed to listen in. I sincerely hope she didn't."

He thanked her and hung up. "Ironic, isn't it?" he said to Wayne. "Most of the time, I have to tell the switchboard girls to butt out of my telephone calls. But this is one case when I wish—"

"Yo, fellas," a male voice said. "Which one of you is the sheriff?"

Buddy turned. A stranger had come into the waiting room— the same man he'd seen at the Diner's back corner table this morning and once or twice the week before. He had heard from Marvin Musgrove over at the hardware store that the man had been hanging around town for a couple of days, asking about this and that and the other thing—seemed pretty nosy, Marvin said. He also said that the stranger had told the desk clerk at the Old Alabama Hotel that he was down from Montgomery on "state business."

"What kind of business is that, I'd like to know," Marvin had said, and Buddy agreed.

But where most state guys were gray and nondescript, this fellow was a snazzy dresser. His shoes looked like they were spit-polished every morning, his suit was brushed and pressed, and he wore a snap-brim hat that made him look like James Cagney in *Public Enemy*. In fact, Buddy thought, the stranger looked a lot like Cagney, who had played an Irish gang member in that movie. All he needed was a grapefruit.

"I'm Sheriff Norris," Buddy said, straightening up. "What can I do for you?"

The man put his hand into his pocket. But instead of a coin he pulled out what looked like a badge wallet. "You can assist me in conducting a criminal investigation."

"Investigation?" Buddy scowled. "Who the devil are you? This is *my* town. You can't conduct a 'criminal investigation' here unless *I* say so." He didn't know if that was true or not. But he was going to lay down the law first—*his* law. They could negotiate later.

"My name is Hobart Mooney." The man flipped the badge wallet open and held it up. "I am a field agent for the Alabama Tax Commission. I'm here to investigate criminal violations of the tax stamp regulations."

Buddy grunted. The Alabama Tax Commission collected liquor and cigarette taxes. He knew what it was, vaguely, but he'd never had dealings with its agents. They were usually after the moonshiners, and they didn't bother with the local sheriff. They came with the federal revenue agent, Chester P. Kinnard. And it was never pretty.

Showing his teeth in a mirthless smile, Mooney closed his badge wallet with a snap. "Let's get down to brass tacks, Sheriff.

My investigation is nearly finished and I'm about ready to make an arrest. Glad to have you tag along, but if you're too busy, no sweat. I can handle it all by myself." He drawled out the last three words, as if that was what he was hoping.

"Oh, yeah?" Buddy wrinkled his nose. What was that smell? Burma-Shave? "And just who are you aiming to arrest?"

"His name is Dickens. Charles Dickens. I'm sure you know him."

"Charlie?" Buddy asked incredulously. "Why, of course I know him. He's the editor of our newspaper. What's he done?"

"What's he *done?*" Mooney chuckled dryly. "How about if you and me sit down for an hour or two, Sheriff, and I'll tell you."

# CHAPTER EIGHT

# LIZZY MAKES A CALL

IN THE LAW OFFICES OF MOSELEY AND MOSELEY, LIZZY put down the phone and returned to her work with a distinct feeling of uneasiness. She had known Buddy Norris since their school days and admired his dedication to the job of sheriff. Unlike his predecessor, who had been dedicated to lining his personal pockets at the expense of Cypress County, Buddy was an honest lawman who was conscientious about getting things right.

In this case, though, Lizzy was convinced that he was headed in the wrong direction—although she had to admit that he had some pretty compelling reasons for going that way. It was true that the Walkers, even more than most Darlingians, were in urgent need of cash in their pockets and a roof over their heads. What's more, it appeared that Alice Ann was in line to inherit Mrs. Randall's house and the money in her account at the Savings and Trust. If the old lady really *had* been poisoned, Buddy couldn't be blamed for putting Alice Ann at the top of his suspect list.

And although Lizzy had just tried to defend her friend to the sheriff, she had to admit that the situation was distinctly troubling. Of course, everyone admired Alice Ann for shouldering the role of breadwinner and the care of her disabled husband and their orphaned grandchildren. She did what had to be done and never uttered a word of complaint about it. But Lizzy—a careful observer of human nature—understood that her friend wasn't always what she seemed. Alice Ann was a woman who knew exactly what she needed and what it took to get it. If she couldn't manage to get it one way, she would try another, all the while appearing to simply sit and wait, sweetly smiling and gentle as could be.

Of course, many Southern women had perfected the subtle arts of secret manipulation. They often had to deal with husbands and fathers and even mothers who seemed determined to thwart them. Lizzy had had to learn some of these skills for herself, for her mother believed to this day that she was not carrying out her full maternal responsibilities if she failed to instruct "her Elizabeth" in managing all the aspects of her life, from what gloves to wear to what romantic goals she should pursue. Lizzy felt that it was to her credit that she usually got around her mother in a nice way, without confrontation.

And it was definitely true that many Darling women were like Alice Ann. They learned early in their lives how to charm, delight, amuse, enchant, and (yes) ensnare—all the while adroitly appearing to be doing nothing at all. Some might view this kind of behavior as underhanded and discreditable or worse, and perhaps it was. It was certainly a subterranean talent that went out of its way not to call attention to itself.

But Lizzy didn't quite see it as reprehensible. Long ago, she had heard the term "steel magnolia" used to describe a Southern woman who smelled like a flower garden, smiled sweetly, and looked like a good wind might blow her petals away—but who was deeply rooted in her principles and carried out her responsibilities without making a big, noisy fuss about it.

That, in Lizzy's considered opinion, was Alice Ann Walker.

A steel magnolia who did what she had to do to support her family.

And for a small, slight woman with mouse-colored hair, a soft expression, and an air of anxious agreeableness, Alice Ann was certainly much shrewder and stronger than she seemed to be. Which of course (Lizzy added hastily to herself) did *not* mean that she had poisoned the woman from whom she was about to inherit a house and a sizeable chunk of money. Even though it might look that way.

*Even though it might look that way.*

Lizzy frowned. If Alice Ann wasn't responsible for Mrs. Randall's death, why did it look that way? Was somebody else making a deliberate effort to *make* it look that way? If so, who? Somebody at the Manor? Somebody in Darling? Or maybe over in Monroeville? Buddy had said that the cake was mailed from there.

But these questions were more complicated than Lizzy had time to untangle right now. She sat down at her desk and pulled out Mr. Moseley's billing ledger. Today was her usual half-day in the office. She planned to spend the afternoon at home, writing her Garden Gate column—on the plants in the Dahlias' magic garden—for the next issue of the *Dispatch*.

And on the way home, she would call on Mr. Clemens and tell him how sorry she was that his sister had died—and try to find out, if she could do it without raising questions, why Emma Jane had written her brother out of her will. She didn't ask herself if this kind of snooping was devious or underhanded. And if you asked her whether *she* was a steel magnolia, she would probably just smile and shake her head at your silly question.

She opened the ledger to the monthly page, picked up the first invoice form, and rolled it into her typewriter. Plenty of people owed Mr. Moseley. He wasn't likely to get it all in cash, even though the office could certainly use cash. Last month, her billing had brought in a bushel of early peas, three gallons of home-canned dill pickles, a couple of bottles of Bodeen Pyle's moonshine, and three hens and a rooster. The hens now resided in Ophelia Snow's backyard, traded for three hours of office help.

The rooster, Ophelia said, had made a starring appearance on the Snows' dinner table.

FOR YEARS, LIZZY HAD DREAMED OF BUYING A CAR LIKE VERNA'S red LaSalle convertible roadster. An automobile seemed to promise the freedom she craved to get away from her mother. Resisting her mother's efforts could be exhausting, and there were days when Lizzy dreamed of simply escaping—driving alone, fast and far, with the wind in her hair, the sun on her face, and no one to tell her which road to take or when to go home.

But instead of using her savings to buy a car, Lizzy had bought a house. True, it wasn't much bigger than a doll's house and it was just across the street from her mother, barely big enough for her and her cat and certainly not far enough away to declare a radical and permanent independence.

But Lizzy loved the neighborhood where she had grown up and didn't want to leave it. Moving across the street allowed her to stay connected with her mother, while buying her very own house (and not telling her mother until the day she moved in) had been her way of insisting on a separation. And ironically, Lizzy's declaration of independence might also have freed her mother, for it wasn't long before—surprise!—Mrs. Lacy married Mr. Dunlap, who owned the dime store on the courthouse square. From what Lizzy could see, the newly-marrieds seemed perfectly happy. And while her mother still considered it her duty to manage her daughter's affairs, she didn't have as much time as she used to, so it happened far less frequently.*

Sometimes Lizzy rode her bicycle to the office, which was just a block south on Jeff Davis and two blocks west on Franklin—a ten-minute ride from her house. But she preferred walking, especially in the spring. Darling's houses might be small and in need of new paint or roof shingles, but every yard was bright with spring flowers. Mr. Wilson's gorgeous rhododendrons and azaleas had been covered for several weeks with clouds of blossoms, from pure white to a deep vibrant red. Mrs. Tomlin's yellow Lady Banks rose draped itself luxuriantly across the front porch roof. Next door, the Andrews' early roses cast a delicate fragrance that wafted out to the sidewalk, while on the other side of the street, Mrs. Langley's irises bloomed in all colors of the rainbow and her tulips were like polished jewels. Lizzy loved gardens, and the walk was a garden-lover's delight.

For Lizzy, though, the most uncomfortable part of the walk was the house where Grady Alexander lived with his little boy, Grady Junior. Liz and Grady had been all-but-engaged when Grady told her he had to marry Sandra Mann. That had been hurtful enough, but then the newlyweds had moved into the old Harrison house just down the block from Lizzy's, and she had to pass it twice a day on her way to and from the office. She could see Sandra's tidy flower beds in the front yard and the baby's diapers on the backyard clothesline and the wooden baby swing that Grady had made and hung in the old oak tree out front—all of it evidence of a happy marriage.

But Sandra had tragically died and after a decent interval, Grady had come knocking on Lizzy's door, asking to see her

---

* Read *The Darling Dahlias and the Naked Ladies* (for the story of the house) and *The Darling Dahlias and the Unlucky Clover* (for Mrs. Lacy's surprising remarriage).

again. She had told him no, but perhaps not firmly enough, because Grady still persisted. And even though she knew that *no* was the right answer—and she *had* said no—she couldn't help wondering what kind of a life she would have had if they had married. *Until death do you part*, the marriage ceremony said, and Liz was romantic enough to hold that promise in her heart. Would she and Grady have lived in that very house until they were old? Until they died?

Today, though, she was intent on making a call on Mr. Clemens, who lived just down the street from her mother's house and cattycornered from Lizzy's own yellow cottage. As far back as she could remember, the little house—home to Mr. and Mrs. Clemens and their daughter Zelda—had been the most ramshackle and untidy of all the houses on the street. It still was. The weathered gray siding hadn't been painted, a board was missing from the front porch steps, and the screen on the front door was ripped where the cat had clawed it.

But there were roses in the front yard. And did Mr. Clemens still have those wonderfully fragrant peach trees in the back? Lizzy remembered herself at eight, standing in the alley, wishing wistfully that Zelda, a pretty flame-haired teenager then, would come outside and toss a peach across the fence. Or that a peach would fall off the tree right in front of her, so she could snatch it and dash away before Mr. Clemens came storming out of the back door, fist in the air, yelling. He had a temper, and he could run faster than she could. Faster than any of the neighborhood kids, whom he regarded as a nuisance.

But the man who answered her knock at the door was no longer in any shape to chase children down the alley. Dressed in baggy bib overalls, he wore a closely clipped gray beard and leaned heavily on a carved wooden walking stick. He couldn't be more than sixty-five, Lizzy thought, but he looked older.

He smiled when he saw her, showing tobacco-stained teeth.

"Why, it's little Miss Liz, who used to live next door. Haven't seen you in donkey's years, girl. Come in and sit a spell, won't you?"

"Who is it, Papa?" a woman's voice called from the back of the house. A radio playing a jazzy chorus of "We're in the Money" was abruptly turned off and the voice repeated, "Who is it, Papa? Who are you talking to?"

"It's little Liz Lacy," Mr. Clemens said loudly, as Lizzy followed him into the small parlor. It was crowded with a sagging sofa, a cane-bottomed rocking chair, and a black parlor stove with a blue-black stovepipe elbowing out of the wall near the ceiling. A colorful crocheted granny afghan was thrown over the back of the sofa, hiding its worn spots, and on a rickety table, a bouquet of purple wax violets bloomed under a round glass dome—relics of Mrs. Clemens, dead now for a dozen years. The room smelled of a disagreeable mix of tobacco, sweat, and dirty feet.

An auburn-haired woman in a cotton print dress and apron came into the room, bringing with her the welcome fragrance of freshly baked bread. She was plain-looking, with a receding chin and a square nose in a face lined with worry wrinkles. Recognizing her, Lizzy was startled. She had to be in her early forties, but her red hair had faded, her face was gray, and her shoulders were stooped. She looked like a tired old woman.

Mr. Clemens said, "You remember my girl Zelda?" Before Lizzy could say "Of course," he added, with an old man's casual cruelty, "Lost her job up there in Chicago and couldn't find another. Too plain to get herself a husband, so she's moved back home to take care of her old dad." He sat down in the rocking chair, both hands clasped on the top of his walking stick, which was encircled by a realistic-looking carved wooden snake.

Zelda had lost her job? Lizzy gave her a sympathetic look. "I'm sorry to hear that," she said, but it wasn't surprising. The

Depression bit deep into everyone's lives, making it hard to find work and harder still to keep it, especially in the cities where there were hundreds of applicants clamoring for every job, for *any* job. But the remark about not getting a husband was especially mean. What was Mr. Clemens thinking? Lizzy had known Zelda only slightly, because the older girl seemed to spend most of her time indoors. What's more, she had left home when Liz was still in grade school and—until now—hadn't come back, not even for a visit. Lizzy smiled and held out her hand.

"How nice to see you, Zelda. It's been a long time."

Silently, the woman took her hand. Her grip was limp, her glance sidelong, and whatever energy she once had seemed dissolved. She was silent as she sat on the sofa farthest from her father's rocking chair, Lizzy at the end closer to him. As they took their seats, a faint memory flickered like a sputtering candle in Lizzy's mind. An unpleasant memory, and painful. What was it?

But then Mr. Clemens began to talk and it was gone. Feeling chatty, he complained about the neighbors' dog digging up his tomato plants, asked about Lizzy's purchase of the old house, and snickered about her mother's unexpected marriage to Mr. Dunlap.

"Hell's bells," he said, "if I'd've known she was in the market for a man. I would've proposed myself. I could do her better'n that that namby-pamby Dunlap."

Zelda shifted. "Now, Papa," she began nervously, then closed her mouth.

Easing the awkward moment, Lizzy leaned forward. "I just stopped by to tell you how sorry I was to hear about your sister's sudden death, Mr. Clemens. If there's anything I can do to help with the funeral service, please don't hesitate to ask."

"A real shock, it was," Mr. Clemens said. "Happened just

like that. When she was here with me, Emma Jane was fit as a fiddle, and now—" He snapped his fingers. "Now she's gone. Gone. Just like that."

Zelda opened her mouth to say something, but her father glanced at her and shook his head slightly.

"Just like *that*," he repeated. "Like the Good Book says, in the blink of an eye. We never know when the end is comin', do we?"

Not sure where this was going, Lizzy said, "I believe that Bessie Bloodworth told me that Mrs. Randall moved to Darling to live with you. Before she moved to the Manor, I mean."

"That was what we agreed to," Mr. Clemens said. "Emma Jane was rattlin' around in that great big house of hers over in Birmingham. She figured on sellin' it and movin' in here with me. With us." He nodded at Zelda. "That was about the time Zelda came back home. We gave it a try, but it didn't work out. Did it, daughter?"

"No, Papa, it didn't work out," Zelda repeated obediently. To Lizzy, she said, "Aunt Emma Jane had very strong ideas about the way things ought to be managed." She gave the impression of choosing her words carefully. "After a while, she decided she'd be happier at the Manor, where she'd be with people who . . . who were more . . . agreeable." She lapsed into silence, as though she had used up all the words she had available.

Her father snorted. "Emma Jane weren't no Mrs. Agreeable herself, you know. Bossy, just like she always was back when we was kids." He seemed to have forgotten that Lizzy was there. "Didn't like this, couldn't stand that, figured on changing every other little thing to suit the way she expected it. Wanted to be waited on hand and foot, like she was a queen or something." He rapped his cane sharply on the floor. "Wanted Zelda to do everything for her, when my girl was already busy, cookin' and cleanin' and washin' and ironin'. I cooked and baked for m'self for years, but when Zelda came back, she took over, just to give me a rest. She didn't have time to wait on that bossy old lady."

"Papa," Zelda said. "You know I didn't mind doing it, when I could. That was just Aunt Emma Jane's way."

Lizzy shivered. For a moment, she could imagine how Zelda felt to be caught in the middle between a demanding aunt and a difficult father. It must have been awful.

Mr. Clemens scowled. "Well, I suppose." He looked at Lizzy and added, "Not to say that Emma Jane left here on bad terms. It was what you could call mutual. And she liked it over there at the Manor. Told me she had a room that looked out on the garden and somebody to do her cookin' and her laundry. And Zelda visited right often. Didn't you, girl?"

"Once or twice," Zelda said, complying. "I went to see her when I could."

The silence lengthened, awkward and strained. In Lizzy's mind, the memory flickered again, elusive and tantalizing, and was gone. Deciding it was time to leave, she said, "Well, if there's anything I can do to help, you'll let me know, won't you?"

Mr. Clemens put his head on one side, regarding her with narrowed eyes. "There is one thing, since you're here and offerin' . . ." He paused. "Zelda, you go in my bedroom and fetch that envelope on top of my dresser. It's your aunt's will."

Zelda's mouth tightened. "Really, Papa, I don't think you should impose on—"

He thumped his walking stick on the floor, hard. "You do what I tell you, girl," he barked.

Wordlessly, Zelda jumped to her feet and scurried out of the room.

He turned back to Lizzy. "You still workin' for Mr. Moseley, ain't you?" When she nodded, he said, "That's good, then. You tell Moseley I want him to represent me again, like he done last time."

"Represent you in what way?" Lizzy asked.

"My sister left me that house of hers I was tellin' you about, the one over in Birmingham. I want Moseley to find somebody to sell it for me. Times is tough and property ain't movin' fast, so I don't want him to let the grass grow under his feet. I'm the executor of Emma Jane's estate, so Moseley can get on it right away. This week."

Left *him* that house? Lizzy stared at him, uncomfortably remembering the will she had seen in Harold Parsons' office—the most recent will. Mr. Clemens must have a copy of an earlier will and was expecting to inherit. He would be sorely disappointed. But she didn't want to be the one to tell him that.

Evasively, she said, "I think Mr. Moseley would advise you to wait."

"Wait for what?" Mr. Clemens demanded. "What should I wait for?"

Lizzy smiled, remembering the challenge her friends Mildred and Earlynne had Lizzy fumbled for an answer. "Well, for one thing, it will be a few weeks before Mrs. Randall's will can go to probate. Mr. Moseley will probably tell you that the property can't be disposed of until—"

"Lawyers always want to *wait*," Mr. Clemens said, as his daughter came back into the room and handed him a long brown envelope. He held it out to Lizzy. "This here is my copy of Emma Jane's will. Harold Parsons has the original, which has got her signature on it, all right and proper. But ol' Harold and me, we don't get along, so I want Moseley to handle this. You tell him to forget waiting for probate. The sooner he gets that house on the market and sold, the sooner he'll get his fee. Oh, and he might oughtta check at the Savings and Trust. I think Emma Jane had an account over there. Could be some money in it."

Lizzy opened the envelope and took out two folded sheets of paper. The date—early January—was at the top of the first page. The will Parsons had shown her was dated just two weeks ago. She refolded the pages and put them back in the envelope. "You see?" Mr. Clemens said, obviously pleased. "All done right and proper. Witnessed by Miz Walker, the notary in Mr. Duffy's office at the bank."

*Witnessed by Alice Ann?* Lizzy frowned at that, but all she said was, "I'll give this to Mr. Moseley and tell him you'd like to talk to him about it."

They spoke for a few moments more. Then she got up, repeated her condolences and her offer of help, and followed Zelda into the hallway.

At the door, the other woman leaned toward her. "My father's bark is a lot worse than his bite," she said in a low voice. She cast a surreptitious look back over her shoulder. "Please don't bother Mr. Moseley with what he's asking. About putting Aunt Emma Jane's house on the market right away, I mean." Managing a smile, she reached for the envelope Lizzy was holding. "I'll just take that back for now and—"

"Oh, I'm sure it's no trouble," Lizzy said brightly, holding on to the envelope. "Mr. Moseley is always glad to be of help. He'll be in touch with your father as soon as he can."

When it was clear that Liz meant to keep the envelope, Zelda dropped her hand. "Well, then," she said awkwardly, and her shoulders slumped.

Lizzy felt a sudden surge of sympathy for the other woman. It must be very hard, losing your job and having to take care of an aging, irascible old man who ordered his daughter around like a slave. Impulsively, she said, "Do you bake, Zelda? When I came in, I thought I smelled fresh bread."

"I do," Zelda said. Her mouth twisted. "I bake bread. It's about the only thing that gives me pleasure these days."

Lizzy smiled, remembering the challenge her friends Mildred and Earlynne had faced when they opened their bakery.

Aunt Hetty Little had made sure that they learned to bake bread, but Earlynne still hated it. Mildred was too busy with the counter. And now, with their radio show, they could never produce enough.

"The owners of The Flour Shop," she said, "are looking for somebody to help in the kitchen three or four hours a day. Their names are Mildred Kilgore and Earlynne Biddle. They might be very happy to meet someone who enjoys baking bread. Maybe you could drop in and talk to them."

"Oh, what a wonderful idea!" Zelda exclaimed, and broke into her first smile. "I've noticed the shop. I'll go and see them as soon as I can. I'd love to earn my own money again," she added, and some of the worry wrinkles smoothed out of her face. "It would be good to get out of the house. When I moved back to Darling, I was hoping to find a place of my own, near enough to my father to help him when he needed me, but far enough away to—" She took a breath. "My father means well but he's rather old-fashioned and . . . dictatorial at times. Perhaps you can understand."

"I'm afraid I do," Lizzy said ruefully, thinking of her mother.

And as she said goodbye and turned to cross the street toward her cottage, the surge of sympathy she'd felt grew even stronger. Zelda's father obviously dominated her in something like the same way that her mother had dominated her—and still did, even though she had declared her independence.

But the situation had to be worse for Zelda, for she had declared her independence long ago. She had become a mature adult and found the freedom of a life of her own in Chicago, but her father—and probably her aunt, as well—still treated her as if she were a half-grown child. And now she had no alternative but to come back to Darling and live with him. At his age, he was unlikely to change. If anything, his habits and attitudes would have hardened. Her life must be exceptionally difficult.

And then, with such a stunning fierceness that it literally stopped her in her tracks, Lizzy remembered what she had forgotten. Zelda's mother, sobbing on the shoulder of Liz's mother, spilling her pain and anger about what her husband had done to their daughter. Herself, only nine or ten, huddled at the hallway door, listening. The next morning, she had seen Zelda trudging down the street toward the railroad station, head bowed, eyes on the ground, a desolate figure carrying a small cardboard suitcase.

Lizzy had been too young to understand all of what she had overheard that afternoon. But she had understood enough to be horrified. So horrified that she had stuffed the memory far down inside her, where it lurked like a seed in the darkness, bursting out now like a malignant blossom. With a bone-chilling clarity, she understood why Zelda had left her home and gone to Chicago. Why it must be excruciatingly painful to come back.

And why, all those years ago, her mother had commanded her to stay away from Mr. Clemens and never, never, never go into his house.

How could she have forgotten *that*? Was it because it was so . . . painfully unthinkable? And now that she had remembered, should she tell Zelda that she knew? Would it help her to know that someone—a friend—recalled and understood her long-ago pain and would like to help now, however she could?

But perhaps Zelda was still trying to forget what had happened. Perhaps a reminder would be too embarrassing. Or too agonizing.

Lizzy was still thinking about this as she went up on the porch, but at the sight of a neatly wrapped package left by Mr. Wilson, the mailman, she put it on a shelf in the back corner of her mind. The package bore several rows of canceled stamps and—most excitingly!—her literary agent's return address in

New York. She unlocked her front door, snatched up the box, and stepped inside.

For Lizzy, her home was not only a place to escape from her mother but also a refuge from the uncertainties of the Depression, and when she shut the door, she closed out the whole world. The house was tiny, just four rooms and a bathroom, converted from a kitchen pantry. On her left as she came in, a flight of polished wooden stairs led up to two small bedrooms. On the right, a double doorway opened into a parlor just large enough for a fireplace and built-in bookcases, a brown leather sofa, a dark brown corduroy-covered chair, and a lamp with a Tiffany-style stained glass shade. Lizzy knew she had paid too much for the lamp—half a week's salary, seven dollars and fifty cents. But she loved the golden glow it shed on her book as she curled up in the chair to read in the evening. It was special.

She carried the box into the kitchen and put it on the table in the dining nook, eying it eagerly. But lunchtime was long past and she was hungry, so she made a cheese sandwich, poured a glass of milk, and sat down for a quick bite. She was just finishing when Daffodil, her orange tabby cat, came in from the screened-in porch at the back of the house and wrapped himself around her ankles, purring throatily. She picked him up and cuddled him against her, loving the soft warmth of his thick orange fur.

"What do you suppose is in that box, Daffy?" she said, putting him down. "Shall we open it or save it for later?"

Daffy flicked his tail, sat up on his haunches, and stared at her with his golden eyes. *Don't be silly*, he was saying. *We'll open it now, of course.*

The box was full of books. On top was a letter from Nadine Fleming, her literary agent—typewritten and brief and breezy as usual.

My very dear Elizabeth—

Herewith your author copies of *Inherit the Flames*, which is due out in just three weeks. I found myself in the Scribner office on an errand yesterday and who should I run into but your editor, Max Perkins. He says he'll send the reviews (*Publishers Weekly, Pictorial,* the new *Kirkus Reviews*, et al.) as soon as they appear. He thinks the book turned out splendidly and of course so do I. A grand achievement for a debut author. We're both quite proud of it and hope you are, too!

Congratulations and felicitations,

Nadine

P.S. Mr. Perkins asked especially after your second book. He has his eye on Scribner's Fall 1936 list, so he would like to see a manuscript from you before the summer is out. We don't want your first book to be your last, so I hope this is possible. Please let me know.

Her heart pounding, her breath catching in her throat, Lizzy pulled out one of the books, inhaling the heady scent of printer's ink and fresh pages. The title, *Inherit the Flames*, was printed in large blood-red letters in a vintage typeface across the top of the dust jacket. Below the title was a drawing of a plantation house engulfed in flames. The woman looking on wore a white dress with puffed sleeves and layers of lace ruffles atop wide Civil War petticoats. Below that, in a narrow bar across the bottom, was her name. *Elizabeth Lacy.*

Ecstatic, Lizzy closed her eyes and sank into a chair, clasping the book. Her very own *first* book, once a dreamed-of hope, now at long last an astonishing reality. It told the story of Sabrina, a passionate, impetuous, and often imprudent young woman whose Alabama family plantation had been plundered by Yankee soldiers during the War Between the States. She was left with only two choices: marrying a wealthy older neighbor who promised her at least some security in the bleak aftermath of the war, or struggling to rebuild on her own.

Lizzy had written the book in the tumultuous months after Grady's abrupt marriage. To help her get away from her curious neighbors and solicitous friends, Mr. Moseley had found her a temporary job with Mr. Jackman, a lawyer he knew in Montgomery. She had rented a small furnished apartment and there, with just Daffy to keep her company, she had put her spare time to use by writing the novel she'd been thinking about for several years. Because she knew the chaotic history of the war so well and the characters and their dilemmas were so clear in her mind, the story had come together almost as fast as she could type.

When the first draft was done and revised, Mrs. Jackman, who had New York connections, had put her in touch with Nadine Fleming, a literary agent in the prominent George Bye Agency. With remarkable dispatch, Miss Fleming had found an editor—Max Perkins at Scribner's—who loved Lizzy's manuscript and was willing to take a chance on a debut author. And now, here it was at last, in her hands. *Inherit the Flames*, a real book! The reality of it nearly took her breath away.

Delighted as she was, though, Lizzy knew that she had to be realistic about the book's chances. It wasn't the usual formulaic Southern novel, the kind that many readers would expect. She had done her best to upend the hackneyed stereotype of a tranquil everybody-happy plantation life that was disrupted by the North's cruel invasion. Her main characters, Sabrina and Sabrina's younger sister Sarah, were no belles; they were strong-minded women who rolled up their sleeves, pinned up their skirts (or put on trousers), and shouldered their postwar burdens with humor and tenacity. Her servant characters were strong and independent and politically savvy. It was an optimistic book that depicted Reconstruction as a hard road, but the only road into the future.

In an ordinary year, Miss Fleming said, *Inherit the Flames* should do quite well. But the Depression had already closed many bookshops and killed off a great many potential bestsellers. Even top-tier writers were forced to find whatever work they could. Mary Margaret McBride, a popular travel writer, was dishing out advice to the lovelorn. F. Scott Fitzgerald, perennially between novels, had tried his hand at writing Hollywood screenplays, not very successfully. Rose Wilder Lane, whose *Let the Hurricane Roar* had been a near-best-seller the previous year, was ghostwriting Lowell Thomas' adventure series and her mother's children's books. Miss Fleming was full of cautionary tales about writers who were struggling to make a living—and not succeeding very well.

"If you've got a job that pays the bills," she advised, "it's not a good time to quit. And do stay in Alabama, where you have friends and relatives. New York is already full of starving writers."

Lizzy agreed. She had a job that not only paid enough to keep her afloat but left her with several free afternoons for writing—and even whole days, when Mr. Moseley was out of town. She loved living in Darling and hoped never to live anywhere else—*especially* not in New York. And she was satisfied with the progress she was making on her second book.

So, yes. She could write to Miss Fleming and let her know that—barring something unforeseen—she would be sending Mr. Perkins another manuscript by the end of summer.

Whether her first book was successful was up to the literary gods.

Whether it was her last book was up to *her.*

# CHAPTER NINE

# FANNIE MAKES LUNCH

In her public life, Fannie Champaign was a milliner whose artistic creations graced the heads of stylish women from New York to Chicago to Los Angeles. If you asked Fannie about this, she would say that it was all due to the kindness of Lilly Daché, the celebrated Viennese-born, Parisian-trained milliner who was leading the way for talented American designers. Madame Daché had moved to New York and built a millinery emporium, with a silver room for her fair-haired clients and a gold room for brunettes.

It was through the supportive Mme. Daché that one of Fannie's chic creations had been chosen for the movie *Grand Hotel*, where it was worn by leading lady Joan Crawford. Miss Crawford had been quoted in the *Hollywood Reporter* as saying that she "just adored" that "clever little hat." Voilà! Fannie was famous, and her hats—still produced in her small studio across from the Darling courthouse—were now in such demand that she could scarcely keep up.

In private life, Fannie Champaign was the recently married Mrs. Charles Dickens, and no matter how busy she was, she loved to make a daily lunch for her new husband and serve it to him in their airy flat over Fannie's studio. Their home boasted lofty ceilings and lovely oak floors and was filled with the simplest of furnishings. The walls were creamy, the perfect background for Fannie's collection of beautifully framed floral prints, and there was plenty of room for shelves of Charlie's books, at last out of the boxes in which they'd been stored for too many years. Her collection of fashion magazines was stacked under the low coffee table in front of the sofa. Several recent issues were open on the table, where she had been studying them: *Vogue, Chatelaine, Delineator*—and the newest, *Mademoiselle*, first published in February, which featured several of Mme. Daché's creations. Fannie followed her own instincts in design, but it was important to keep up with what other designers were doing and—whether you liked them or not—what trends might be developing.

The living room window looked out on the courthouse square, and in front of it stood their luncheon table, covered with an embroidered cloth and set with real china and silver and a small bouquet of sweet peas. On the table, Fannie had already laid their Monday lunch: tomato soup; a salad of fresh lettuce, tomato, and early cucumber from the Dahlias' garden; and a chicken salad sandwich. A member of the Dahlias, she tended the miniature flower garden in front of Darling's little public library next door, and the sweet peas she had gathered added their enchanting scent to the pretty scene.

Fannie was an inventive cook, and Charlie, a longtime bachelor, always applauded her efforts. And well he might, for he had boarded at Mrs. Beedle's for the past six or seven years and had eaten most of his meals at the Diner. He made it clear that he appreciated Fannie's efforts on the domestic side of their marriage and did what he could to help out.

Of course, the domestic side wasn't the only pleasing thing about the marriage, for Fannie and Charlie were compatible in many ways. They spent their mealtimes sharing what had happened in their work—in Fannie's millinery studio and at Charlie's newspaper. After dinner, Charlie helped with the dishes and then they sat down together in the living room to read or do puzzles or play cards while they listened to the radio (Jack Benny was a favorite), pausing now and then to discuss interesting bits of this and that. They also liked to turn the lights down low and dance, especially when Guy Lombardo's CBS radio show came on, or when they played Ted Weems' records on the Victrola. And then there was bedtime.

Fannie colored, smiling a little. She had regarded that part of marriage with trepidation, because of her earlier painful experience. Jason, her nine-year-old son, lived (for the time being) at Warm Springs, in Georgia, where President Roosevelt had built his Little White House and where Jason, a polio victim like FDR, was learning to do many things for himself. Jason's father had been a . . .

Fannie's mouth tightened. Jason's father had been a fraud. She had been completely fooled by him, which was part of the reason she had been so hesitant when Charlie Dickens began courting her. Charlie was a dry, ironic sort of person who could wield a destructively sarcastic remark like a gangster wielded a knife, and with the same fatal effect. She had been more than a little afraid of him—and afraid to tell him about Jason and why she had never been legally married to Jason's father. How would he react when he knew that she had a son, a boy who would never run and play like other children? What would he think of her, when he found out that she had been foolish enough to fall in love with a charlatan, a *scoundrel*?

But Charlie had opened his heart to her and to Jason, and he was respectful and surprisingly gentle with both of them. For him, the marriage seemed to be a safe harbor from the things he dealt with every day, and he almost always left his dark, ironic self at the door. In fact, when the lights were turned off and they went into their bedroom together, he could be quite the tender romantic. He—

But that was his footstep on the stair, and she turned toward the door to welcome him. Instead of a smile, he wore an unusually grim expression, which she thought might be due to this morning's launch of Darling's new radio station. He had explained to her his fears that WDAR would siphon off the *Dispatch*'s advertisers and subscribers. So Fannie had decided that she'd better not tell him how much she had enjoyed the morning's programs, especially *The Flour Hour*, which originated in the new bakery right next door. She had been glad that Mildred Kilgore had announced the Dahlias' quilting session at the clubhouse that night. She'd almost forgotten that she promised to be there. She was working on a fanciful appliqued iris.

But it wasn't Radio WDAR that was dragging on Charlie's spirits, and when they sat down to their lunch, he told her what was on his mind.

"Mickey LeDoux is back in Darling."

She looked up from her soup. "But I thought . . ." She felt a sharp flare of concern. Everyone knew that when Mickey got out of prison, there would be trouble—serious trouble. "I thought he wasn't due to be released until the end of August."

"That's what we all thought. They let him out early for good behavior. He came to the newspaper this morning, loaded for bear. He wanted to talk to Baby Mann."

"Oh, dear," Fannie whispered. Everybody in town knew that it was Baby who had spilled the location of Mickey's still to Agent Kinnard, and that Mickey would be out for revenge. "What are you going to do?"

"*Me?*" Charlie barked a rough laugh. "*I* am going to do exactly nothing. This is between Mickey and Baby. I hope it's not going to be another gunfight at the O.K. Corral, but I'm afraid there's likely to be fireworks. It might not involve just

Mickey and Baby, either. If the two sides of the Mann clan are going to battle it out on the streets of Darling, I for one don't intend to get caught in the crossfire. It could be deadly."

"You don't really think it will come to that, do you, Charlie?" Fannie asked.

"I doubt it." He gave her a half-reassuring smile. "More likely, a lot of name calling and taunts thrown back and forth." His face darkened. "But there's more."

Fannie saw that he hadn't taken more than a spoonful or two of soup and not a single bite of his sandwich, even though both were favorites. She put her spoon down and reached across the small table to take his hand. "What is it, dear? What's wrong?"

"I just had a visit from Buddy Norris." Charlie squeezed her hand and let it go. "And an agent from the Alabama Tax Commission. Mooney is his name. Hobart Mooney."

"The Tax Commission?" She was startled. "But what—"

"He's here in Darling to investigate criminal violations of the tax stamp regulations. The cigarette tax stamp."

"Cigarette tax?" Fannie asked, frowning. "I don't understand. You pay the tax every time you buy a pack, don't you?" Charlie still smoked his Camels—at least a pack every day. But before they married he had agreed not to smoke in their apartment and he was standing by his word. He went out to the library garden to smoke.

"Of course I pay it. Everybody does. That's how come a pack of cigarettes costs thirteen cents instead of a dime. Cigarette distributors and dealers buy the tax stamps from the state and stick a stamp on every pack, then add the price of the three-cent stamp to the price of the pack. Same thing with the liquor tax. Both are a way for the state to make some money. Big money, in fact—hundreds of thousands of dollars every year, in fact. It's supposed to go to the schools. Whether it does or not . . ." He shrugged.

"But I don't understand what *you*—" She stopped, helplessly.

"Where there's that kind of money, my love, there are crooks." Charlie's mouth twisted. "Little crooks, big crooks, an aggregation of crooks. The mob."

Fannie's hand flew to her mouth. "The *mob*? But how—"

"It's easy. Instead of buying legitimate tax stamps from the state, the crooks simply print their own."

"*Print* them?"

"Counterfeit them. Instead of the money going to the state of Alabama, it's going into the mob's pocket."

"Oh." Fannie shook her head, her eyes wide. "But I still don't see what that has to do with *you*, Charlie. *You're* not a counterfeiter. You don't print—"

"Apparently, I am a counterfeiter," Charlie said sourly. "That's what Agent Mooney says, anyway."

Fannie was staring at him, nearly speechless. She pulled in her breath and managed, "A . . . counterfeiter? You?"

"Yeah." In a musing tone he added, "Remember when we saw *Public Enemy* last winter? This guy looks just like Jimmy Cagney. If you didn't know better, you'd think Mooney was trying out for Cagney's double. Give him a grapefruit and the studio will hire him."

Fannie was aghast. "But you couldn't possibly be a *counterfeiter*, Charlie!" she whispered. "You *couldn't*."

"You know I'm not and I know I'm not," he replied bleakly. "Buddy Norris probably knows I'm not, too. But Mooney's got a different opinion. And I have to say that the stamps he showed me were very professionally done. An expert who knows what he's looking for could probably tell the difference, but they'll fool the average Joe—and maybe even the average stamp inspector." Charlie picked up his spoon and went to work on his soup.

"Well," Fannie asked, after a moment. "Are you going to tell me what happened?"

"The sheriff brought a search warrant," Charlie said. "By the time they'd finished poking around, Mooney had found what he was looking for."

"What?" Fannie pushed her bowl away. She had suddenly lost her appetite. "What did he find?"

Charlie didn't look up. "The specialty paper the stamps are printed on. Red ink. That old stamp perforating machine of my dad's, which I had completely forgotten about." He put his spoon down. "And the engraved plate. The tax stamp engraving. Along with a stack of printed tax cigarette stamps."

"Oh, no," Fannie said, eyes wide.

"Oh, yes. The paper, the ink, the engraving—all stowed in various places around the shop, not really hidden but not out in plain sight, either. And of course, there was the Kelsey, big as life and twice as natural. The perfect press for this kind of job. Mooney was all set to wrap up his investigation. In fact, if it hadn't been for Buddy Norris, I'd be in jail right now."

Fannie's heart was beating fast. "What did the sheriff do?"

"He told Mooney he wasn't satisfied. That there were other possibilities. That if Mooney intended to arrest somebody, he'd better have evidence. And not just circumstantial evidence, either."

Fannie had always liked Buddy, who wasn't much older than a boy but seemed to care very deeply about the well-being of Darling and its citizens.

"Well, thank goodness for Buddy," she said, feeling a deep relief. She leaned forward on her folded arms. "But if you're not the counterfeiter, then—"

"Yeah." Charlie sighed heavily. "If I'm not the counterfeiter, somebody else is. And there are only three possibilities."

Fannie's heart went out to her husband. When his father had

died and left him the Darling *Dispatch*, he intended to sell it and go back to one of the big-city newspapers he had worked for earlier in his career: the *Cleveland Plain Dealer*, the *Fort Worth Star-Telegram*, the *Baltimore Sun*. But the Depression made that impossible. Like every other business in the country, newspapers were shedding jobs. So Charlie had been stuck in Darling, trying to keep the *Dispatch* afloat all by himself, feeling increasingly frustrated and drinking a lot of (too much of, in Fannie's opinion) the local moonshine.

Their marriage had helped him feel more contented, she knew. And he had been so pleased when he was able to assemble a small staff he could trust to get the newspaper out and give him a little breathing room. Wilber, the new reporter and Linotype operator, also sold advertising. Osgood managed the print run on the big newspaper press and did the job printing, with help from the others. And Baby Mann kept things clean and straight and made the office a pleasant place to work—and now had to face the wrath of the man he had sent to jail.

Poor Charlie, Fannie thought sympathetically. She was no mind reader, but she knew that he must suspect that one of his three staff members was the counterfeiter.

Which one was it?

Or maybe it was two.

Or even all three.

# CHAPTER TEN

# VIOLET IS CHARMED

VIOLET SIMS WAS NOT A BRAVE PERSON, AND SHE KNEW IT. EVER since she had come to Darling, she had been hearing people talk in hushed whispers about the Voodoo Lily—Big Lil, she was called—who lived in a weathered board-and-batten shanty out on Little Bigtooth Creek, in the spookiest part of Briar Swamp. The Voodoo Lily was a conjure queen who was reputed to be able to call up anything you wanted or needed, if you asked in the right way.

Violet, who was always intrigued by a mystery, had long wanted to pay Big Lil a visit. Roseanne had agreed to take her several times, and once she had even gotten partway there before she twisted her ankle (at least, that's what she *said*) and had to go back.

But the real truth was that Big Lil spooked her. In Violet's vivid imagination, the conjure queen was a threatening figure, large and fierce and all-powerful, like a witch or an enchantress. So she had yet to make her first visit. Her cowardice had always won out.

Tonight was different. Tonight, Violet felt more desperate than cowardly, for there was something she wanted. She was going to ask for a conjure spell, one potent enough to guarantee that Cupcake would win first prize in the Shirley Temple look-alike contest in Nashville, so they could be on their way to Hollywood.

Violet had been terrified the previous winter when Cupcake's father showed up with a scheme to take the little girl to Hollywood and make her his partner in a father-daughter movie dance team. Of *course* he wasn't going to take her Cupcake away! Neither she nor Myra May would stand for it.

But at the same time, Violet had been tantalized by the notion that Cupcake had the potential to be a child movie star. She just *knew* that if the big movie producers—David O. Selznick, for one, or Darryl Zanuck or Louis B. Mayer—could see little Cupcake dance and sing, they would cast her in a starring role in their very next movie. But the trick was getting Cupcake and herself to Hollywood. Myra May had made it crystal clear that she was strongly opposed, so Violet didn't think it was right to ask her to fork over the money.

Then she had read in the Nashville newspaper about the look-alike contest and its stunning first prize of a two-week, all-expense-paid trip to Hollywood. She sent in the two-dollar entrance fee, which left her with just enough money for Greyhound tickets to Nashville and back and a bed in a cheap hotel for Friday night, after the competition. Then they could start planning their trip to Hollywood. They would be on their way to stardom!

But there was always the chance that Cupcake *wouldn't* win—that some other little girl would be cuter or dance better or have more curls. (From all reports, the Shirley-style curls were even more important than the talent.)

Which brings us to Big Lil. The Voodoo Lily was reputed to be able to conjure up anything you needed, if you asked in the right way. If anyone doubted her magic, all they had to do was look at Miss Tallulah's intact family fortune, which didn't disappear in the Crash of '29. So considering this powerful testimonial to Big Lil's voodoo skill and others that were whispered around Darling every now and then, Violet was sure that the conjure queen had what it took to ensure that Cupcake would win that trip to Hollywood. Her confidence was buoyed by the fact that Lil (who had been told why Violet was asking to see her) instructed her to bring Cupcake's Shirley Temple doll, which bore an uncanny resemblance to the real Shirley, from her glorious golden curls down to her lacy white stockings and white Mary Janes and doll-sized pocket book outfitted with a tiny comb and mirror.

Getting the doll had proved difficult, because Shirley Temple seemed to have cast a spell over Cupcake, who slept with Shirley every night and wouldn't let go of her all day long. But tonight, Violet had put Cupcake to bed a bit early and managed to extricate the doll from the little girl's embrace after she fell asleep. She hoped Lil didn't plan to stick Shirley full of pins, the way it was done with other voodoo dolls. But whatever the magic, it had to be worked very soon, because the contest was Friday night. And this was Monday. There wasn't much time left.

So Violet tucked Shirley Temple in her sewing bag and told Myra May that she was going to meet Ophelia and a few of the other Dahlias to work on the appliqued flower quilt. Violet hated to fib to Myra May, who was her dearest friend in all the world. But she knew that Myra May, a very practical person, would not approve of her visit to Big Lil.

So she swallowed her guilt and told Myra May that she might be late, so don't bother to wait up. She walked over to Magnolia Manor, where Roseanne (Bessie's cook-housekeeper) and her cousin Sally-Lou were waiting. Sally-Lou, who over the years had worked for just about every housewife in Darling, had borrowed a jalopy from her brother, Fremon Hawkins. All three of them climbed in—Violet in the rumble seat—and Sally-Lou drove south on the Jericho Road, past the prison farm to the point where the road ended in a marshy morass at the edge of Briar Swamp.

The swamp was a couple of thousand acres of quagmire in a horseshoe bend in the river, nothing but bald cypress standing knee-deep in the dark, still water, surrounded by hummocks of buttonbush and black willow and pawpaw and dense patches of cordgrass. It was a good place for Bodeen Pyle and Mickey LeDoux to hide their moonshine operations from Chester P. Kinnard, the revenue agent, and a wonderful place to get lost. If you didn't know for sure where you were going and the least-hazardous way to get there, all you'd find would be cottonmouths and copperheads, mosquitos the size of jaybirds, and alligators hungry enough to take your foot off—some of them so big they didn't have to stop with a foot.

By the time Sally-Lou parked the jalopy at the end of the road and turned off the engine, the sunset was a salmon-pink glow in the west. Night had sucked almost all the light out of the eastern sky, the stars were beginning to sparkle, and an impossibly large and luminous moon, round and full, was climbing silently out of the dark trees. They got out of the car and Violet wrinkled her nose, smelling the swamp's unmistakably sulfurous odor of decaying vegetation and sour mud and hearing the distant *jug-o'-rummm* of a lusty bullfrog.

"We walkin' back in the deep country 'bout half a mile," Roseanne said briskly, taking out her flashlight. "Best we go single-file."

Violet found herself in the middle. Sally-Lou, carrying a bundle of rosemary, brought up the rear. Roseanne, a basket over one arm and her flashlight in the other hand, took the lead. They started off into the swamp, Violet carrying Shirley

Temple in her sewing bag and wishing that she'd worn low-heeled shoes.

The other two women seemed cheerful and untroubled, but for Violet, what was illuminated by the flashlight's wobbly beam was not at all reassuring. No more than an arms-length wide, the path (if you could call it a path) looped along the spine of a low ridge. The steep banks on either side sloped down to long, narrow fingers of black water, the bayou's still surface laced with green tendrils of bladderwort and pennywort. It was dark under the sweetgum and beech, and the night was rich with the sounds of frogs, whippoorwills, screech owls, and a bittern's soft, booming *pump-er-lunk*. Every now and then something splashed loud in the water, and Violet cringed, imagining a gator grabbing a swamp beaver as it swam by.

Another step farther, something small and brown darted swiftly across the path in front of her. Startled, she jumped away, grabbing the nearest branch to keep from falling into the water and dislodging a furry brown spider the size of a half dollar. It landed on her arm. She screamed and tried to shake it off.

"Nev' mind, Violet," Sally-Lou said. "She just a big ol' swamp spider. She won't hurt you none." She brushed it off, smiling. "See there? Mrs. Spider, she got mo' impo'tant things on her mind than bitin' you, however tasty you be. She go on 'bout her bus'ness now."

"Could be that's Big Lil herse'f," Roseanne offered matter-of-factly. "The Voodoo Lily is a shape-shifter, y'know. Folks say they've seen her in the form of a big black panther goin' straight up a sweetgum tree. Myself, I've seen her as a fox. And I've heard she likes to tarry in the buttonwoods right 'bout here, to see who's comin' to visit her."

Violet didn't believe this, exactly. But in the dimness, with the eerie *who-whoo-who-who* of an owl in her ears, the moist, earthy smell of the swamp in her nose, and the ghostly moon rising into the darkening sky, it was possible to believe almost anything. She shuddered at the possibility that Roseanne was right—that the spider was Big Lil, going to some trouble to get a preview peek at tonight's visitors.

But spider or no spider, Violet's determination was stronger than ever. Clutching her bag and the doll, she took a deep, steadying breath and they started off again, following the path around mounds of green resurrection ferns and under tree branches draped with ribbons of Spanish moss and through thickets of silver-willow, the leaves glittering like tiny scraps of moonlight that had snagged on the branches. Deeper and deeper the three women went, into the remote reaches of the swamp where everything lay under a spell, although what kind of spell, good or bad or both, nobody could say. It was a mystery, that was all they knew. A mystery framed in green shadows and haunted by the silent, secret knowing of wild things.

And by ghosts. Ghosts of the Choctaw and Chickasaw who refused to leave in the Indian Removals. Of the slaves who fled to the swamp for refuge and the slave hunters who tracked them down. Of moonshiners and the revenue agents who aimed to put them out of business. Of timber cutters, the victims of their own careless saws, of trees falling with a vengeance, of yellow fever and malaria.

Oh, yes, the swamp was haunted, and not just in people's imaginations. It was an enchanted place that existed in a space between the Darling world, where everything was known, and the world of the completely unknowable. That's where the Voodoo Lily ruled, ruled all the animals and birds and trees and ferns and, yes, the ghosts. Which was all anybody knew, and all they wanted to know. It was enough.

Night had fallen and Violet was breathless and shivering by the time they saw the glimmer from the red-shaded kerosene lamp burning in the window of Big Lil's shanty. Off to the left was the bayou, a ribbon of silver in the moonlight. A shallow-sided pole boat was moored to a wooden dock perched precariously over the water. The front yard was fenced with white-painted wooden pickets, and the scent of roses and sweet peas hung heavy on the air. Their fragrance was mixed with a strong, distinctive odor—the profoundly disagreeable odor of decaying flesh—that Violet recognized with foreboding. Somewhere in the tangle of blooming flowers was a voodoo lily, like the one in the Dahlias' magic garden. Or maybe more than one, since the odor was so strong. That flower was supposed to be bad luck, death, even. Why would Big Lil want to grow it? Why would *anybody* want to grow it?

Violet was glad to take Sally-Lou's reassuring arm when it was offered and was grateful to Roseanne when she said, with a chuckle, "You don't need to be skeered, Miz Violet. It's just Lil we're goin' to see, not the devil."

But first they had to get past the pigs. There were two of them, enormous and muddy, lying across the porch steps. They lifted their heads and snorted suspiciously but allowed Roseanne, who had visited Big Lil many times before, to step over them. Violet shrank back fearfully.

"Nev' mind them pigs," Roseanne said. "They the laziest ol' things." She stamped her foot on the floor. "You git outa the way, y'all." The pigs lumbered to their feet, moved a yard away, and flopped down again.

"Thank'ee, pigs," Roseanne said. She was about to rap on the door when they were all startled by a question: *Who-looks-for-you,* deep and breathy, like somebody blowing across the mouth of a jug.

Stifling a scream, Violet turned to see a large dark creature with golden eyes perched on the porch railing. Sally-Lou patted her arm. "Lil's owl," she said.

"Or Lil herse'f," Roseanne remarked. "You never can tell." She flapped a hand at the owl. "G'wan now. Git." The owl flew away. To Violet, Roseanne confided, "Just an owl tonight. When she's Lil, she don't budge. Just sits there an' hoots while we go in."

Turning back to the door, she rapped three times lightly, paused, then rapped three times more. The door obediently swung open. Sally-Lou reached for Violet's hand and they followed Roseanne inside.

In addition to the red-shaded lamp in the window, four fat white candles flickered on tall wooden stands in the corners of the room. They gave off a rich, smoky perfume, like incense, spiked with a bright orange scent that tickled Violet's nose. One wall was filled with shelves that held old books and containers of various sorts—bottles and boxes and wicker baskets—and against another wall was a large wooden chest, carelessly covered with a crimson velveteen shawl. On the wall above it was a large calendar with a picture of a placid brown cow and the words *Snow's Farm Supply*. Straight wooden chairs stood at either end of the chest.

Against a third wall was an altar, under a mirror draped with a giant snakeskin and a string of polished buckeyes and another string of dried peppers of various sizes. A pot of incense sat smoking in front of the mirror, along with three colored candles—purple, silver, and gold—and a crystal bowl filled with three white roses. A massive black cat with inscrutable golden eyes was curled up on an upholstered purple chair beside the altar. Violet wished she could see if this was the cat with nine toes, but its front paws were folded invisibly under its regal ruff.

*Or maybe that's Lil herself*, Violet guessed, and knew immediately that she would prefer the cat or the owl to the spider on the path or the panther going straight up a sweetgum.

But no, the cat definitely wasn't Lil, for in the next moment, the Voodoo Lily herself swept through a curtain of colored glass beads strung across a doorway in the fourth wall. She was a large woman, heavy and majestic in her dimensions, all of six feet tall and wide across her shoulders and broad in her hips, with skin the color of richly polished mahogany. She wore a purple blouse and a yellow and red silk scarf and a flounced red skirt. Her hair was hidden under a madras tignon that was wrapped like a turban around her head, its large bow pinned with a striking snake-shaped brooch. The tignon added another twelve inches to her height, so that she seemed an astonishing seven feet tall. Golden hoop earrings the size of saucers hung from her ears and silver and copper bracelets jangled at both wrists. Her eyes were watchful under dark, heavy brows, her expression grave and unsmiling. It was impossible to guess her age. Was she forty? Seventy? A hundred? Violet shifted nervously.

Arms akimbo, fists on her hips, Lil surveyed the three of them. Her eyes fastened on Roseanne. "What do you bring me tonight, daughter?" In its timbre, her voice was as deep as any man's but musical and smooth, like the richest cream. It was an attractive voice. Hearing it, Violet felt a little easier.

Roseanne held out the basket she had been carrying over her arm. "A quart jar of mustard pickles," she said, "with them little pearl onions you like. Two dozen coconut meringues with almonds. A jar of quince jelly." She put the jars and the bag of meringues on the altar and dropped a coin into a woven twig basket. "And a Liberty quarter."

"I brought a quarter, too," Sally-Lou said, following suit. "Got a picture of old George Washington on it. And some rosemary." She put a bundle of fragrant rosemary on the altar. "A body can always use more rosemary."

Violet had been told that a quarter was the usual tariff, but since she was feeling urgent, she'd brought more. She hadn't thought to see whose picture was on them, and it was too dark in the room to see them now.

"Two quarters," she said, dropping them in the basket. It was already full of silver coins, as well as what looked like a twenty-dollar Indian Head gold piece and another gold coin Violet couldn't quite see.

Lil picked up the cat from the purple chair and took its place, settling it on her lap and resting her feet on a small stool in front of the chair. She arranged her red skirt, stroked the cat, and turned her attention to Violet. Her eyes were enormous, as deep and dark as swamp pools, and hypnotic. Violet could not escape her gaze.

After a moment, Lil held out her hand. Her fingers were long, the sharp-pointed nails painted a startling scarlet. "Come here, chil'."

"Yes, ma'am," Violet whispered. Clutching her bag, she stepped forward.

Lil looked past her to Roseanne and Sally-Lou. "You gals might's well sit in them chairs over there. This is goin' to take some while." To Violet, she said, "Lemme see that doll you brought."

Violet pulled it out. It was the smallest Shirley doll, although at three dollars at Mann's Mercantile, it hadn't been cheap. Dressed in a flirty red-polka-dotted dress with a red silk sash, red and white panties, white shoes and white stockings, it looked uncannily like the real Shirley, down to the big red bow atop the banana curls.

"Huh." Lil turned the doll over in her hands. "This what all the fuss be 'bout? In the movies an' all?"

"Yes, ma'am," Violet said humbly. "You've seen her? The real Shirley, I mean. On the screen."

Everybody knew that Lil was no recluse. Once every few weeks, she poled her boat to the edge of the swamp and walked to Darling to buy groceries at Hancock's and pick up a copy of the *Dispatch*. She had never stopped at the Diner, but Violet couldn't see any reason why she couldn't go to the movies if she wanted to.

Lil was squinting at the doll. "Your little gal—you tellin' me she look like *this*? She got no color in her face."

"Well, yes, ma'am." Violet straightened. "Cupcake does look like Shirley, almost exactly. Everybody says so."

"Huh." The pride in Violet's voice did not seem to impress Lil. "There ain't no black Shirleys, I reckon."

*Black* Shirleys? But Shirley wasn't black, so how could there be—

But Violet didn't want to get into that. "Not that I know of," she said.

Lil poked a finger at the doll's abundant golden curls. "An' this here hair. Your gal's head got curls like this all over?"

"Well, it's sorta straight now that she's a little older, but it curls real nice when I twist it up in muslin rags. I do that every night. But not fifty-six," she added hastily. "Only thirty-two. Cupcake's hair is finer."

Which wasn't the whole truth. Cupcake began to whine by the time Violet got fifteen of the little rag knots wound tight, and by twenty-two she was in full-scale rebellion. The rest of the thirty-six curls were done to the accompaniment of Cupcake's loud wails and beating of heels against the chair legs. Violet had no idea how Shirley Temple's mother got her little girl to sit still for fifty-six, night in and night out. (She knew this was true because she had read it in *Silver Screen*.)

Lil leaned forward, frowning. "Fifty-six *whut?*"

"Fifty-six curls. That's what Shirley Temple's mother does. She peroxides it, too." (Also true, according to *Silver Screen*, although Violet didn't approve of it. She hoped that the studios would like the color of Cupcake's hair as it was.)

Lil rolled her eyes. "What some folks'll do for money is hard to credit," she muttered under her breath. "I hear tell you're wantin' to put your little gal into some kinda *con-test*." She drew out the word. "That right?"

"Yes, ma'am. In Nashville. She'll sing and dance 'On the Good Ship Lollipop.' It's her favorite song, and she does it just like Shirley. She'll have a dress like Shirley's, too. It's blue plaid, with a white collar and a dark blue bow—just like the dress Shirley wears in *Bright Eyes*."

A flickering shadow fell across Lil's face. "So whut're you askin' for from me?"

Violet took a deep breath and spoke fast. "I want Cupcake to win the first prize in Nashville and then go to Hollywood, where she can get into the movies and be a big star." She knew she was supposed to ask for only one thing, but she had practiced bundling her requests and was hoping that Lil wouldn't notice that she had tucked three into it.

The Voodoo Lily gave her a *spare me* look and a dismissive wave of her hand. "Whether a body can get whut they want depends on whether it's a good want." She frowned. "Not everything a body wants is a good want. You understand whut I'm sayin,' chil'?"

Wordlessly, Violet nodded.

Lil's eyes, fastened on her, seemed to grow larger and darker, her voice deeper and more resonant. "When whut a body wants is for another body to want the same thing an' want it jes' as much an' for a long time, it's not always a good want. You understand that?" The cat on her lap lifted its head, sniffed, and then leapt onto the floor.

Violet shifted uncertainly, beginning to see where this was going. "But it's *not* just what I want," she said. "Cupcake wants this every bit as much as I do. Honest, she does. She—"

Big Lil held up the doll. "How old is this little gal of yours?"

"Five," Violet said, and qualified it. "Well, almost."

"Four-and-a-half. She have any notion how hard it is to be in the pictures? Whut she'd have to do, day in, day out, in front of cameras, with folks watching her ever' move?"

Violet considered. "Actually, I think she would enjoy—"

"She don't know," Lil said in an authoritative tone. "Four-and-a-half ain't old enough to know somethin' like that." She frowned. "She know she'd have to live somewheres else, like out there in Hollowood?"

"Hollywood," Violet said.

"*Hollowood*," Lil repeated emphatically. "Away from all her friends and kinfolk."

"Actually, there's just me and Myra May. We've adopted her. We're her only kin. And Myra May wants what I—" She stopped herself. She'd heard that it was dangerous to lie to Big Lil.

"Myra May don't want to live in no Hollowood," Lil said sternly. "Myra May wants to live in Darling, where she's satisfied. Where she got friends. Got her mama. You need to make it up with her."

*Make it up?* Was Lil telling her to give in and do what Myra May wants? And how did this woman know what Myra May wants?

Violet swallowed. "I really don't think I—"

"Yes, you do." Lil raised her chin, her eyes hard as marbles and glinting in the candles' flickering light. "How come you walk all the way out here to ask me for hoodoo if you think I don't know what I'm talkin' 'bout? How come, huh?"

"Well, I . . ." Violet's mouth was suddenly dry as a desert. "I'm sorry. I didn't mean to—"

"Be quiet," Lil commanded irritably. "I gotta decide whut's best to do with you."

Violet's heart sank. Big Lil was known to be particular about whose wants would be granted and whose would be denied. Was the conjure queen about to send her home empty-handed—or worse?

Lil looked down at the doll, studying it. Then she looked up and stared at Violet for a moment, her eyes narrowed. Then she leaned toward the altar beside her chair, took up a candle and used it to light another. The flame blossomed into a curl of smoke and a new, spicier fragrance filled the air. She picked up a very small brown glass jar from the altar, unscrewed the lid, and dipped her finger into the jar. She smeared a swath of what appeared to be ointment across the doll's forehead. She brought the doll up to her face, pressed her forehead against its forehead and held it there, muttering something incomprehensible.

It had to be a voodoo chant, Violet decided, as the fragrance grew stronger. She felt a surge of almost giddy exultation. Lil must be granting her wish!

The muttering went on. Chanting, her voice rising and falling, Lil began to rock back and forth in time with the rhythmic incantation. The cat had stalked into the shadows in a corner of the room, where he sat, glaring balefully at Violet. Lil's voice grew louder and her words (if that's what they were) blurred all together as Violet watched, her heart beating fast.

Suddenly Lil fell silent. She dropped Shirley on the altar, then got up and went to the shelf of bottles and boxes, where she rustled around for a few moments. Curiously, Violet tried to peer around her, but she couldn't quite see what the conjure woman was doing. When Lil finally returned, she handed Violet a small satin brocade pouch with a drawstring closure.

Gingerly, Violet turned the pouch over in her fingers. "What is it?"

Lil took her seat again, looking peeved. "Why you gotta know every little thing?"

"Well, because—"

"Be quiet. What you got in that there mojo bag is some

traveler's herbs—mugwort, comfrey, sweet bay, wormwood. They's for gettin' you where you need to go and bringin' you home again safe and sound. There's a little vial of bammygilly oil in there, too, and some Road Opening oil and a few other hoodoo odds and ends." Her eyes darkened. "You tuck that bag into your pocket right now and keep it there. It'll do you good."

"Bammygilly oil?" Violet asked.

Lil made an impatient noise. "Reconciliation. Bury the hatchet."

"Bury the hatchet?" Violet frowned. "What does that mean? What I want is—"

"A drop in a cup of coffee. That'll bury it good." Lil waved her hand, bracelets jangling. "You'll know what to do when the time comes."

Violet took a breath. This didn't sound at all like what she had come for. "But what I *want* is for Cupcake and me to go to Hollywood. I don't need to bury any—"

"Who said it was for you, girl?" Lil thundered. "You be doin' a little chore for me. And didn't I tell you *be quiet*?"

"Yes, ma'am," Violet whispered.

Lil held out the doll and Violet took it. "Now you listen to me and you listen good. There's four pink candles on that shelf over there. You take them candles home with you. Tomorrow, you go out and look around and find yourse'f a young ash tree. You cut yourse'f a limber ash switch about two foot long and you bend it into a circle. Tie the ends together with red thread. Then you lay the ash circle down and put the doll on it, with the candles around it in four places, top and bottom and both sides. Light the candles and say this charm: 'Safe we go, safe we come back, and may we get whut we need.' Say it five times, no more." She fixed her eyes on Violet. "You understand? Five times. Less ain't enough. More is too many. You follow orders."

"Does it have to be an ash switch?" Violet asked. "How

about a willow?" She was thinking about the willow tree in the backyard of the Diner. All she had to do was walk out the back door and—

"Lord deliver us," Lil said. "Didn't I tell you to follow orders?"

"Well, okay," Violet said. She tucked the mojo bag into the pocket of her blouse. Hoping she could remember the charm until she got home, she whispered, "Safe we go, safe we return, and may we get what we need." She didn't want to forget the magical words that would take her and Cupcake to Nashville and then to Hollywood and a life in the movies. "Thank you."

Lil regarded her, her face stern. "Be wise," she said. "And listen to your little gal."

Violet wanted to ask her what "be wise" was supposed to mean, but Lil was looking past her to Roseanne, who was seated on one of the straight chairs.

"Next," she called, and Roseanne stood. In a kindly tone, Lil said, "Whut you come to ask me for this time, Rosie?"

Violet collected her candles and took the empty chair as Roseanne stepped forward. "Me and Miz Bloodworth was wonderin' if you could give us a spell and maybe some goofer dust to send a spirit back to the cemetery. We had us a dyin' at Magnolia Manor on Sunday and we may need to keep her from coming back."

"Keep her?" Lil asked, interested. "Who died? Whut kind of a dyin' was it?"

"An old lady by the name of Emma Jane Randall," Roseanne said. She wrinkled her brow. "As for what kind of dyin', that's hard to say. The sheriff says maybe some bad person put a poison into some cake she ate. That's why we think goofer dust—"

"Poison!" Lil leaned forward, all ears. "You don't say!"

*Poison?* Violet thought, and instantly remembered what Myra May had told her about the conversation between the sheriff and Doc Roberts, over their pie that morning. *Murder*, Myra May had said. This must be the story they'd been talking about.

"Yes'm. Miz Emma Jane was a perverse lady when she was alive, and Miz Bessie and me are worryin' that she'll be jes' as perverse now she's dead. She might feel like hangin' round the place a bit longer."

"Which she could very well feel like doin'," Lil said, "if she was taken early and unprepared."

"Yes," Roseanne agreed. "We don't want Miz Emma Jane's spirit plaguing the new lady who'll be movin' into her bedroom. Have you got something that'll send her back to the graveyard and keep her there?"

"Prob'ly so," Lil said. "Lemme look."

She hoisted herself out of the chair, went to a shelf, and ran her finger across a row of small earthenware jars. She chose one, pulled out the cork, and tipped a little of the yellowish powder into the palm of her hand, holding it out for Roseanne to see.

"This here is good goofer dust. Graveyard dirt mixed with salt and a little powdered sulfur, for driving away spirits who are makin' a nuisance of theirselves. It's also got some powdered snake skin sheds, red and black pepper, and powdered bones. It's already been blessed," she added.

"I reckon that'll send her back where she belongs," Roseanne said. "We was also thinkin' about purification. Any good way to purify the death room?"

"Well, yes. You start with a good sweep, back to front, then you can do a floor wash. I'm outa the powder, but you can mix up your own. All you need is some red pepper, garlic, salt, black pepper, Mrs. Stewart's bluing, and some saltpeter—but not too much saltpeter, just a pinch. Be generous with the bluing, though."

Roseanne frowned. "I never understood about bluing in a floor wash. How does that work?"

Lil seemed pleased by the question. "Well, you maybe know that lots of hoodoo is in the magical way of 'like makes like.' What something does in the real world, it can also do in the world of the spirits. Bluing in the wash makes white clothes whiter, don't it? So we use it to purify. So you put it in a bucket of warm water with the peppers and garlic and salt, and you scrub. When you got your floor good and clean, sprinkle goofer dust on four white candles and burn 'em in the four corners of the room. Wrap up a nice tight bundle of dried garden sage with blue thread and burn it, too. While you're doing that, keep saying over and over again, 'Spirit be gone. Spirit be gone.' If Miz Emma Jane give you any trouble, you get out that goofer dust again and sprinkle it around."

"Seems like that should 'bout take care of it," Roseanne said. "Thank you very much."

"Always glad to help." The Voodoo Lily looked over at Sally-Lou and beckoned. "Next."

# CHAPTER ELEVEN

# CHARLIE CUTS A DEAL

IT WAS AFTER THREE O'CLOCK ON TUESDAY MORNING WHEN Charlie got in from the stakeout at the Dispatch office. He was frustrated, exasperated, and completely out of patience. Nothing had come of the long and boring six hours he and Hobart Mooney had spent waiting for the tax stamp counterfeiter to show up so they could catch him in the act.

But Mooney—still hopped up on the hope of springing a trap on a criminal—was not in the least discouraged. As he swaggered off to his room at the Old Alabama, his last words had been confident.

"We'll have another go at it tonight, Dickens. I'm going to nab that crooked sonofagun if it's the last thing I do. That boy is going to *jail*."

Another night of being stuffed into the Dispatch storage closet with Hobart Mooney, who dressed like a dandy but smelled like stale beer, cheap cigars, garlic sausage, and Burma-Shave?

Charlie didn't think so. He'd had enough. And now that he'd had time to reflect on the situation, he was ninety-nine-point-nine-nine-nine percent certain that Wilber Casey was not their counterfeiter. Wilber had too good a shot at a career in journalism to risk it all for dirty money—not to mention that Charlie knew for a fact that the boy hadn't been out of Darling since he came to work for the *Dispatch* in December. How could he have gotten hooked up with a syndicate-controlled counterfeit scheme when he hadn't set foot out of town?

Charlie was just as certain that their crook wasn't Baby Mann, who (in his view) was barely smart enough to tie his shoelaces. While Baby might be able to run off a flyer for the Ladies Guild bake sale if somebody loaded the plate and the paper for him, he could never in a million years manage the complicated registrations required to produce a multicolored counterfeit tax stamp on that old Kelsey. No, the counterfeiter that Hobart Mooney was looking to nab was *not* Baby Mann.

Which—to Charlie's wholehearted dismay—left only Osgood Fairchild. The young man who had cheerfully halved Charlie's workload at the *Dispatch*, who had the touch of genius when it came to that misbegotten letterpress, and who (in very short order) had mastered all the Babcock's antique intricacies and was now managing the print run single-handed. Young Osgood might be Mooney's criminal, but he was Charlie's angel.

And Charlie did *not* want to see the boy (for he was *very* young) shipped off to the penitentiary. Which he would be, if Mooney had anything to say about it. And since Mooney would clearly have something to say about the charges, he'd want to see that Osgood was put away for as long as the law would allow.

And therein lay the problem.

Charlie's problem.

"Where have you *been?*" Fannie asked, when Charlie crawled into bed sometime after three a.m. She sniffed. "At the Cotton Gin, smells like."

"I've been shut up in a closet with Hobart Mooney for six

hours," Charlie said darkly. "You're smelling Mooney's cigars and Burma-Shave. And that's all I'm going to say about *that*."

"Good, because I'm going back to sleep," Fannie said sensibly, and rolled over.

But for Charlie, sleep was elusive. For the next hour, he turned over options and plans and scenarios in his head, trying this and testing that. Finally satisfied that he had reached the only possible conclusion and had concocted the only viable plan, he reset the alarm clock for six-thirty instead of eight. When it went off, he stumbled out of bed, dressed, and gulped a cup of coffee. Fannie was still sleeping and he didn't want to wake her, so he silently found her purse, took out two ten-dollar bills, and penciled an IOU, signed with his name and a lopsided heart.

Then he went out to his old green Pontiac, which was parked, as usual, behind Fannie's millinery shop. The sun was just rising over the eastern horizon and the early birds were cheerfully getting their early worms.

Which was why Charlie was up at this obscene hour of the morning. He had a plan for getting his own early worm.

He went first to the Dispatch office, to pick something up. Back in the car, his route took him around the corner and past the post office, so he stopped to mail the monthly subscription check to the Western Newspaper Union for the ready-print and pick up the previous day's delivery from crabby old Caleb Thorpe, who never had a good word to say to anybody.

That's where he ran into Sheriff Norris, who asked how the surveillance had gone. Charlie told the sheriff that nothing much had come of it but a stiff neck and a marked dislike for Mooney's aftershave. However, he might have something for the sheriff later, if things worked out—no promises, though.

"You look like death warmed over," the sheriff said, eyeing him critically. "Something like what?"

Charlie told him.

The sheriff thought for a moment. "Believe we can work it out," he said finally. "But no guarantees. And I gotta hear it myself. In detail."

That's where they left it.

OSGOOD FAIRCHILD HAD A ROOM AT MRS. MEEKS' BOARDINGHOUSE on Railroad Street, two blocks from the Louisville & Nashville railyard and depot. Since it was only a little after seven, Charlie thought Osgood was probably still there, having breakfast.

Charlie knew the Widow Meeks' boarding house well, since he'd had a room there for a couple of months after he sold his dad's place. It was a plain, no-nonsense two-story frame structure painted a noxious shade of green, with darker green trim on the windows and porch rails. Busy indoors from before dawn until after dark, Mrs. Meeks had no time for flowers, so the front yard was a patch of weeds. She boarded men only, no women, no children, no families. Most of her boarders were railroad men or worked at Ozzie Sherman's sawmill or on one of the timber crews. Or at the Vanity Fair plant on the Monroeville highway, which made women's underwear and had just announced that they were about to hire another dozen people. It was well known in the area that if a man needed a place to sleep and couldn't afford the Old Alabama (the cheapest bed was a buck-fifty a night and meals started at a pricey six bits), Mrs. Meeks' was a satisfactory alternative.

Downstairs, there was a pleasant, lace-curtained parlor where the men could read a newspaper, listen to the radio, and grouse about politics or women or the weather. Through a double door was a large dining room (breakfast and supper were included in the board bill), and the massive oak table could accommodate up to sixteen hearty eaters—if there were more, they ate in shifts.

Mrs. Meeks served bountiful breakfasts—eggs, bacon, oatmeal, pancakes, hot buttered biscuits, and coffee—which was enough to stick to your ribs until supper, if you had two bowls of oatmeal. If you wanted lunch, you could keep baloney in the ice box and pack your own, or one of the kitchen girls would pack one for you (sandwich, cheese and crackers, a cookie, and an apple) for twenty cents.

Mrs. Meeks' suppers were definitely worth coming home for, although you had to be there on the dot of five or risk finding an empty plate. It could be meatloaf and mashed potatoes with gravy and Mrs. Meeks' famous overnight icebox rolls. Or maybe beef stew and dumplings or chicken and cornbread dressing or fried catfish and hush puppies. There was always dessert, too: green apple pie or stewed pears or cake. And not one of those newfangled mixes, either, with water and fake eggs and butter. *Real* cake, sometimes with coconut frosting.

And all this, including the bed, for eleven dollars a week plus laundry. Or forty dollars, if you took it by the month and did your own washing and ironing. The rules were minimal but stern: no drinking in the house, no coming in pie-eyed, and the doors were locked at midnight. If you missed curfew, you were welcome to sleep on the porch swing. No refunds for missed meals or for nights when you didn't occupy your bed.

It was about seven-fifteen when Charlie parked his Pontiac a half-block away from Mrs. Meeks' house on the opposite side of Railroad Street. He lit a cigarette, stretched out his legs, and waited. Sam Rose drove by in a Blue Ribbon Dairy truck, on his way to his morning deliveries. A towheaded boy on a rusty old bicycle went whizzing down the middle of the paved street, a Popsicle in one hand. Mrs. Meeks' old cocker spaniel clambered down the front steps and wandered across the street to do his business in a neighbor's yard.

At 7:15, just when Charlie was wondering if he'd somehow missed his quarry, Osgood Fairchild came down the front steps. His shaggy black hair flopped over his forehead the way it always did, his wrists stuck out past the cuffs of his blue work shirt, and white socks showed between his too-short pants and his brown leather shoes. He was carrying a lunch bucket.

Charlie tapped the horn briefly. Osgood saw him and came to the car, breaking out in a friendly grin. "Hey, Mr. Dickens. What're you doin' here?"

"Waiting for you, Osgood," Charlie said, and leaned over to open the passenger door. "Come on, get in."

"Sure thing," Osgood said warmly. "Save me ten blocks on shank's mare." Too tall for the Pontiac, he had to fold himself into thirds to get in. "Nice car," he added appreciatively, although Charlie's Pontiac was almost ten years old and mottled with a patchwork of ancient green paint and rust. "Maybe someday I'll have enough saved up to buy me one."

He could use some of the money from his counterfeiting business, Charlie thought ironically. But he only grunted as he put the Pontiac in gear and pulled away from the curb. At the end of the block, he turned right, toward the depot.

"Got railroad business this morning?" Osgood asked curiously, as Charlie parked at the end of the platform nearest the ticket window. Alvin O'Reilly had just opened up, the way he did every morning, a half hour before the morning train. The local spur went to Monroeville. From there, you could go south to Mobile or north to Montgomery and beyond. You could be in Cincinnati tomorrow.

"*You* have railroad business," Charlie said, turning off the ignition. "At least, that's one of your options."

"My . . . options?" Osgood asked uncertainly.

Charlie reached into the glove box and pulled out the item he'd picked up at the newspaper office that morning. A sheet of tax stamps from the three-inch stack Mooney had found in a box in a dark corner and confiscated as evidence—all but this one, which Charlie had surreptitiously kept.

"Yours, isn't it?" Charlie held it up.

Osgood's face paled. He swallowed, and his prominent Adam's apple bobbed up and down. "Mine?" he whispered. "I don't think I—"

"Yours," Charlie repeated roughly. "Damn it, Osgood, don't make a bad thing worse by lying about it. I know what you've been doing those nights when you claim to be working on job printing orders. You've been running counterfeit tax stamps."

"I don't . . . I—" Osgood swallowed again, then spread his large hands. They were red and chapped, the fingers ink-stained, the knuckles scabbed from encounters with the unforgiving Babcock.

"Yeah. Mine," he said finally, in a dull, despairing voice.

"Well, good." Charlie wadded the sheet into a tight ball and tossed it on the floorboard. "At least we're on the same page. We both know what you've been doing. Now I want to hear the story behind it."

"There isn't—"

"The whole story, Osgood. *All* of it."

It came out, haltingly, accompanied by jerky motions and gulps and throat clearings and long, awkward pauses. It was pretty much the way Mooney had it figured, although there was more to it than Mooney—Charlie, too, for that matter—could have guessed.

Forget the story Osgood had told when Charlie hired him, about Pinetucky and an English teacher and not knowing anything about presses. The boy had grown up in a small town south of Tuscaloosa, on the southern rim of the ridge-and-valley

Appalachians. His father packed up his banjo and went off to play bluegrass with the Boll Weevils in Nashville, joined a band that took off for California, and never came back. His mother fed the family by doing laundry for folks in the washhouse in the back yard.

Most of the boys in Osgood's extended family stayed in Tuscaloosa County, except for his older cousin Abner. As a kid, Abner had been an inveterate tormenter and a bully, in and out of trouble with the law. Once, he'd stolen Osgood's bicycle and wrecked it at the bottom of the gravel pit. Another time, he set fire to a shed at the school. When he got a local girl pregnant, he left town. Osgood was not a bit surprised when he heard that he'd ended up in Georgia, working for Eddie Guyol. Osgood himself didn't leave the county, at least not then. He only went as far as—

"Wait a minute," Charlie interrupted. "Eddie Guyol. Isn't he the bootlegger who got gunned down outside his mansion in Atlanta? Just in the last couple of weeks or so?"

"That's him." Osgood made a face. "Guyol. The 'liquor king' of Atlanta. Head of his own syndicate."

Charlie had read about the sensational murder, which had been all over the wire services for days. Dressed fit to kill, on their way to a party, Guyol and his wife had climbed into their Cadillac in front of their home in an affluent Atlanta neighborhood. A man jumped out of the shrubbery, stuck a .45 through the driver's window, snarled "You've got it coming, Eddie," and pulled the trigger. Eddie's wife, Myrtle, splattered with her husband's blood, had passed out. When she came to, she telephoned Eddie's right-hand man, Walter Cutcliffe, before she phoned the cops. Unsurprisingly, the killer had not yet been found.

Since the first years of Prohibition, Guyol had run one of the biggest bootlegging operations in the country. But the illicit liquor business had taken a big hit when Repeal came along and sent bootleggers scrambling for a new career. Guyol had moved into the numbers racket—illegal bets, placed in illegal betting parlors scattered across the state—bulldozing his competition along the way. His lottery syndicate, the Home Company, was reported to be the largest and most successful of all the Atlanta crime syndicates, employing as many as fifteen thousand people and putting some $50,000 a day into Guyol's pockets.

But Repeal had taught Eddie Guyol that it was prudent to have more than one line of business. He broadened out to the counterfeiting of alcohol and cigarette tax stamps, setting up a network of various engravers, print shops, and liquor and tobacco distributors around the state. People needed work, Guyol said, so he spread out the jobs and paid well, counting on loyalty to keep folks' mouths shut. He told his employees that it was smart to involve their family members whenever they could. When it came to the nut-cutting, your brother or your cousin or your father-in-law could be counted on. Blood was thicker than water any day of the week.

That's where Osgood came in. While he was still in high school, he got a job in a print shop in Tuscaloosa, where he had learned how to operate several letterpresses. He was good at the work, he enjoyed it, and after he graduated from high school, his boss put him in charge of the shop's entire print operation. He kept enough from his salary to pay his rent and buy his meals, but most of it went back home to support his mother (who was sick half the time) and his three younger sisters.

And then Abner showed up. Osgood hadn't heard from his cousin since he took off for Atlanta, but there he was, out of the blue and with a lucrative proposal. Guyol was expanding his syndicate into Alabama. He had set up an office in Birmingham and wanted to hire a good Alabama counterfeiter. Using the materials and engravings supplied by Guyol's syndicate,

Osgood could print the tax stamps at night, when the shop was closed and nobody else was around to snoop. He would earn a dollar for every sheet of Alabama stamps he sent to the tobacco distributor, and he could expect to get an order for a print run every couple of weeks. And what would he get in return? Moonlighting for the syndicate, he could earn maybe five hundred a month—four times as much as the twenty-five dollars a week he was getting from his day job. The chances of getting caught, Abner said, were very small, because neither Georgia nor Alabama had the manpower to go poking around in small print shops.

Abner had a good line. Easy production, easy money, low risk. If you asked most folks, he said, they'd tell you that counterfeiting wasn't a crime. It was simply screwing the system, which was okay with just about everybody. If you could make a few dollars that way, well, have at it. Screw the system.

Osgood wasn't averse to screwing the system and he didn't think he was likely to get caught. But he wasn't keen on the idea of getting tangled up with Abner and the syndicate, even if the money was good. His cousin was pushy, even aggressive, but Osgood held out against his intimidation. He told him no—not just once, but several times.

But then his mother was diagnosed with lung cancer, could no longer support herself and Osgood's younger sisters, and desperately needed doctoring. So the next time Abner came around and began hounding him to say yes, Osgood agreed and the thing was all set. He would get a message by mail from Abner, who would also ship him the supplies—the special watermarked paper, the ink, and any new engravings. Osgood would print the job and put the package on the next Greyhound, shipping it to the Birmingham address Abner had given him.

And the money? Yeah, that was what he was doing it for—to

see that his mother got the medical treatment she needed. He arranged with Abner to send the payoff directly to his family, keeping nothing for himself.

"I didn't want it, y'see," Osgood said grimly. "It was dirty money. But it did for Mother what needed to be done. Bought her some time, anyway."

This went on without incident until the owner of the print shop died. The shop closed and Osgood was out of a job. By this time, his mother had died and his sisters were old enough to work. Osgood found himself hating his bullying cousin and was desperate to escape from the clutches of the syndicate. So he changed his name (his real name: Daryl Goodwin), and looked around for a small town where he could lay low for a while, keeping his head down. All he wanted was a job and a clean place to sleep.

He finally found what he was looking for in Darling.

And then, just a week ago, his cousin Abner caught up with him. With Eddie dead, Walter Cutcliffe had seized control of the syndicate, and Abner said he needed to secure a place in Cutcliffe's criminal empire. He told Osgood that if he would do just one more print run of the counterfeit stamps—a big run, big enough to show Cutcliffe what Abner could produce—that would be the end of it. He'd stop badgering and go away. Osgood would never hear from him again.

And if he refused? Trouble. Bad trouble. And not just trouble for Osgood, either. Trouble for the *Dispatch*, like maybe a fire. Or something.

"So the story you sold me—about a passion for the printed word, wanting to be a printer—that was all just so many lies," Charlie said.

Osgood sighed. "Well, the Pinetucky part was lies. The rest of it is true, sorta. There's nothin' on this earth I'd rather be than a printer. But there was my mother's doctor bills stacked up to the ceiling and no way of paying them. What I was doing for Abner was wrong, but how else was I gonna pay those bills?" His mouth twisted and tears came into his eyes. "And now I'm stuck with him and the syndicate. I'm like a bobcat caught in a trap. I can't get out."

Charlie sighed. A true story? Of course, it could be checked out, but Osgood had the manner of a young man finally telling the truth.

He searched Osgood's face. "Do you want to get out?"

"Oh, Lord, do I want to get out?" Osgood rolled his eyes. "You're the third print shop where I've worked in the past twelve months, and Darling is the third little town. But this is the first time I've had a clean place to sleep, good food to eat, and my clothes washed regular. And every day, I get to work on that wonderful old Babcock. And the Kelsey—man, those presses are like my friends. And there's Wilber and Baby and . . . and *you*. And maybe even a girl." He ducked his head.

"A girl?" Charlie asked.

"Yeah. Katy. We both sing in the Methodist choir. We went for a walk a couple of evenings ago. She's . . . nice."

Charlie liked to be known as a crusty old newsman, detached, dispassionate, objective. But there was something under that exterior—something softer, more compassionate, something that loved the human side of every story. That was the part of Charlie that had lain awake until nearly four a.m., trying out alternatives. He sat for a moment, in silence.

Then he said, "Okay, Osgood, here's what you need to know. There's a man in town, Hobart Mooney, from Montgomery. He's a state tax agent, and he's been following the trail of the tax stamps you've been printing. He's traced them back here, to the *Dispatch*. He doesn't know if the counterfeiter is you, Wilber, or Baby—or two of you or all three."

Osgood started to say something, but Charlie held up his

hand. "Mooney and I staked the place out last night, waiting for one of you to show up and start running the Kelsey. When that didn't pan out, he said we'd repeat the surveillance tonight, and he went back to the hotel where he'll no doubt sleep all day. So if you want to get away, you've got at least a full day's start." He reached into his pocket and pulled out the money he'd taken from Fannie's billfold. "Here's twenty. It's enough to buy yourself a ticket up north someplace."

Charlie put the money on the dash, then pointed to his watch. "You've got time to get on the morning train, which leaves in twenty-two minutes. Mooney won't hear about this from me. And neither will Abner, if he shows up looking for you. You'll want to get a new name. A new job. You're a good printer. You'll find work."

"Options." Licking his lips, Osgood stared at the money. "You said options, plural. You got something else in mind?"

"Yeah." This was the hard part, the thing that Osgood would be reluctant to do. This was what Charlie had told Buddy about this morning, in front of the post office. No promises, he'd said, because he wouldn't blame Osgood for picking up that pair of tens and getting on the train.

"You can go back into town with me. To the sheriff's office. You can sit down with him and tell your story, voluntarily. Everything you've told me, plus the names of the syndicate guys. Abner's name, his buddies' names, the addresses you used to mail the stamps. The sheriff will come up with a charge—I don't know what it'll be, a felony or a misdemeanor. Something that will hold you here locally. In jail."

"And that tax agent? Mooney?"

The Burma-Shave guy. Charlie smiled bleakly. "When Mooney wakes up and wanders over to the sheriff's office, he'll be informed that you've come in voluntarily and told the full story. That you've named names and described procedures and that your information will be turned over to him so he can go after the members of the syndicate. They're the ones he's really after." He paused. "He'll probably want to get on it right away. Maybe he'll take the afternoon train."

Osgood was chewing on his lip. "You said jail. How long, d'you reckon?"

"That I can't tell you. You'll have a lawyer. There'll be a bond hearing and Judge McHenry will set bail. The bail will be met—out of your salary—and you can go back to living at Mrs. Meeks' and working at the *Dispatch* until the case is settled. Could be your lawyer will work out a plea bargain." He paused. "No promises, though."

"I understand." Osgood sat very still for a moment, his eyes on the two ten-dollar bills on the dashboard. At last, he said, "You've got a deal, Mr. Dickens. Let's go see the sheriff."

"Good idea," Charlie said, and started the car. He was shifting into gear when Osgood put a hand on his arm.

"Before we go," he said. "I need to say thank you. I really don't know why you're doing this for me. I don't deserve it."

Charlie turned to give him a straight look. "Let's just say that I like you, Osgood. And that I don't much like Mr. Mooney— or his methods." Or his Burma-Shave.

And that he *did* like the way Osgood managed that newspaper print run on Thursday nights—all by himself.

# CHAPTER TWELVE

# BUDDY GETS A BREAK

BUDDY NORRIS FROWNED DOWN AT THE REPORT HE WAS WRITing. He was not the most competent writer in the world, so reports were a chore that required his full attention. This morning, he had come in early to take care of a few things, one of which involved checking with the Diner to see if Myra May had any information for him about yesterday's anonymous phone call.

So when the telephone rang at seven-thirty, he thought it was Myra May, calling back. It wasn't. Hearing the caller's name, he straightened in his chair, pulled his notebook out of his pocket, and began penciling rapid notes. At one point he asked, "What was that again, Doc?" and later, "How do you spell that?"

But mostly he listened, trying to make sure he was getting it straight because there were several scientific-sounding words he wasn't sure he understood and several more that were pure Greek to him. Or maybe Latin. How was he to know?

When the call was finished, he hung up, got up from his desk, and took his empty coffee mug into the kitchen at the rear of the sheriff's office, where Deputy Springer had fired up Mrs. Crumpler's wood-burning kitchen range and was standing over a cast iron griddle with a pancake flipper in his hand.

"Want some?" Wayne asked over his shoulder. "I got extra batter here. And there's maple syrup."

The sight of Wayne's pancakes, crisp around the edges and brown all over, made Buddy's mouth water. "Well, sure," he said. "If you don't mind fryin' up a few more."

He had eaten breakfast at Mrs. Beedle's as usual (his seven-fifty-a-week board bill included five free breakfasts), but his landlady wasn't any too generous with her helpings. Two strips of bacon, a teacup-size bowl of oatmeal, a couple of slices of toast, and a cup of coffee was all he got. He didn't complain because he knew Mrs. Beedle was trying to make ends meet when there wasn't near enough slack in the middle. Hard to put a decent breakfast on the table when the price of bacon had rocketed up to thirty-three cents a pound. Mr. Parrish had ought to keep a more watchful eye on Ruby, or somebody would turn her into hams.

"No trouble," Wayne said, and flipped a pancake. "There's more'n I can eat, and the Beast doesn't like pancakes." Sleeves rolled up, cigarette dangling from one corner of his mouth, he looked comfortably at home with the pancake flipper. "Was that Doc Roberts you were talking to just now?"

"Yep," Buddy said. "He just got off the phone with Doc Martin over in Monroeville—the one who did the testing on Miz Randall." He filled his mug from the coffee pot that was perking merrily on the back of the stove. As usual, it was black as tar and strong enough to float a battleship. "Looks like we got us a murder."

Wayne transferred the four pancakes from the griddle to a stack keeping warm on a plate next to the percolator. He added a dollop of butter to the griddle and poured four more puddles of batter, sizzling in the hot butter.

Around his cigarette, he said, "It was nicotine, then." It wasn't a question.

"Yeah, nicotine," Buddy replied. The autopsy report Doc Roberts had read to him in detail had been full of complicated scientific terms—something about alkaloids and precipitates and Mayer's test and milligrams, 210 of them (whatever milligrams were), when it only took 60 of them to kill a person. There'd been no tobacco fiber, so the nicotine was in some sort of liquid form. But nicotine was the bottom line. Doc Roberts promised that the autopsy report would spell it out so that even the dumbest juror—or the sheriff—could understand.

"The doc said it could've been that Black Leaf Forty you were talking about yesterday," Buddy added. "It's concentrated. Doesn't have much of an odor, 'slightly fishy,' if anything. But it tastes bitter. I'm remembering the note that came with the cake. It said there was coffee and chicory in the recipe, which would cover up the taste of the poison."

Buddy made a face. He'd never understood why folks liked chicory in their coffee or coffee and chicory with their chocolate. A good way to spoil chocolate, to his way of thinking.

Wayne flipped the first two pancakes. "So you're going to have a little talk with Miz Walker? Get her prints, too?"

Buddy glanced at the windup clock that sat on top of the icebox. Ten minutes to eight. Mrs. Walker was Duffy's secretary. The bank didn't open until ten, but she would likely be at her desk in another hour. He'd bring her over to the office for their conversation. Wayne had found a couple of clear prints on the wrapping paper. When they printed her, chances were good that they'd find a match. And of course, her name and return address was on the wrapping paper in nice, clear block letters, big as life. He wondered what she would say when she saw *that*.

"I'm talking to her this morning," he said. "Moseley's out of the office today, so we'll likely have this all wrapped up by the time he gets back. While I'm dealing with Miz Walker, here's what I want you to do."

Wayne listened to what Buddy told him, nodded, and said, "I can do that, soon as I can get hold of Judge McHenry."

"He's never in his chambers until the middle of the morning. Just go over to his house and tell him what you need. He won't give you any trouble."

"I'll do it." Wayne picked up the pitcher. "How many pancakes you want?"

"How many you got?"

Wayne squinted into the pitcher. "Five, six maybe." He took another pull on his cigarette, raised a lid on the range, and dropped the butt into the fire.

"Might as well fry 'em all up," Buddy said. "I doubt they'll go to waste." He pulled out a chair and sat down at the table, watching Wayne pour more pancakes. "I ran into Charlie Dickens, getting into his car in front of the post office just now. He said nothing came of the stakeout last night. Him and that field agent stayed with it until nearly three a.m., then called it quits."

Wayne chuckled. "If Charlie stayed up that late, I'm surprised he was out of bed this morning."

"I told him he looked like death warmed over," Buddy said. "Said he might have something for us later today."

"Something like what? Information?" Wayne took several dishes to the sink and ran cold water over them.

Buddy reported what Charlie had said. "I told him no guarantees," he added. "But I gotta come up with a charge. Any ideas?"

"How about unauthorized use of property?" Wayne went back to the stove and flipped a pancake. "Or maybe theft of services? Fourth degree would get the kid a fine but no jail time."

Buddy looked at him with admiration. "That's why I hired you."

"Huh," Wayne said, but he looked pleased. "Well, you'd best watch out. Mooney won't be any too happy if he has to leave

Darling without making his very own personal arrest. And taking his prisoner with him—in handcuffs. That fella has a yen to play cops and robbers."

"You're right about that," Buddy said. "But we're getting ahead of ourselves here. Gotta see what Charlie comes up with first."

"If Mooney was expecting the stakeout to work, it would probably take a few nights." Wayne put the pancakes on the table, found a couple of plates and forks and refilled his coffee mug. "He was willing to stick around?"

"He had to be, if he wanted to catch his counterfeiter." Buddy forked several pancakes onto his plate and lathered on the butter. "And make him squeal, which I figure is the point of this exercise."

"Right." Wayne sat down and sluiced syrup onto his pancakes. "Mooney wants the big boys. The sharks behind the little fish."

"The sharks who are calling the shots," Buddy added. "He wants names."

That's how he had put it together, anyway. He was mostly guessing and maybe he wasn't right, since nothing like this had ever happened in Darling. He just knew he didn't much appreciate Hobart Mooney barging in and demanding an arrest. Didn't trust him much, either.

So what Charlie had in mind—if it worked out, which it probably wouldn't—was a much more attractive proposition, as far as Buddy was concerned. Mooney wouldn't get his arrest, but he'd get his information. Whether that made him happy was his lookout.

Wayne glanced up, his fork loaded with pancake bites. "Been meaning to ask if you know what's going on with Mickey LeDoux. I hear he's been asking around town for Baby

Mann, but no dice. Everybody is stonewalling him and Baby is nowhere to be seen."

Thinking that Darling was seeing more than its usual allotment of trouble this week, Buddy picked up his coffee mug. "You heard right," he said grimly. "Early release. I don't know what he's got in mind, but he's making everybody nervous."

Wayne chewed thoughtfully. "That debacle out at Dead Cow Creek happened before I got to Darling, but I've heard the story so many times from so many people that I've got every detail memorized. Every version names Baby as the stool pigeon and blames him for Rider's dyin'. If I was that boy, I'd find myself a good hidey-hole somewhere, pull the lid over on top of me, and play like I'm dead until LeDoux goes away."

Buddy nodded, agreeing. "I sure wouldn't want Mickey to find me. Wouldn't be healthy." He went back to his pancakes.

"What if he did?" Wayne chewed and swallowed. "Find Baby, I mean. What would Mickey do?"

"Do?" Buddy chuckled darkly. "Why, I reckon he'd shoot him." He drained his coffee mug. "Mickey's a crack shot. None of the Manns are man enough to stop him. Ain't *nobody* goin' to stop him—unless it's you or me." Pointedly, he eyed Wayne's gun belt and gun hanging on the coat hooks beside the door. "You're better with that thing than I am," he added casually. "If it looks like there's going to be shooting, I'll let you arrest him."

"Druther it be you," Wayne said. "Then if he shoots you, I'll shoot him."

There was a rap at the kitchen door and both turned to see Charlie Dickens standing there, accompanied by a young man with loose dark hair and a shirt with sleeves too short for his long arms.

"Got somebody here you can arrest," Charlie said cheerfully. He stepped back. "This is Osgood Fairchild."

The young man pulled his mouth down. "If you're going to

arrest me, better use my real name, I guess. I'm Daryl Goodwin. I'm the counterfeiter you're looking for."

"I believe," Charlie said quietly, "that Daryl has several names for you, Sheriff. Big names."

"Glad to hear that." Buddy pushed back his chair and stood, coffee cup in his hand. "Let's you and me sit down in the office and have us a little talk, Daryl." He turned to Wayne. "Got some coffee in that pot for our friend here?"

"Sure thing," Wayne said. He filled a mug and handed it to Daryl. "You better have a cup, too, Charlie." He frowned as the sheriff and Daryl left the room. "You look like death warmed over."

"Somebody else already said that to me this morning." Charlie pulled out a chair and eyed the plate in the middle of the table. "I see you got a couple of pancakes left. I skipped breakfast. How about if I finish them off? Be a shame if they sat here and got cold while I went hungry."

"All yours," Wayne said, pushing his chair back and standing up. "I have to go and get the judge to sign a search warrant." He went to the coat hooks by the door and took down his gun belt and gun. "Stack your dishes in the sink when you're done," he said, buckling the gun belt. He put on a dusty black cowboy hat. "I'll wash 'em up when I get back."

# CHAPTER THIRTEEN

# BEULAH DOES HAIR

BEULAH TRIVETTE HAD GOTTEN UP EARLY ON TUESDAY MORN-
ing to do an early-bird client, Alice Ann Walker. Alice Ann
didn't like to ask Mr. Duffy for time off during the day and
her family responsibilities made it impossible to come in after
work. So once a month, she came in at seven-forty-five for
a quick trim. Beulah, who liked to accommodate her clients
whenever she could (especially another Dahlia, like Alice Ann),
was always glad to do hair early when hair needed to be done.

This was a special appointment, though. Alice Ann, who
usually pinched every penny until it squeaked, had decided to
splurge on a thirty-five-cent shampoo and set, and Beulah was
combing her out. Which was the best part of the process, as
far as Beulah was concerned. She viewed herself as an artist,
every bit like Michelangelo or that guy who was carving the
presidents up north somewhere—in the Dakotas, maybe? Men
made beautiful things out of big chunks of rock, while she
made beautiful hair.

Beulah was combing out Alice Ann's newly curly back hair
when the bell over the front door tinkled and she looked up to
see Bessie Bloodworth, a little early for her usual eight-fifteen
with Bettina Higgens. Bettina, who had been Beulah's beauty

associate for several years now, was especially talented when it came to making the teensy-weensy pin curls that Bessie liked so much. When Bettina was finished doing her, Bessie always looked like she was wearing a gray Persian lamb hat on her head.

"Well, hello there, Bessie," Beulah said with a welcoming smile. "Bettina called a few minutes ago and said she was running late. She forgot to wind her alarm clock. You doin' okay this mornin'?"

"Well as can be expected," Bessie said. She blinked. "Is that Alice Ann Walker under all those curls?"

"It's me, all right," Alice Ann said in a sprightly tone, admiring herself in the mirror. "Do you like it? I thought I'd better get it done before the funeral." She looked up to meet Bessie's eyes in the big mirror on the wall, her own eyes wide. "I was just so *shocked* when I learned that Emma Jane died on Sunday, Bessie. Really, you could have knocked me over with a feather! And to think it happened while we were all at the Dahlias' clubhouse, having a party. A stroke is what I heard—is that right?"

This was more than Alice Ann usually said in a half hour, but when Bessie just stood there like a stone, without a word to say, she went on.

"Well, all I can tell you is that she seemed perfectly well the last time I saw her—full up with pickled ginger, as my grandma used to say. We had such a nice conversation at the picnic table in your backyard." She heaved a dramatic sigh. "But then, the two of us have always gotten along pretty well. We were cousins, you know. Second cousins once removed." Another sigh. "I only wish I could have spent more time with her toward the end. She'd been abandoned by her brother and her niece. She was a lonely soul."

"If you say so," Bessie replied crisply, and took a seat in one of the chairs along the wall. To Beulah, she added, "Don't mind me. I'll just sit over here and read a *Ladies Home Journal* until Bettina is ready to do me."

Which was curious, Beulah thought. Bessie usually talked up a storm, especially when it came to something interesting, like somebody dying or having a baby or getting a new living room suite. The Bower was gossip central for all the Darling ladies, who couldn't resist the temptation to pass along the juicy story they had just heard and had promised not to tell anybody. Sometimes people said things that you didn't want to believe. That you *couldn't* believe.

For example, Leona Ruth Adcock had said just yesterday afternoon that she had seen Violet Sims buying two Greyhound bus tickets to Nashville, and heard her say that little Cupcake was going to win the Shirley Temple look-alike contest so the two of them could go right straight to Hollywood. They were leaving on Thursday and never coming back.

*Never coming back?* Beulah had been so surprised that she nearly dropped her scissors. *Never coming back?* she wanted to shriek. *You're not saying that Violet is taking dear little Cupcake away from Darling forever?*

But she didn't, of course. She just said "Mmm," and somehow managed to snag the comb in Leona Ruth's stringy wet hair. Just a little.

"And it's a *secret*, naturally," Leona Ruth had said, in a stage whisper that could have been heard as far away as the courthouse. "So don't you go and tell it on *The Flour Hour* the next time you're on the radio, Beulah."

Beulah had no intention of saying a word on the radio about Violet taking Cupcake away forever. When Mildred Kilgore asked her to share the local news during *The Flour Hour* on Darling's new radio station, Beulah had promised both Mildred and herself that she would deliver only the *good* news—interesting tidbits about local doings that weren't likely to cause anybody any heartburn or hurt anybody's feelings. And only the news she knew without a doubt to be true. Nobody was ever going to accuse her of peddling *fake* news. (Of course, you couldn't avoid mentioning it when somebody lost a pig or broke a leg or died. Things like that were just a natural part of life and everybody ought to know about them.)

Even though Beulah didn't contribute to the constant stream of gossip that flowed through the Bower like the mighty Mississippi in an April flood, just listening was sometimes enough to curl a person's hair. For instance, what she had heard yesterday afternoon from Mrs. Sedalius (one of Bessie's Magnolia ladies) about poor old Mrs. Randall. Mrs. Sedalius didn't always remember things exactly the way they happened and her stories were sometimes like a kudzu vine, all twisted up and hard to follow.

Once Beulah got it untwisted, the gist of it seemed to be that Mrs. Randall—who had gotten a permanent wave at the Bower just last week—had died after eating (all by herself, without sharing a single bite) most of a chocolate cake baked by Alice Ann Walker—the very lady whose hair she was doing right now. Of course, Beulah wasn't going to mention this to Alice Ann, who must feel bad enough already, especially since she couldn't have guessed that Mrs. Randall would be such a pig.

Beulah was troubled. Why in the world hadn't somebody warned Mrs. Randall that eating a whole, entire chocolate cake was definitely *not* a good idea?

But nothing much could disturb Beulah's contentment this morning, or any other morning, for that matter. She had everything she had ever wanted. Darling friends and a lovely little town to live in. A devoted husband (Hank) and two quite remarkable children (Hank Junior and Spoonie). And good work to do, for it was Beulah's very great privilege to spend all day every day (except Sunday, of course), using her

God-given talent as an artist to make plain women pretty and pretty women beautiful.

Beulah had spruced up that God-given talent somewhat. The day after her high graduation, she had gone to Montgomery and worked her way through the Montgomery College of Cosmetology. Her diploma and the accompanying certificate, framed and hung right at eye-level next to the mirror at her hair-cutting station, testified to the fact that she could cut the latest bob, manage a marcel, work miracles with a curling iron, and color hair in all shades of auburn, blond, and brunette. As Beulah saw it, bringing out the beauty in people was one of the worthiest vocations on the face of God's beautiful earth, especially when she could do it in her very own beauty shop.

The Beauty Bower used to be a screened-in back porch at their house on Dauphin Street. Hank, who might not be much to look at but was the most supportive, cooperative husband in all the world, had enclosed the porch to make it comfortable during the winter and wired it for electricity so Beulah could have the latest beauty equipment. The new Kenmore hand-held hair dryer, for instance, and the permanent-wave machine with amazing drop-down curlers that electrically heated hair to create a curl that lasted for weeks, and the new electric hot water heater, so the water came straight out of the faucet at the perfect temperature to shampoo every head. Hank installed side-by-side sinks and hair-cutting chairs and large wall mirrors in front of the chairs. Beulah painted the wainscoting her favorite peppermint pink, wallpapered the walls with fat pink roses, and spatter-painted the pink enamel floor with gray, blue, and yellow. It was her intention to make the Bower so enticing that ladies simply could not wait to come and get beautiful.

And there was no point in waiting for Bettina this morning. So when Alice Ann hurried off to her job at the bank, she said to Bessie, "My nine-thirty won't be here for a while yet, hon, so just come on over here and I'll shampoo you. That way, you'll be all ready for Bettina to put in your pin curls when she gets here." She paused. "Of course, if you'd rather read . . ."

"I'm ready if you are," Bessie said, putting down the *Ladies Home Journal*. She had only been turning the pages, not reading at all, since she had so much on her mind—especially with Alice Ann Walker sitting right there in front of her, getting all dolled up so she could look beautiful for poor Emma Jane's funeral. It was a scandal, that's what it was.

Bessie got up and followed Beulah to the shampoo chair. The Bower was empty now, except for her and Beulah. The radio on the shelf beside the shampoo station was tuned to WDAR, which was playing one of Bessie's favorite songs: the Carter Family singing "Keep On the Sunny Side."

And when she sat down and leaned her head back in the sink, Bessie heard herself talking about what was first and foremost on her mind, which was—who else?—Alice Ann and Emma Jane. And Beulah was such a quietly attentive listener that Bessie found herself saying far more than she had intended.

In fact, while Beulah shampooed and rinsed her hair and used her special hair-beautification ointment to smooth away any split ends, Bessie related the entire story, beginning with Roseanne's startling announcement, "Miz Emma Jane, she's dead," and continuing with the sheriff's visit to Magnolia Manor and what he had found in Emma Jane's bedroom—the last piece of cake in the box under the bed and the card saying who had sent it (Alice Ann)—plus Roseanne's report of what she had overheard of the conversation at the picnic table while she was doing dishes.

"Alice Ann's going to inherit Mrs. Randall's *house?*" Beulah exclaimed with a delighted smile. "Why, that's wonderful news, Bessie! She and Arnold can sell it and use the money to buy a house here in Darling and—oops, sorry, sweetie."

She had gotten so excited that she splashed water on Bessie's face. She began patting Bessie's wet forehead with a dry washcloth.

Bessie closed her eyes. "I'm afraid it's not that simple, Beulah."

And then, because she had already spilled so many beans that she might as well spill the rest, she told Beulah about the autopsy report from Dr. Martin, over in Monroeville. She had heard the awful news that very morning, from Doc Roberts' wife and office nurse, Edna Fay.

She had happened to run into Edna Fay at Lima's Drugs, where she had gone early to buy several items for the Magnolia ladies. She had already picked up a can of Mack's Foot Life cream for Miss Rogers and a Staywave invisible hairnet for Leticia Wiggens. She was reaching for Maxine Bechtel's Mum (*No smart woman risks offending. Make sure of your charm with MUM!*) when she looked up and saw Edna Fay.

Edna Fay, who had come to Lima's to pick up a box of surgical gauze, had just heard from her husband, Doc Roberts, what the doctor in Monroeville had said about Mrs. Randall and that chocolate cake. She had it on her mind, so it just came tumbling out.

And why not? Mrs. Randall had been one of Bessie's Magnolia ladies and had died in Bessie's upstairs bedroom. Bessie would hear it soon enough, anyway. She might as well hear it from the horse's mouth.

And now Bessie herself couldn't keep this secret for another second, especially since she knew that Beulah (who was constitutionally unable to say a bad thing about anybody, no matter how wicked they were) would not tell a soul.

Beulah was so shocked she stopped massaging Bessie's scalp and stood stone still, her eyes wide.

"*Nicotine poison?*" she exclaimed. "Why, I read about that just last week, Bessie! Seems like smoking cigarettes won't kill you. But if you don't watch what you're doing, you can get accidentally poisoned by that Black Leaf Forty I use to kill those mean old aphids on my big cabbage roses. So I marched straight out to the shed, got the can, and flushed the poison down the toilet. I was afraid the kids might get their hands on it."

"That was smart," Bessie replied. "Edna Fay said that the doctor said that there was enough poison in that cake to kill anybody who ate more than a couple of pieces. Emma Jane loved chocolate so much that she ate the whole thing all by herself—all but the very last piece, which we found under her bed, still in the box it came in. The sheriff is the one who sent it to the doctor to be tested," she added, lest Beulah think it was *her* idea.

"Oh, my goodness," Beulah murmured. "So it *was* the cake that killed her." She began working on Bessie's scalp again. "But Mrs. Sedalius told me yesterday that the cake was a gift from . . ." Her voice died away.

"From Alice Ann," Bessie said grimly. "Yes, I'm afraid it's true."

"No!" Beulah shook her head. "Alice Ann Walker is a Dahlia, like you and me. I have been doing her once a month for as long as I can remember. You will *not* convince me that she would deliberately poison somebody."

Privately, Bessie thought that Beulah was so sweet and good-hearted that she couldn't bring herself to think ill of Bonnie and Clyde, so her defense of Alice Ann didn't count for much.

But of course she didn't say that. Instead, she said, "I felt the same way in the beginning, Beulah. I didn't want to believe that Alice Ann had anything to do with this. But there was a card with the cake. 'With dearest love from your cousin, Alice Ann.' And Roseanne overheard Emma Jane telling Alice Ann that she had changed her will and that *she* was going to inherit a house over in Birmingham."

"Oh, dear," Beulah whispered. "That's going to look like she knew what she was getting. Which gives her a whaddyacallit. A motive."

"Yes." Bessie sighed. "As Verna would say, it looks like an open-and-shut case. Everybody knows that the Walkers are having a terrible time. With Arnold's medical bills and the three grandchildren, Alice Ann's paycheck just isn't enough to cover everything. And now she has to find another place for them to live." Another sigh. "I can't blame her for being terribly excited when she heard that Emma Jane was leaving her that house."

Beulah looked stricken, as if she wanted to come to Alice Ann's defense but couldn't think of anything to say. Wordlessly, she turned on the faucet and began to rinse Bessie's hair.

But Bessie wasn't quite finished threshing the whole thing out in her mind.

"You know," she said pensively, "the one I feel sorry for is old George Clemens, Emma Jane's brother. He thought he was going to inherit his sister's property. They didn't get on all that well, especially in the past few months. But in a family, fault always goes both ways. It wasn't right for Emma Jane to cut out her brother in favor of somebody way out on a twig of the family tree."

"I can agree with that," Beulah said. She finished rinsing Bessie's hair, squeezed out the water, and wrapped her head in a white towel, turban style. "But it's . . ." She was going to say *impossible*, but she chose another word. "It's hard for me to feature Alice Ann doing such a thing. She's so quiet. And, well, kind of timid."

"She isn't, really," Bessie said. "She just likes people to think of her that way." She pushed herself into a sitting position. "She has a determined streak a mile wide and half a mile deep. She has to, to manage that family of hers and all its troubles. And if some deviousness is needed, well . . ." She reached up and straightened her turban on her head. "*Somebody* did this awful thing, Beulah. Every time I think about it, I keep coming back to just one question. If Alice Ann didn't bake that cake and send it to Emma Jane, who did, and why? And I can't think of a single soul. Not one."

Now, Beulah was not usually a very reflective person. She believed that if you went looking for trouble, you were likely to put your foot on a rattlesnake with a longstanding objection to being disturbed. But she had to admit that Bessie was right: there was an occasional calculating shrewdness in Alice Ann, like a poker player who knew exactly where the aces were. She seemed to have been born with the ability to pull a rabbit out of a hat when everybody else was expecting an empty hat.

And something else. Beulah supposed that Alice Ann couldn't be blamed for wanting to splurge on a shampoo and set, since she was expecting to come into Mrs. Randall's money. But it almost seemed like *celebrating*, didn't it? Was it right to be glad that you were inheriting a house, when the gift was the very last act of a person who died? Worse, had Alice Ann decided that the lives of five people were worth more than the life of one old, cantankerous lady?

These were complicated thoughts, and Beulah didn't like complications. But she couldn't seem to let go of them. They kept coming into her mind as Bettina arrived, twirled up Bessie's pin curls quickly, then put her under the dryer and went off to plop the Bower's towels into the Maytag wringer washer in the wash house out back.

Beulah was still thinking about them when Liz Lacy, bright and cheerful as usual, arrived for her once-a-month eight-thirty appointment. Liz made arrangements with her boss, Mr. Moseley, to open the office a little later on those days.

"My goodness, Beulah," Liz said, hanging her pink sweater

on the coat hooks near the door. "You look like you're chewing on a big wad of worry. What's wrong?"

Beulah glanced over at Bessie, who was engrossed in the latest issue of *Good Housekeeping* under the dryer and couldn't hear a thing. Bettina was in the wash house, and it was just the two of them in the shop. In a low voice, she said, "You sit right down in that chair, Liz. I'll tell you the whole thing while I do you. Are we going short today, or medium long?"

Normally, of course, Beulah wouldn't have breathed a word of what Bessie had told her. But Liz Lacy worked in Mr. Moseley's office and dealt with legal matters every day. Alice Ann looked to be in a big pot of trouble. Was she going to end up needing a lawyer? Could Mr. Moseley help?

So, while Beulah snipped and combed and combed and snipped, she told Liz every scrap of what she knew about Alice Ann, Emma Jane, and the poisoned chocolate cake.

She concluded with the question that was most on her mind. "Do you think Alice Ann could have done it, Liz?"

Lizzy had already learned one part of the story from Sheriff Norris and another part from her reading of Mrs. Randall's will in Harold Parsons' office. But the description of what the sheriff had found under the bed and the autopsy report from Dr. Martin were news to her, and she listened carefully.

So it was nicotine poisoning, she thought sadly, watching in the mirror as Beulah snipped another inch off the top. Emma Jane Randall's death would soon be ruled a murder, and Alice Ann Walker, who stood to benefit most, would be the sheriff's prime suspect. In fact, she was probably the *only* suspect, at least so far. The card that came with the cake had Alice Ann's name on it. And nobody else had a motive, at least as far as Lizzy could see.

*Could Alice Ann have done it?* Lizzy didn't have an answer to that question.

"But that's not the only worrisome thing," Beulah said with a sigh, still snipping. "Have you heard about Violet Sims taking Cupcake to Nashville for a Shirley Temple contest? Mrs. Adcock said she's leaving on Friday and then going straight out to Hollywood. And never coming back."

"Well," Lizzy said in a practical tone, "if the story came from Leona Ruth, you might want to take it with a grain of salt."

"I suppose," Beulah said. "Not to be critical, but Leona Ruth's stories are close enough to the truth so that you can believe just about half of what she tells you."

"That's right," Lizzy agreed. "If you only knew which half."

# CHAPTER FOURTEEN

# BUDDY HAS THE EVIDENCE

BUDDY NORRIS KNEW HE WASN'T VERY GOOD WHEN IT CAME TO dealing with women, especially when they took out their little white hankies and began to cry. Sometimes the tears were real, sometimes they were fake. Buddy, who had trouble telling the difference, had long ago decided that a real sheriff would probably suspect that they were all fake.

Alice Ann Walker hadn't been sitting in his office for more than five minutes that Tuesday morning before the little white hanky came out, and by the time Buddy finished reciting all the facts he knew in the case, she had broken out in loud sobs. The Beast, who was sitting on the windowsill staring out at a squirrel, flicked his tail, gave an irritated *mmmrrr*, and stalked out of the office. Buddy wished he could leave, too.

"But I didn't do *any* of that!" Mrs. Walker wailed. "I didn't bake a chocolate cake and send it to Emma Jane. I don't know a thing about nicotine poison." She balled up her hanky in her fist. "I wouldn't even know what to ask for if I went to the store to buy it."

"Well, I—" Buddy began. But Mrs. Walker wasn't finished. She was looking straight at him, scrunching up her eyes and her mouth in a look of tearful defiance.

"I am very sorry that my cousin is dead," she said, "but if you want to know God's honest truth, I couldn't be happier that she left me that house. I have no idea in the world why she didn't leave it to Cousin George the way she intended to. I had nothing to do with that, but I am deeply, deeply grateful. I'm going to put it up for sale as soon as I can and when it's sold, I'm using the money to buy a house here in Darling." Tears welled up in her eyes again. "It'll be a home for Arnold and me and our grandchildren. The first real home those poor little children have ever had."

When she mentioned the children, Buddy couldn't help feeling sorry for her, although he was sure that a real sheriff wouldn't have that problem. He also wanted to tell her not to count on the Birmingham house. It would be in legal limbo until this whole murky affair was cleaned up. And if she was convicted of Mrs. Randall's murder or pleaded guilty to bargain for a lighter sentence, there wouldn't be any inheritance. A criminal can't benefit from her crime.

But of course he didn't say a word. It was for her lawyer to explain things like that, and she apparently didn't have one. Yet. He cleared his throat.

"You, uh, you might want to think about getting yourself a lawyer." Not Mr. Moseley, of course. As county attorney, he would be prosecuting her. And not Parsons, who had drawn up the Randall will. There were only a couple left. "How about Jimmy Ray Ricketts?" he asked tentatively. "You could call him and ask him to come over."

"A lawyer!" she wailed. "I can barely afford a shampoo and set over at the Beauty Bower. How can I afford a lawyer?" Her mouth twisted bitterly. "Unless Jimmy Ray Ricketts will work for eggs. My chickens are laying pretty well."

Buddy didn't think Jimmy Ray would work for eggs. He stood up. "I'll get the fingerprint kit. I gotta take your prints."

Another wail.

Escaping into the workroom to look for the fingerprint kit, he discovered that Wayne had come in the back way.

"You got something?" Buddy asked hopefully. "From the Walkers'?"

"Yep." Wayne put a paper sack on the workroom table. "Like you said, Judge McHenry signed the search warrant as quick as I asked him, and Arnold cooperated with the search. I think this is what we're looking for." Careful not to smudge any fingerprints, he pulled a glass bottle out of the sack and held it up for Buddy to see. Black Leaf Forty.

"Well, whaddaya know," Buddy said.

"'For spraying garden crops,'" Wayne read from the label. "'Repelling dogs. Drenching sheep. Delousing chickens.'" He put the bottle down. "An all-purpose poison."

"Where'd you find it?"

"In the shed where the Walkers keep their garden tools. Sitting on a shelf beside a window, right out in plain sight."

"I don't suppose she suspected we might come looking for it," Buddy said. In his experience, few criminals gave much thought to trying to hide their tracks. They just did whatever they did and hoped that nobody noticed.

Like Daryl Goodwin, aka Osgood Fairchild, who'd hoped that nobody would notice his late-night forgery routine. But that little matter had turned out reasonably well—at least for now. Daryl had been interrogated, charged with a couple of minor infractions, and released to Charlie Dickens' custody. What happened after that depended on whether Hobart Mooney was satisfied with the names that Daryl had provided. Buddy liked Daryl, who seemed like a good kid working his way out of a rough patch. He hoped Mooney would get enough to make him happy—and send him back where he came from.

"I turned up something else that might be important."

Wayne reached into the sack and pulled out a one-pound metal can with a blue and yellow label that read, "Charmer's Ground Coffee and Chicory." He set the can on the table beside the poison bottle.

"Found it in the Walkers' kitchen cupboard, next to the flour and sugar. Didn't find any chocolate, though. She must have used up what she had and thrown the container away." He looked again at the can. "You said the cake had coffee and chicory in it, right? I figure this about clinches it."

Buddy had to agree that Wayne's evidence just about settled the matter. "Good work," he said without enthusiasm. He began rummaging around on the shelf over the worktable. "Where are we keeping the fingerprint kit?"

"Here." Wayne opened a drawer and pulled it out. "I'll get to work on these two items, pronto. Then I'll do a comparison to the prints I found on the box and the wrapping paper, and then to her prints, when you've got 'em. You and Moseley will want to get an expert to double-check my results, though. I'm an amateur when it comes to this stuff." Still, he looked eager. "You arresting Miz Walker this morning? If we're gonna lock her in the pokey, I'll need to get over there and do some cleaning. After the weekend, it ain't fit for a lady."

"I reckon." Buddy took the fingerprint kit. He had already thought about this. "I was going to let her go back to work this morning. But now that I see what you've found, I think there's more than enough evidence for an arrest. Of course, it'll be better when we've got the fingerprint evidence pulled together. But this"—he nodded at the can and the bottle on the table—"pretty much does it. We can add the rest later."

Wayne nodded approvingly. "Fast, clean job, sheriff."

Buddy agreed. He had the whole picture now, he thought. All he had to do was get Mrs. Walker to confess, which would make it easier for everybody, herself included. She seemed like a nice but unfortunate lady who'd been dealt nothing but bad hands in life, while the victim, by all accounts, had been a bullying old lady who liked to lord it over people whenever she could. Buddy usually tried to reserve judgment about people's moral shortcomings. He had so many of his own that it would be the pot calling the kettle black.

But in this case, he had no trouble seeing why Mrs. Walker had done what she did. He wasn't going to blame her for it. Still, he had a job to do, like it or not. He had to arrest a killer.

And he had the evidence.

# CHAPTER FIFTEEN

# VIOLET HAS MOJO

VIOLET WAS UTTERLY WORN OUT WHEN SHE GOT BACK HOME after her Monday-night visit to Big Lil's shack in the depths of Briar Swamp. She returned Shirley Temple to Cupcake's damp grasp as quietly as she could, and then tiptoed into the bedroom she shared with Myra May, who was already asleep with the pillow over her head. When she finally fell asleep, her dreams were unpleasantly vivid: a basket of snakes, a black panther with amber eyes, a pair of massive red pigs, and a surly spider as big as a washtub. She was glad when the alarm clock went off at six-thirty and she could get up and begin the day.

Which started off in an unpromising way. When she went to dress Cupcake, she found that her little girl had been awake for some time—long enough to pull all the rag curlers out of her hair and hide them, or try to. She had stuffed them into a split seam under her teddy bear's arm and cried when Violet saw one dangling end and pulled them all out.

"Why did you take them out?" Violet asked, irritated. "They need to come out carefully, when I comb you. Otherwise, it's nothing but tangles."

"I don't like to sleep with rag knots all over my head." Cupcake stuck out her lower lip. "They *hurt*. I'm not going to do them anymore."

Violet brushed the hair back from Cupcake's face. "Well, honey, if you want your hair to look like Shirley's, you'll have to—"

"I don't *want* to look like Shirley!" Cupcake put out her lower lip. "And I don't want my doll to look like Shirley, either. I want her to look like *me*!"

Violet frowned. "But baby, we have to—"

"Like *this*!" Cupcake reached under her pillow and pulled out her Shirley doll. "See? She's all better now. She looks like me. She has a new name, too. It's Cupcake, same as me. But we'll call her Little Cupcake, so nobody will mix us up."

Violet was disconcerted. Cupcake had combed all the curl out of Shirley's beautiful golden wig. The beauty of the doll was in its hair—and now it was spoiled!

She started to scold but something made her stop. If Cupcake wanted a doll that looked like her, well, that was understandable, wasn't it? And while it was surprising that she didn't want her doll named for the most famous child in the world, of course she could choose any name she wanted.

But the stubbornness about the curls—that was more troublesome, especially now, with the contest coming at the end of the week. Frowning, she pulled a pair of red bib overalls and a yellow cotton shirt out of a drawer.

"Let's get dressed and comb your hair and take little Cupcake down to see Gramma Ray."

Violet also wanted to see Raylene, for she had some questions about the mojo bag Big Lil had given her the night before. The brocaded bag held a smaller muslin sack filled with dried herbs that Violet guessed were the traveler's herbs. There was also a piece of a shriveled tuber, a silky gray rabbit's foot, the small glass vial of bammygilly oil—whatever that was—and another tiny vial, corked. It was labeled "Road Opening" in a miniature script. It contained a yellowish powder.

Violet understood that the traveler's herbs represented good luck and a safe journey. She also understood the rabbit's foot, which brought luck in traveling and gambling. Since the trip to Nashville was definitely a gamble, it scored on both counts. But she still didn't understand how to use the bammygilly oil.

And what was this "Road Opening" powder? Raylene knew about magical things, and so did Euphoria. One of them might help.

It was almost seven when Violet took Cupcake downstairs. Myra May was in the Exchange and Gramma Raylene and Euphoria were at work in the kitchen. The fragrance of frying bacon and percolating coffee filled the air. On a usual weekday, the breakfast regulars would go through a large urn of coffee, six quarts of orange juice, a four-quart pot of grits, three dozen eggs, a couple of pounds of thick-sliced bacon, four pounds of smoked ham and an equal amount of thin-sliced red potatoes, three dozen biscuits, and several quarts of Raylene's redeye gravy. And that was just breakfast.

Euphoria turned from the stove, where she was stirring a large pot of grits. "Well, there's my Cupcake," she said, beaming. "My, you look purty this mornin', little gal."

Cupcake ran to her and clutched her around the knees. Euphoria had mothered a couple of dozen children, black and white. She was generous with her affection.

"See my doll?" Cupcake cried, and held her up. "I combed out all her curls and now she looks just like me. So I changed her name. She's not Shirley anymore. She's Little Cupcake, 'cuz I'm bigger than she is." She pulled herself up to her full height of a little over three feet. "I'm *Big* Cupcake."

Euphoria smiled down at her. "She shore do look like you and that's a *fact*, honey."

"She'd look more like you if she had some clothes like you," Raylene remarked. "How about if we make some on your mama's sewing machine?"

Cupcake looked critically at her doll's Shirley Temple dress. "Red overalls, like mine," she pronounced. "And a yellow shirt. She can keep her shoes, but she wants them to be red." She pointed down to her red Mary Janes. "Like mine."

"You bet," Raylene said. "You ready for some breakfast?" When Cupcake nodded happily, she settled the little girl and her doll on a stool at the worktable, ladled strawberry syrup over a short stack of pancakes, and poured a glass of orange juice.

When Cupcake was busy with her pancakes, Raylene turned to Violet. "How was your session with Lil last night?"

While Myra May wouldn't have approved of a visit to Big Lil, Raylene was a different matter. Violet had a strong bond with Myra May's mother, who sometimes served as a bridge between her strong-willed, hot-tempered daughter and Violet. And in truth, Raylene made it a habit to visit Big Lil every few months. They had been introduced by Euphoria, who had known Lil since they were both girls.

Now, Euphoria turned a bowl of biscuit dough upside down on the table and began to flatten it gently with a rolling pin. Without looking at Violet, she said, "Did Big Lil say she gonna give you whut you want?"

"Yes." Violet hesitated. "At least, I think so." She reached into the pocket of her skirt. "She gave me this mojo bag after I asked her to—"

"That's all right, dear," Raylene said, putting a hand on Violet's arm. "What you asked for is between you and Lil, and private. It'll weaken the magic if you share it with someone who wasn't there." She paused, smiling. "Of course, if you want to ask me about some of the things in the bag, I'll be glad to tell you what I know."

"Oh, swell," Violet said. "Lil told me about the travelers' herbs—the mugwort and stuff. But what's this?" She opened the bag and took out the piece of shriveled tuber.

Raylene took the tuber, turned it over in her fingers, and handed it back. "It's John the Conqueror root. It comes from a wild morning glory vine. In African folklore, John is called 'High John.' He's a tricky character who always turns the tables on anybody who's trying to trick him."

Euphoria picked up a round biscuit cutter, dipped the rim in the flour canister, and began cutting circles of dough. "My grandma used to say that John the Conqueror root always has something to teach you, but you won't know whut it is until you got the seein' eye."

"The seeing eye?" Violet frowned.

Euphoria cut out a few more circles. "Meanin' sometimes things ain't what they seem, so you gotta look *through* 'em. See 'em from the backside, like. When you can do that, you got the seein' eye."

"Mmm," said Violet, thinking that Euphoria's explanation wasn't quite clear but not wanting to confess that she didn't understand. She held up one of the tiny vials. "What's this? The label says 'Road Opening,' but there aren't any directions for use."

Raylene raised an eyebrow. "Lil gave you that? She must like you, Violet."

"Like me?" Violet chuckled ruefully. "I'm afraid I didn't make a very good impression."

"Huh." Euphoria began putting the biscuit rounds into a baking pan. "Lil don't give her Road Openin' powder to just any old body."

Violet peered at the powder in the vial. "What's in it?"

"Lil's Road Openin' powder is five-finger grass, camphor, citronella, and sage." Euphoria opened the oven and took out another pan of biscuits, beautifully browned. She put it on the stove and slid the unbaked biscuits into the oven. "And abre camino, o' course. Which is the leaves off of a wild bush," she added. "Dried and powdered."

"Abre camino means 'road opener' in Spanish, Violet," Raylene said. "Conjure often starts with clearing away obstacles and opening new paths. There are often a lot of things in the way of what we want. Old habits, old hopes, old desires—a person can feel like she's going up blind alleys all the time. She can't see the road ahead, which means it's time for a change."

Violet was startled. That description fit her to a T, from her girlhood in Florida to the time she'd spent as a dancer in the chorus line at the Orpheum—all her life, really, until she'd come to Darling, met Myra May, and adopted Cupcake. She was always looking for a change, a way out of wherever she was.

And now she was thinking that it was time for a change again. A new road lay ahead. All she had to do was get past a few obstacles. She studied the powder in the vial.

"So how does it work?"

"Well, conjure magic is mostly believing," Raylene said. "If you asked Lil that question, I'm sure she would tell you that when your wants are good and you believe that you can have what you want, you can have it." The corner of her lip tipped up. "That is, if what you truly want is to become yourself. Your best self."

Which sounded like a riddle. "And this?" Violet held up the vial.

"It affirms your belief in the possibilities of change. Sprinkle a bit on a burning candle, on a doorsill, in your shoe. See if it shows you the way to what you truly want."

"Thank you," Violet said, and smiled. "I understand—I

guess. Sort of." But to herself, she was saying, *I don't need a couple of spoonsful of dried powder to tell me what I want. It's very simple. I want Cupcake to win first prize in that contest, so we can go to Hollywood.* Still, she knew she'd be putting a sprinkle of "Road Opener" in her shoe, first chance she got.

As she put the vial back into her mojo bag, her fingers touched the glass vial of oil. "Oh, there's this one." She wrinkled her nose as she pulled it out. "Big Lil called it bammygilly oil."

"That's Balm of Gilead oil." Euphoria slid the baked biscuits into a basket, covered it with a red-checked cloth, and set it on the pass-through to the Diner. "My grandmammy used to make it."

Raylene took the vial from Violet and held it up to the light. "It's not the same balm of Gilead that's mentioned in the Bible, if that's what you're thinking, Violet. This is made from the buds of our native cottonwood trees, steeped in oil. The cottonwood is really a medicinal tree, you know. There's a compound called salicin in the leaves and bark and especially in the buds—the same compound that's in the aspirin you buy over at Lima's Drugs. This oil can be used in the same way, to reduce inflammation and pain." She smiled. "Just a little bit of herbal healing."

Violet frowned. "But I'm not sick. I didn't ask Lil for medicine."

Euphoria snorted. "Lil didn't give it to you for no *medicine*, girl. She give it to you for a diff'rent kind of healin'. Inflammation ain't just in your joints, you know. They's all kinds of heat."

"Euphoria's right." Raylene regarded her thoughtfully. "Did Lil tell you why she was giving you this?"

"Not really." Violet frowned down at the vial. "She used the word 'reconciliation.' And she said something about a little chore I was supposed to do for her. A drop in a cup of coffee—

that's what I think she said. But she didn't tell me whose coffee. Or why. Or even when."

Raylene chuckled. "That's Lil for you. She's given you an assignment, for reasons of her own. I'm sure you'll figure it out when the time comes." She paused. "I hope you enjoyed your visit with her."

"I suppose I did," Violet said, "once I got past the spider and the pigs and the owl." She put everything back in her mojo bag. "Lil is impressive. But a little . . . well, strange."

"In more ways than you know, my dear," Raylene said cheerfully, and turned to Euphoria. "Euphoria, when we start on the pies, let's make an extra lemon meringue. I have the feeling that Purley Mann may be wanting a couple of pieces. And while you're at it, how about another buttermilk pie. Twyla Sue might want something special for dessert tonight. I believe she's having company."

Leaving Cupcake to finish her pancakes, Violet went out of the kitchen, heading for the Telephone Exchange office at the back of the Diner. Behind the counter, she saw Myra May, dressed in her usual red plaid shirt, khaki trousers, and white bib apron. She was putting a fresh cup of coffee in front of Marvin Musgrove, who was hunched over a plate of bacon, eggs, and pancakes.

"Hang on a sec, Violet." Myra May came over to her.

Violet paused nervously. She hoped Myra May wasn't going to ask her about her so-called time with the Dahlias last night. But that wasn't what Myra May had in mind.

"Do you remember the question the sheriff was asking yesterday?" she asked.

"About somebody who called his office yesterday morning?"

"Right. About seven-thirty. Well, Buddy called again a few minutes ago, wondering if we had anything to report. I was busy when Opal came in a little while ago. Could you ask her if she remembers?"

"Sure thing," Violet said, heading for the exchange.

Not long before, she and Myra May had acquired a badly needed new switchboard to replace the antique system that had been installed sometime before the War to End All Wars, just after Wilson got elected to the White House. Frustrated Darling telephone subscribers had been delighted by the new system, for the old one was totally inadequate. Everybody complained about calls being dropped, or not going through, or going through to the wrong person. And the party lines? Well, we'd better not get into that.

It had taken a while and cost more money than they could count, but at long last, the Darling Telephone Exchange could boast that it now operated with a larger, more modern switchboard—sold and installed by the Kellogg Switchboard Company of Chicago—that could handle calls without dropping them or connecting callers with the wrong people. While the new board was still a "number, please" board, it could handle three times more calls than the old one, in just a little more space. Which meant that there was still plenty of room for a desk for the supervisor (Violet, this morning), an extra chair, and a cot for Lenore Looper, who worked the board all night and was allowed to nap between calls when the traffic slacked off. The Exchange was now in operation around the clock, which made the Darling night owls happy.*

The new board also meant that a single operator could do the work of two, so it reduced the number of operators at work at any one time. In the long run, that alone would save a pretty

---

* You can read about the Exchange's equipment problems in two previous books: *The Darling Dahlias and the Four-Leaf Clover* and *The Darling Dahlias and the Poinsettia Puzzle.*

penny. And—just as importantly—it had a "secret service" feature that kept the operators from listening in. At least that's what it was supposed to do.

But it wasn't long before every one of the "Number-Please Girls," as the Darlingians liked to call them, knew how to bypass that "secret service" feature. It was still very easy to notice who was calling who, and it wasn't hard to listen in, either—always a temptation in a small town where everybody felt that everybody else's business was *their* business, too. Of course, this was a no-no as big as an elephant where Myra May was concerned, and she had made the strictest rules against it. If she caught you eavesdropping, you were done for.

On the other hand, it was really impossible for the girls not to know who was calling whom. Let's say that you're sitting at the board, ready to go to work. You are wearing a headset like earmuffs over your ears and a big black funnel-shaped microphone that hangs around your neck under your chin. The contraption in front of you consists of two panels: a vertical panel, some five feet long and four feet high, with rows of lighted sockets; and a horizontal board with rows of plugs. When Gladys Smucker picks up her receiver to call the Beauty Bower and make an appointment, the light next to her plug and number label flashes. You flip a switch so you can talk to Mrs. Smucker. You ask her for the number she's calling and she gives it to you. Or sometimes she asks you to put her through to the Beauty Bower, or just says, 'Honey, will you connect me with Beulah, please? I'd love it if she could do me this afternoon.'"

You plug Mrs. Smucker's plug into the Bower's socket and the Bower's little light goes on. Meanwhile, the switch you flipped to talk to Mrs. Smucker automatically flips shut, so you can't hear what she and Beulah are saying to each other. This is the "secret service" feature of the new board. However, it doesn't take long for you and all the other operators to discover that the automatic cutoff can be overridden with a quick side-to-side toggle, allowing you to listen in and learn that Mrs. Smucker now has a three o'clock with Beulah. This is naturally considered unprofessional and unethical and will get you fired, if Myra May catches you at it.

But it is also extremely tempting, for instance when Homer Giddings is calling the Widow Hovick at eleven at night for the third time in a week, and you don't have anything else to do but read the *Ladies Home Journal* and polish your nails. Then that little toggle can be almost too tantalizing to resist.

But let's say that you're *not* listening in. You're busy answering other calls and connecting other callers, and you're also keeping an eye on that pair of lights. When they go out, the conversation is finished. Gladys Smucker is now washing the breakfast dishes and Beulah has gone back to cutting Verna Tidwell's hair. You can pull the plug and disconnect them.

It's as easy as that, most of the time. Unless of course there's a fire somewhere in Darling and Hezekiah Potts rings the court-house bell to warn the town, in which case three or four dozen Darlingians will call the switchboard in a panic, wanting to know what's burning and where and how it started and which way is the wind blowing. Then the Exchange is likely to get overloaded. You might even feel like throwing the switch and cutting everybody off.

This is the process that Violet was asking Opal about when she went into the Exchange that morning. "Opal, the sheriff would like to know about a call that came into his office yesterday morning about seven-thirty. The caller didn't give a name." She added hopefully, "I don't suppose you happened to notice who it was."

In her mid-forties, Opal Kagle was the oldest of the generally young crew of operators who worked the board. Tall and painfully thin, with brown hair pulled back into a bun and steel-rimmed eyeglasses with lenses thick as the bottoms of soda pop bottles, she sat hunched over the switchboard like a mother stork brooding over a nest full of eggs, scrutinizing each for signs of life. But for all her awkward posture, Opal was unusually skilled at managing the board and was able to connect more people faster and more reliably than any of the other girls. Violet had never seen her listening in on a conversation.

"A call to Sheriff Norris?" Opal asked. She screwed her eyes shut behind her glasses, concentrating. "Well, actually I do remember it—sort of." She opened her eyes and peered down at the horizontal board in front of her. "It came from . . ." her hand hovered over the upper right of the board. "About . . . here," she said finally, and pointed to three plugs in a row. "It was one of these, I think."

Violet was impressed that Opal could narrow it down so precisely. But maybe . . .

"Of the three," she asked, "you can't be sure which one?"

Opal shook her head. "I remember that I had just plugged in the call when Mrs. Butcher wanted to know how she could reach WDAR. She was trying to find out if they could play the happy birthday song for her little girl, Brenda, who's having a birthday next week. WDAR's phone number is new, and I had to look for it. And then Leona Ruth Adcock called the switchboard to say that Mr. Parrish's red pig Ruby was threatening to get into her garden and Mr. Parrish should come and get her *right away*. You were busy, so I had to ask one of the men who was eating breakfast to go to the hardware store next door and holler up at Mr. Parrish—he was working on the roof—and tell him where his pig was. By the time I got all that sorted out, the lights were out on the call to the sheriff, so I disconnected it." She gave Violet a querulous look. "If I'd known it was important, I would have paid more attention."

"I'm sure it's no big thing, Opal," Violet said in a comforting tone. With a pad in her hand, she leaned over Opal's shoulder and wrote down the numbers associated with each of the three jacks. One of them seemed familiar to her, and she frowned, trying to think whose it was. But another question had occurred to her.

"Did the caller give you the sheriff's number, or ask you to ring him, or what?"

"Whoever it was asked for the sheriff's office," Opal said promptly.

"A man or a woman?"

"To tell the truth, I'm not sure," Opal said. "It was pretty muffled, and I wasn't paying a lot of attention. Could have been either."

Violet thought for a moment. "Let's try a little experiment. How about if we ring each of those numbers. When someone answers, you can tell them you're just testing the line. Then tell me if one of them sounds like the voice you heard." She looked down at the pad again, suddenly remembering.

"But don't bother calling this one." She pointed to the first of the numbers she had written down. "That's Liz Lacy's telephone number. I'm sure *she* didn't put in an anonymous call to the sheriff."

Opal's experiment didn't prove anything, however. No one was at home at either of the other two numbers. So they were no wiser than they had been when Violet asked her question.

But while Opal was conducting her experiment, Violet was looking elsewhere for an answer. Her efforts, as it turned out, were rather more successful.

# CHAPTER SIXTEEN

# EDNA FAY MAKES A REQUEST

IT WAS JUST AFTER NINE WHEN LIZZY LEFT THE BEAUTY BOWER, feeling lighter now that she'd gotten a haircut. The morning sun was warm on her shoulders, although clouds were piling up in the south and the air smelled sweet and clean, as if it were raining not far away. She had a couple of errands to do before she went to the office and she would be a few minutes later today. But Mr. Moseley wouldn't care, since he had driven to Mobile and wouldn't be back until tomorrow.

As she walked, Lizzy was still thinking about what Beulah had told her about Mrs. Randall and the chocolate cake, most of which dovetailed fairly neatly with what she already knew. She would have to report these developments to Mr. Moseley when he called later that day. But Beulah had gotten the news from Bessie, who had gotten it from Edna Fay Roberts, and details could have changed in the process. Lizzy needed to hear it directly from the source.

So she was aiming to stop in at the doctor's office, which was located in a three-room frame addition tacked to the back of the Roberts' house on Jefferson Davis Street. Doc Roberts' father and *his* father had both been doctors, which meant that every Darling child had been delivered by one of the three Dr.

Roberts since before Secession. The present Dr. Roberts and his wife Edna Fay had three daughters, so everybody was expecting this venerable tradition to come to an end—or at least skip a generation.

But the eldest, Lavinia, was in her last year of medical school, so maybe Darling was in for a change. Lizzy smiled as she thought about it. A female doctor in Darling would be a sign that their little town was about to enter the era of the Modern Woman.

Doc Roberts was at the Oldfields', delivering Mrs. Oldfield's seventh baby, and the waiting room was empty. But Edna Fay, dressed in her usual starched white uniform, white stockings, and white shoes, with a neat white cap topping her prim brown curls, took Lizzy into an examining room so they could talk without being interrupted.

It was not a congenial room. There was a white metal examining table (cold and terribly uncomfortable, as Lizzy knew from experience), several glass-fronted cabinets filled with shiny instruments and supplies, a pair of straight chairs, and a large wall-mounted poster of a naked person, with organs and skeleton exposed. The air had an antiseptic smell. Lizzy shivered. Doc Roberts himself was gentle and gentlemanly, but being examined in this room was like being stripped of all your privacy.

When Lizzy told her what she had heard, Edna Fay shook her head. "Gracious sakes. I spoke to Bessie not an hour ago. News certainly travels fast in this little town, doesn't it?"

Then, in her usual competent way, Edna Fay confirmed what Lizzy had heard. Yes, Dr. Martin's autopsy report, when it was released, would say that Mrs. Randall had died from acute nicotine poisoning. The doctor had performed something called a Mayer's test and calculated that the victim had ingested nearly four times as much nicotine as it took to kill a person.

There was no tobacco fiber in the cake, so the nicotine would have been in a concentrated liquid form, like Black Leaf Forty, which was commonly available.

"The sheriff's office has been informed," she added. "The doctor himself called Buddy early this morning, as soon as he got the word." She sighed. "We've seen several accidental poisonings of various sorts in the last few years—kids eating castor beans or chinaberries, for example. But nothing like *this*. It seems like it has to have been deliberate."

"I'm afraid so," Lizzy said. "I think I heard you say that Mrs. Randall might not have died if she hadn't eaten *all* the cake—all but that last piece. Is that correct?"

"That's what Doc Martin said. She was dying for chocolate, I guess." Edna Fay rolled her eyes. "Forget I said that. It was unkind. The poor lady is dead."

It may have been unkind, Lizzy thought, but it was accurate, in more ways than one. "Can you think of anything else I should report to Mr. Moseley?"

"I believe that pretty much covers it." Edna Fay regarded her with a half-teasing smile. "Speaking of Bent Moseley, didn't I see the two of you at the Palace week before last? *Night Flight*. John Barrymore and Helen Hayes. Pretty good movie, if you like airplanes."

Lizzy nodded, blushing a little. Edna Fay was an old friend—and just a little nosey. Or to put it more charitably, Edna Fay had lived in Darling her whole life and took an almost proprietary interest in the life story of every patient who came through her husband's examining room.

And since that was everybody in Darling who could afford to pay a dollar for an office visit, Edna Fay's interest in life stories was quite broad and inclusive. What's more, she was interested in every chapter of everybody's story, including those secret little paragraphs you'd rather keep to yourself. So she asked all sorts of questions about how you felt and why you felt that way and when she heard the answers, she asked some more, until you felt as if she had just about pumped you dry.

Acknowledging this, some people said that while Doc Roberts had all the necessary credentials, Edna Fay liked to practice psychology without a license. Some people liked it, because she made you feel like somebody (other than your nearest and dearest) really cared about you. And if you didn't like it, you could drive over to Monroeville, where the doctors (there were three of them) would treat your sore throat or your arthritis and ignore the rest of you.

Edna Fay smiled thoughtfully. "So you and Bent have been seeing one another outside the office," she prompted. "How long?"

"Oh, just a few months," Lizzy said in what she hoped was a careless tone. "When the legislature is in session, Mr. Moseley has to spend a lot of time in Montgomery." Four dates, she reminded herself. January, February, March, April. Pleasant outings to the movies, a spring picnic, a party at the country club. There had been a few prim goodnight kisses, but no repetition of the bone-rattling Christmas kiss. It was now May. Would there be a date *this* month?

"Mr. Moseley? Isn't that a bit old-fashioned?" Edna Fay asked curiously. "I call Eugene the doctor or Doctor Roberts here in the office. But I call him Eugene at home."

"I'm sure it is." Lizzy sighed. "But I call him that at the office, and it's hard to make the switch."

It *was* hard, now that she considered it. Even on their dates, she might call him Bent but she still thought of him as Mr. Benton Moseley. Did that tell her something about their relationship? She wasn't sure.

Edna Fay persisted. "And didn't Eugene and I see you and your other young man out for a walk a couple of weeks ago?

A stranger and quite good-looking, I must say." She seemed to be eyeing Lizzy closely. "The two of you looked rather . . . intensely interested in one another."

*Your other young man?* Lizzy blushed even brighter. These romantic interludes, if that's what they could be called, were new to her, and not something she talked about lightly, even to friends. She wasn't sure she was ready to share her experiences with Edna Fay, but from the deeply inquisitive expression on her friend's face, there was no escaping it.

So she tried for a casual little laugh. "Oh, you must have seen me with Ryan. Ryan Nichols. He's the regional director of the new Writers' Project, which is part of the WPA. We were—"

She was talking too fast. She took a breath, forcing herself to slow down. "You probably saw us when we were discussing the project, which interests both of us intensely—especially the story collection."

That much was true. Ryan had plans for something even more significant than just Southern stories, though. He wasn't satisfied with the idea of a regional collection of folklore and local legends, the way it was being done in other parts of the country. He wanted to create a collection of slave narratives, true stories about the experiences of Negro slaves, told by the old people who had lived before and after the War Between the States and still remembered them. The lived experience of slavery and of emancipation was especially unique to the southern tier of states—Florida, Georgia, Alabama, Mississippi, Louisiana, Texas—but nobody had ever attempted to collect the stories. It would be an incredibly difficult and brave thing to do. And perhaps even futile, if all the stories were collected by white people. Colored people would be afraid to tell the truth. The next time she saw Ryan, she had some ideas she intended to suggest.

But of course, that wasn't all there was to the relationship she had with Ryan. There was the powerful physical attraction. She was perceptive enough to recognize it for what it was and not to confuse it with love. Still, she—

But Edna Fay was regarding her curiously, and she hurried on.

"Ryan has a pretty big territory, the whole South, really. He's based in Montgomery, but he does a lot of traveling. He's only gotten to Darling a couple of times." She looked away, wanting to sidestep this oddly threatening subject. "Have you heard that Ophelia Snow is working for him? She's already gotten started on the guidebook project. Bessie and Verna—well, all the Dahlias, really—are going to help."

"Yes, Ophelia told me. She's glad to have a job and she seems quite happy about the guidebook. And she'll be good at it, too. She likes to organize things." But Edna Fay was obviously determined not to be deterred. She leaned forward and put a hand on Lizzy's arm.

"I have to say that it did my heart good to see you with Benton Moseley the other night, Liz. I know how hard it was for you after Grady Alexander married. I hope that's all over now." She tilted her head to one side, her gaze intent on Lizzy. "It *is* over, isn't it, my dear? If you don't mind my asking."

"Of course it's over," Lizzy replied confidently. She met Edna Fay's inquiring eyes. "I care for Grady and want to see him happy. But both of us need to move forward. I think we understand that."

Edna Fay smiled, and Lizzy thought she was genuinely pleased to hear this. In the next moment, she understood why.

"Grady has suffered too much unhappiness in the past couple of years," Edna Fay said. "Sandra's death and his little boy being sick so often—well, it's obviously been difficult for him." Her tone became confidential. "Actually, I was thinking of introducing him to my niece, who will be visiting us next month. Amelia is a smart young woman, very pretty, with a year of college and a great many interests. She was engaged but recently broke it off. I was thinking that she and Grady might take an interest in one another, but I wanted to be sure that you . . ." She waved a hand, a gesture that filled in the rest of the sentence.

So that was it, Lizzy thought, understanding. Edna Fay was matchmaking—her attractive young niece, available now after a broken engagement, and the recently widowed Grady Alexander. She had been asking about Mr. Moseley and Ryan Nichols because she wanted to be assured that Liz was no longer in love with Grady.

And really, she ought to be delighted, oughtn't she? And not just delighted, of course, but relieved. If something came of it, she would no longer have to say no to Grady's repeated persistence.

And she was. Delighted. *And* relieved. Why wouldn't she be?

Just for an instant, though, she felt a painful wrench, as if something were twisting inside her.

Or untwisting. Which was it? Hard to tell.

She summoned a smile. "I think that would be lovely, Edna Fay. Grady needs somebody. And I don't want to . . ."

Really, this was ridiculous. She didn't need to go into that. She straightened her shoulders. "My book will be out next month, you know. And that will keep me busy. And in addition to working for Mr. Moseley, I have another book underway."

"I *do* know," Edna Fay said, "and we are all very proud of Darling's favorite author. We all expect her to be famous one day very soon." She was smiling, but there was a serious look in her eyes. "Work isn't everything, though. I hope you don't mind my being frank, my dear, and I hope you'll forgive me for meddling where I shouldn't. But I believe it would be good for both you and Bent Moseley if it became more than just an 'occasional' thing. Between the two of you, I mean."

Lizzy was startled. She knew, of course, that Dr. Roberts and Edna Fay were longtime friends of Mr. Moseley, a friendship that went back to his marriage with Adabelle, long before their divorce. Edna Fay had been close to Adabelle until she moved back to Birmingham with the two girls, and Dr. Roberts and Bent still went fishing together when they could both find the time. Did Edna Fay assume that this long friendship conferred a special privilege, perhaps even a special responsibility? Or maybe she was just an inveterate matchmaker.

Lizzy wasn't quite sure what to say. She just waited for whatever was coming next. She didn't have to wait long.

"You see, I have several friends in Montgomery." Edna Fay leaned closer and dropped her voice, although they were the only people in the room. "From what I've been told, that woman Bent has been seeing there isn't . . . well, shall we say, not terribly well suited to him. Moira Skelton is very much a social butterfly, and frivolous." Her mouth tightened. "Not only that, but she has some—how shall I put it? Some dangerous liaisons?"

Lizzy stared at her. *Dangerous liaisons? What in the world was that about?*

But maybe she didn't want to know. Mr. Moseley was involved in a great many things, both in Darling and in the state capital, that didn't include her. Some of them she knew about. Some, she knew only by the dark shadows they cast across the landscape or by the fragments of messages that she caught on the phone.

Edna Fay seemed to reconsider. "Well, perhaps not *dangerous,* exactly. But Moira certainly keeps the wrong sort of friends." She waved a hand. "I'm sure you've been reading about the latest bribery scandal."

"I haven't, really," Lizzy said slowly. Politics had never interested her, especially state politics, which always seemed to be about one scandal after another, each one twice as ugly as the one before.

But she had read about this one. The previous Friday, she'd happened to pick up the copy of the Montgomery *Advertiser* that Mr. Moseley had been reading at his desk, folded open to an article about two attorneys and a power company executive who had been indicted on charges of mail fraud, wire fraud, and bribery, three very serious felonies that could result in heavy fines and long prison terms. One of the attorney's names had been circled in black ink, and it almost took her breath away. It was Jeremy Jackman, the attorney for whom she had worked after Grady's marriage to Sandra. Mr. Jackman, a law school friend of Mr. Moseley's, had been kind enough to hire her for a few months so she could escape from Darling and its inevitable gossip. And it had been Mrs. Jackman, with her New York connections, who had brought Lizzy's novel to the attention of Nadine Fleming, now Lizzy's literary agent—a happy combination of accidents.

When she read that, Lizzy's heart had sunk. Mr. Jackman was obviously in some serious trouble. Now, hearing Edna Fay, her heart sank even further. Bent—Mr. Moseley—couldn't be involved as well, could he? If he was, what did Edna Fay think *she* could do about it?

Edna Fay sighed. "I've probably said too much." She leaned back in her chair. "The doctor tells me that my nose is too long and I poke it into other people's business. I'm repeating what I've been told, and maybe it's not all entirely accurate. To tell the truth, I suppose I was hoping . . ."

She gave a rueful chuckle. "Actually, I was hoping that you could rescue Bent—snatch him out of Moira Skelton's clutches. He is such a smart man in so many ways, and everybody looks up to him. But he is *so* susceptible to women—and especially to duplicitous women." She hesitated, then added, half under her breath, "What is there about some men that makes them act like naïve schoolboys where women are concerned?"

"*Rescue* him?" Lizzy asked, feeling almost appalled. "I'm afraid you seriously overestimate my powers." She tried to say this lightly, but her heart was doing a sad flip-flop. She had known that Bent had been involved with Moira Skelton some months ago, but she had thought—or perhaps had only hoped—that he had stopped seeing her. She had never pried into his personal life, of course. It was none of her business whom he dated when he was working in Montgomery—or here in Darling, for that matter. But after their Christmas kiss and the evenings together when he was in town, she had begun to think . . .

What had she begun to think? Whatever it was, it was obviously wrong, if he was still seeing Moira Skelton. She was the daughter of an Alabama state senator and very well connected politically. And strikingly beautiful, Lizzy had heard, with a gorgeous figure, exquisite taste in clothes, and a reputation for putting on fabulous parties. But *duplicitous*? And what was this about the wrong sort of friends?

"I don't think I'm overestimating your powers, Liz." With a smile, Edna Fay got up from her chair, and as Lizzy stood, she put an arm around her shoulders. "I think Bent is seriously smitten with you. That he needs somebody like you. Somebody who can settle him down, make him happy right here in Darling. Give him what's been missing from his life for all these years."

There was that word again, Lizzy thought. *Need*. As if it were a woman's job to meet the emotional needs of the men in her life. As if their needs were more important—and far more imperative—than hers. Was it so wrong to wonder whether there was more to a relationship than meeting the other person's needs? Didn't anybody ever think about *love*?

But she didn't say that. How could she? She might be Bent's friend, or even more than that. But first of all, she was Mr. Moseley's assistant, and she spent her working hours doing whatever he asked of her. And wasn't Edna Fay in the very same situation, working as her husband's nurse? Was that what she had *wanted* to do with her life? If Doc Roberts hadn't needed her, would she have chosen to do something different?

Too many questions, too many complications. So she only returned her friend's hug and said, "Thanks for the advice, Edna Fay. I appreciate it very much. And I promise to give it some serious thought."

"Always glad to help," Edna Fay said, and smiled brightly. Then she pulled her brows together and her frown faded. "On another subject—what do you know about Violet Sims? I heard that she is taking Cupcake and going to Nashville for some sort of contest. After that, they're going to Hollywood and . . ." Her voice trailed away.

"And never coming back." With a sigh, Lizzy finished the sentence for her. "That's what I've heard, too. All I can say is that I hope it's not true."

# CHAPTER SEVENTEEN

# TWYLA SUE MAKES AN APPEAL

It was past nine-thirty by the time Lizzy left Edna Fay, and the clouds had risen from the south to cover half the sky. She needed to hurry to do her errands—a stop at the Mercantile and another at The Flour Shop—and get to the office before the rain came.

Mann's Mercantile was on the east side of the square, next door to Kilgore Motors. Lizzy needed some burgundy floss to finish the voodoo lily quilt block she was embroidering for the Dahlias' applique quilt. She could have turned at the corner of Robert E. Lee and Dauphin and gone a half-block to Dunlap's, now managed by Liz's mother, the new Mrs. Dunlap. Like other dime stores across the country, Dunlap's sold just about anything anyone's heart desired, as long as it was under a dollar. In fact, the embroidery floss Lizzy wanted might even be a penny or two cheaper there.

But she didn't have time this morning to deal with her mother, who would criticize her haircut or her frilly pink blouse or whisper the latest episode in the continuing soap-opera saga that Lizzy privately titled "The Improbably Passionate Adventures of Mr. and Mrs. Dunlap." She found these tales touchingly ironic, for her mother was a stout, heavy-bosomed woman with a formidable manner, while Mr. Dunlap was slight and mild-mannered, with gray hair and thick spectacles. But appearances were apparently deceiving. When they were alone together, her mother had confided on several occasions, Mr. Dunlap was a "tiger."

Liz turned, opened the door, and went into Mann's Mercantile.

The oldest store in Darling, the Mercantile was said to have been built on the site of the original Darling General Store, a log cabin erected around 1810 by the town's founder, Joseph P. Darling. Mr. Darling was a Virginian who trekked into the area with his wife, five children, three laying hens and a rooster, two slaves, a team of oxen, an obliging milk cow, and a horse. As his journal from that year testifies, he intended to travel on to the Mississippi River, another 150 miles to the west. Mr. Darling had his eye firmly fixed on the farthest horizon.

But Mrs. Darling had other ideas. Over the past hundred or so miles, she had begun to feel that she and the children had been on the road quite long enough. As Bessie Bloodworth (Darling's resident historian) tells the story, Mrs. Darling put her foot down. Firmly.

"I am not ridin' another mile in this gol-durned wagon, Mr. Darling, and that is all there is to it. If you want your meals and your washin' done reg'lar, right here is where you'll find it."

And with that (Bessie says, embellishing the story a little) she got out of the wagon and refused to get back in again. Mr. Darling—who was naturally fond of his eggs and grits and liked fresh socks once a week—bowed to the inevitable. He unhitched the team, turned the cow and horse out to grass, and built a cooking fire. Within the month, he had constructed two log cabins (one for the family, the other for the slaves) and a barn. As more folks settled in the vicinity, he built the general store. Which, through four or five generations, two wars, and several serious Depressions, passed from the Darlings to the Derflingers to the Manns and most recently, to Archie and Twyla Sue Mann.

Darling had long ago learned that, while some black sheep are blacker than others, every family has at least one, and you just have to learn to live with him—or her. The Mann family had two. Archie and Twyla's eldest boy, Leroy, belonged to Tiny French's gang of notorious bank robbers and had been on the lam for so long that Twyla Sue had given up all hope of ever seeing him again. Archie's nephew, Mickey LeDoux, had spent the last couple of years in prison and was at this moment looking to take revenge on Archie and Twyla Sue's youngest boy, Baby, for his part in the Chester P. Kinnard moonshine fiasco.

But black sheep or not, the Manns were solid citizens and the Mercantile was where Darlingians found most of what they needed in the way of practical necessities. The store's front room was large, lofty, and difficult to heat in the winter, even when the shiny black Red Cross parlor stove was roaring away, stoked to the gills with good oak cordwood. The ceiling-high pine shelves that lined the walls were stacked with clothing for every member of the family, as well as shoes and hats and rubber boots and bolts of yard goods and kitchenware and garden tools and just about anything else you ever wanted. You could have a cider mill for $6.50 or a wooden kraut cutter for $1.30 or a crank-powered coffee grinder for $1.20. If you aimed to order a couple of dozen Barred Rock or Leghorn chicks from the hatchery over at Geneva, the Mercantile had an oil-fueled chick brooder you could install in your coop for just $2.25. Or a cover for your cow or a blanket or bridle or even a full leather harness for your team of draft horses. There was even a tall wooden ladder on wheels that allowed Twyla Sue or Archie to climb up and get whatever you wanted off that very top shelf.

And in the Mercantile's back room, behind the tack racks

and the bins of nuts and bolts and nails and screws, you could also find a few bottles of Mickey LeDoux's finest, left from that last, tragic batch of mash.

The Mercantile had it all, although it was sometimes a little hard to locate what you were looking for. The store was large and the lighting was minimal—just a few bare electric bulbs dangling from the ceiling. So if you finally found what you planned to buy and you wanted to actually *see* it first, you took it to the window up front, which was likely to be so dusty that the light was gray. A sign beside the cash register read ALL SALES ARE FINAL. So if you were serious about wanting to look at what you were buying before you paid for it, you took it outside into the sunshine.

Inside, the air smelled of leather and furniture polish and rubber boots and the coffee that was percolating in a pot on the back of the Red Cross stove. On chilly days, the old Confederate veterans from the courthouse bench liked to come across the street to the Mercantile for a cup of coffee and a spell around the warm stove, where you could hear them refighting the Battle of Day's Gap or the Skirmish at Paint Rock Bridge. Twyla Sue kept their mugs on a shelf behind the stove and pointed out the basket where they could drop in a nickel for the coffee, if they had one.

Twyla Sue was a heavyset woman with ample hips, multiple chins, and saggy upper arms. She hadn't always been this way, though. As a young woman, she had never intended to marry a Darling boy, let alone marry a Mann. She had planned to pack her roller skates and go to Birmingham to compete in the amateur roller-skating championship, hoping to get a place on one of the exciting women's roller-racing teams then being formed. She would have done that, too, if Archie hadn't fallen off the roof and broken his arm in three places and looked so noble and distinguished in his cast that she found herself saying yes instead of entering the championship. And then the kids came along one-two-three and old Mr. Augustus Mann died and Archie inherited the Mercantile and Twyla Sue had herself an eight-to-five job six days a week with no vacations. And no pay, either—just whatever Archie took out of the cash register on Saturday night.

Twyla Sue never quite forgot her disappointed dream of touring America as a roller-racing champion, but she had learned that people liked her better (and spent a little more money) if she made an effort to smile. Not this morning, though. Her gestures were hurried and jerky and her plump face was furrowed in a frown that lightened only when she saw that the customer who was picking through the tray of embroidery floss was the very person she had been thinking about at that very moment.

"Help you find something special, Miz Lacy?" she asked, from her place behind the cash register. She reached for the radio on the shelf behind her. It was tuned to WDAR, and somebody—it sounded like Clyde Barlow—was reading the morning market report. She turned it off. Who cared about pork bellies, anyway? The market was like the weather. It went whatever way it wanted to go and you couldn't do a blessed thing about it.

"I found it!" Lizzy said triumphantly, holding up a skein of deep burgundy floss. "Exactly what I was looking for." Going to the counter, she fished in her coin purse for a dime and a nickel and handed them to Twyla Sue.

Twyla Sue rang up the sale on the old National cash register, which had been an antique when Mr. Augustus Mann inherited the Mercantile from *his* father. "Would you like a bag for that?" she asked.

"No, thank you, Mrs. Mann," Lizzy said. "I'll just put it in my purse."

Twyla Sue took four pennies out of the register and handed

them to Lizzy. "I was just thinkin' of you, Miz Lacy. I've been worryin' my head over what can be done about Mickey and Baby—Purley, I mean. My boy. And you came to mind."

"I did?" Lizzy asked doubtfully, not at all sure why Twyla Sue Mann should think of *her* in connection with Baby and Mickey.

"Well, you and Mr. Moseley," Twyla Sue amended. She folded her arms across her substantial bosom. "I was wonderin' if maybe you could ask Mr. Moseley to . . . well, sit them boys down for a lesson. Purley and Mickey, I mean. Talk some sense into them."

"A lesson?" Lizzy frowned. "What kind of lesson?"

"Why, a lesson in gettin' along, that's what kind." Twyla Sue had been making this appeal in her mind for a while and she couldn't hold the words back any longer. They came rattling out like gumballs out of a broken gumball machine.

"It's not right, you know. What's happ'nin', I mean. What Mickey's doin'. It wasn't Purley's fault he got saved the very same day that federal agent came askin' him where he could find Mickey's still. Purley couldn't tell if it was God's voice whisperin' in his ear or the devil." She took a breath. "And Mickey? Well, he knowed that his little brother Rider was barely fifteen and too young to be out there makin' mash. He should've said no when Rider started in askin'. And Rider, too—his mother told him he couldn't go and he went anyway and that's why he got shot. Purley and Mickey and Rider—they was all at fault, one way or t'other. And Agent Kinnard, too, o'course." She snorted. "There's enough blame to go twice around and plenty lapped over."

"Well, I would certainly agree with that," Lizzy said, thinking that Mrs. Mann had more than enough justification for what she'd just said. "But I don't know why Mr. Moseley should be involved. What about Purley's father? Or Mickey's brother?"

"Because when it comes from fam'ly, it goes in one ear and

out the other," Twyla Sue said crossly. "Mr. Moseley is the *law*. When he says something, both those boys gotta listen."

Lizzy might have said that Mickey (now an ex-con) was scarcely a boy and Baby (who was off in his own world most of the time) wasn't very good at listening. Instead, she objected again.

"But it's Sheriff Norris who is the law, not Mr. Moseley. Why shouldn't *he* be the one to have a talk with them?"

Twyla Sue clucked impatiently. "Buddy Norris is still a kid himself. What he says won't cut no ice with Mickey." She shook her head definitively. "But Mr. Moseley is a lawyer. He's got a way with words. He could get Purley to say 'I'm real sorry I ratted you out' to Mickey and tell Mickey to say, "I'm real sorry I let Rider work that still,' and make the two of them shake hands on it." She paused apprehensively. "If he don't, I'm afraid that somebody is going to get kilt. And I don't reckon it will be Mickey."

"Well, I suppose I could talk to him about it," Lizzy said, feeling pretty sure that Mr. Moseley would not want to get involved. "But I heard that Baby—Purley, I mean—is hiding out. If Mr. Moseley wants to talk to them, can you get him to come out of wherever he is?"

"If I can't, his daddy can," Twyla Sue said. "But Mickey's gotta swear that he won't jump Purley the minute he's out. No guns, neither. Nor knives."

Lizzy sighed, seeing the difficulties. "I can't promise anything. But I'll do what I can." She turned to go. "Thanks for the floss, Mrs. Mann."

"Don't mention it." Twyla Sue said. "Say, what do you know about Violet Sims taking her little girl to Nashville to be in that Shirley Temple contest? I heard she's leaving on the Greyhound Friday morning and she's never coming back. You think it's true?"

But Liz, pretending that she didn't hear, was halfway to the door. If it was true, she didn't want to discuss it with Twyla Sue Mann. And if it wasn't—

Well, if it wasn't, she'd be glad.

# CHAPTER EIGHTEEN

# VERNA MAKES THE CASE

IT WAS A FEW MINUTES BEFORE TEN AND THE MORNING SKY WAS now nearly completely covered by thick gray clouds, like a layer of dirty cotton quilt batting. A brisk southern breeze was bringing with it the smell of wet leaves. Somewhere nearby, Verna Tidwell thought, it was raining.

Sniffing the air, Verna came down the courthouse steps with a file folder in her hand. She looked up to see Liz Lacy, dressed in a pink sweater, a frilly pink blouse, and trim gray skirt, come out of Mann's Mercantile and walk across the courthouse lawn.

Verna was on her usual Tuesday morning errand to the Dispatch office, just across Franklin Street from the courthouse. As the elected Cypress County clerk and treasurer (the *only* woman in that role in the entire state of Alabama), it was her job to see that the weekly legal notices were published in the newspaper. She could have sent Madge Shoemaker, her assistant, but she liked to do it herself. It gave her a chance to get out of the office for a few minutes—and out of earshot of Bing Crosby.

Madge had inherited Bing last year from her sister. He was such a fervent and frequent songster that Madge's husband refused to allow her to keep him. So Bing's cage now hung in the south window of the county clerk's office, where—all day long—he enthusiastically trilled his bright canary songs. Verna, who liked music as much as anybody, wished that Bing could turn down the volume a little. But everybody else enjoyed him, so she put up with it until she couldn't, at which point she either asked Madge to throw the cover over his cage or escaped on an errand.

"Good morning, Verna." Liz tilted her head with a smile. "What a pretty red dress. I love that swingy skirt!"

"My new favorite," Verna said. "Rayon crepe. Doesn't need a lot of ironing."

To save time and money, Verna bought all her wearables from the Sears and Roebuck catalog, and she never bought anything that required lots of extra care. She had better things to do than stand at the ironing board with a damp pressing cloth for fifteen or twenty minutes every morning. She kept hoping that somebody would come up with a fabric you could just wash and wear or an electric iron that had some steam in it. But those inventions must be off in the future—they weren't available today.

When her friend got closer, Verna added, "I was going to stop at your office after I turned in the legal notices. We need to talk."

She took Liz's arm and led her to a nearby wooden bench where they sat down, a few paces from the circular flowerbed at the foot of the flagpole. Last week, the Dahlias had filled it with petunias they had raised from seed in Voleen Johnson's greenhouse—one of their "Delightful Darling" projects. The plants would bloom in a few weeks: a bountiful, patriotic red, white, and blue.

"What's up?" Liz asked.

Verna gave her a questioning look. "Have you heard about Alice Ann?"

Liz rolled her eyes. "I've been hearing about Alice Ann all

morning. And about Violet Sims and Cupcake, too. What's happened *now?*"

Quickly, Verna told her. Before work that morning, she had stopped at Alvin Duffy's office at the Darling Savings and Trust, cattycornered from the courthouse, to deposit last week's property tax collection—a business visit with a personal footnote.

Verna and Al had been seeing one another for quite some time, and her friends were starting to ask when they were going to tie the knot. A widow (her absent-minded husband had stepped out in front of a Greyhound bus), she was in no hurry to remarry. Her job paid the bills and left a little extra for a rainy day. Her garden kept her busy and the mysteries she borrowed from the Darling library (her current favorites: Earl Stanley Gardner's Perry Mason mysteries and Rex Stout's Nero Wolfe) kept her entertained.

And best of all, her black Scottie Clyde gave her plenty of snuggling, didn't argue, and didn't require any laundry. Unfortunately, Clyde was an extremely territorial dog, and he had long ago claimed Verna as his personal territory. He continued to refuse all diplomatic relations with Mr. Duffy. They barely maintained an armed truce.

But Al, not one to suffer defeat at the paws of a dog (and a small one, at that), continued to visit. When he came in for a nightcap after Saturday night's dinner at the Old Alabama Hotel, he had left his silk necktie hanging over the chintz-covered chair in Verna's bedroom. When Verna and Al were otherwise occupied, Clyde made off with it and refused to tell where it had gone.

But the next morning, Verna had spotted him carrying Al's tie into the backyard with all the panache of a soldier capturing an enemy flag. She retrieved his prize, washed and dried and put it in an envelope and, this morning, took it to Al's office. He hadn't come in yet, but Alice Ann was at work at her desk, her hair freshly cut and curled from an early morning visit to the Bower. Verna had been about to leave the necktie with her when the sheriff walked in.

It was well known that Buddy Norris had few social graces. This morning, for instance, he might have spared Alice Ann some embarrassment if he had waited until Verna left before he told her why he had come. But he didn't. Verna was standing right there when he announced that Alice Ann was wanted for questioning, in his office, right this minute. When she asked what it was about, he looked nervously at Verna, hemmed and hawed for a moment, and finally said, "It's got to do with Miz Randall's dyin', that's what. And your inheritance. And that cake you baked."

Verna had to admire Alice Ann. Her expression didn't change. She didn't so much as blink. "What cake?" she asked.

At this point, the sheriff obviously decided he'd said too much. "Come on," he said. "I don't want to have to drag you."

"Am I under arrest?" Alice Ann asked.

"Not yet," the sheriff replied grimly.

"You'll have to excuse me, Verna," Alice Ann said. "I need to talk with this . . ." She paused. "Gentleman." With great dignity, she put on her hat, took her purse out of the desk drawer, and followed the sheriff out of the office, her back ramrod straight.

The other employees at the bank were watching curiously, and Verna knew that the story would be all over Darling within the hour. It might not be the true story, either. Gossip had a way of playing fast and loose with the details.

"And that's it," Verna said. "Off she went with the sheriff, like Joan of Arc marching to the stake."

"Oh, *poor* Alice Ann," Liz said. A large grackle landed on the lawn in front of them and began hopping through the grass, its dark blue head iridescent in the sunlight flickering through the clouds.

They watched the bird for a moment, then Liz turned to Verna. "Well, since you saw her being taken to the sheriff's office, I suppose you should hear what I learned from Beulah and Edna Fay this morning."

Verna listened attentively. When Liz finished, she whistled between her teeth. "Nicotine poison—in a cake? It sounds like a Perry Mason plot."

No, that wasn't right. It had been Robert J. Casey who used nicotine to kill Cyrus Bradley in *The Secret of 37 Hardy Street*, a believable tale with an entirely plausible plot. Nicotine was a powerful poison—colorless, with only a bit of an odor. Plus, it was widely available. Anybody who had a garden had a can of Black Leaf Forty.

"According to Edna Fay," Liz said, "the doctor who did the autopsy believes that a slice or two might not have been fatal. But Mrs. Randall ate the whole thing—all but the very last slice."

"So maybe the cake wasn't intended to kill her? Just make her sick?"

Across the street, Old Zeke Clayton came out of the front door of Hancock's Groceries, pulling a red wagon piled high with somebody's grocery order. There had been rumors that A&P might build a self-service store—a super market, it was called—on the vacant lot next to Dunlap's Dime Store, but most Darlingians didn't want it. They preferred Hancock's, where they could pay for their groceries once a month and Zeke would deliver them.

"Maybe," Liz said after a moment. "But I can't see Alice Ann intending to poison anybody, fatally or not. Can you?"

Slowly, Verna shook her head. "Not really. You never know about people, though. I can't think of anyone who is in greater need of a house. This lady—Mrs. Randall—conveniently dies, and suddenly Alice Ann has exactly what she needs." She paused, raising one eyebrow. "On the other hand, if somebody else put Alice Ann's name on that cake, it was done for a reason. Trying to frame her?"

By nature skeptical and suspicious, Verna appreciated a mystery even more when she was able to figure out whodunit before the detective. "Why?" was the question that always came to her mind, followed closely by "Who says?" and "What's that got to do with it?" In fact, she had just finished reading *The Case of the Howling Dog*, a Perry Mason mystery involving two versions of a will. The plot was a bit farfetched, but so was nicotine poisoning.

"So Mrs. Randall made a new will," Verna said. "Who was supposed to inherit under the *old* will?"

A second grackle joined the first, and the two of them began fluffing their feathers, exchanging a series of raspy squawks.

"George Clemens," Liz replied. "He's Mrs. Randall's brother. I don't know why he was cut off. His sister had come to live with him, but there was some sort of family fuss, and she moved to Magnolia Manor. Mr. Clemens isn't an easy man to get along with. He was a client of Mr. Moseley's and he—"

"George Clemens, here in Darling?" Verna interrupted. When Liz nodded, she said, "I've had a few dealings with that fellow. I don't trust him."

A farmer in bib overalls and a straw hat drove past in a wagon pulled by a team of brown horses. He stopped in front of Musgrove's Hardware, tied them to the railing next to a battered old Ford Model T, and went into the store.

"Untrustworthy is right," Liz said ruefully. "But he already has a house, if that's what you're thinking. And anyway, he's not going to inherit. Mr. Mosely will have to tell him that Mrs. Randall rewrote her will, giving her property to—"

"But if Alice Ann is convicted of killing Mrs. Randall, *she* can't inherit," Verna said. "Is George Clemens next in line?"

"I suppose so, but . . ."

A distinctly troubled look crossed Liz's face, as if she had just thought of something ugly—something she didn't want to think about. Verna wondered what it was, but her friend didn't elaborate. All she said was, "In fact, when I talked to him yesterday, Mr. Clemens still thought the old will was in effect and that he was going to inherit his sister's estate. He didn't appear to know anything about the new will. He even wanted me to ask Mr. Moseley to expedite the sale of the house in Birmingham."

Feeling just like Perry Mason, Verna said triumphantly, "Well, there you have it, Liz. George Clemens *thinks* he's in line to inherit, which gives him as strong a motive as Alice Ann's. Doesn't matter that he's wrong about the will." There. She had made the case.

"But the card—"

Verna shrugged. "If George thought his sister was mad at him, he might have figured that she wouldn't accept a cake that came from him." Overhead, the clock in the courthouse bell tower began to strike and she raised her voice. "If the sheriff doesn't already know about George, he should." She glanced up. It was ten o'clock. She needed to take the legals to the newspaper and get back to the office.

Startled by the clock, both grackles flew away. "Oh, gosh," Liz said, getting to her feet. "I'd better move on. I have one more errand to run." She looked up at the sky, now an ominous gray. "I don't have an umbrella. I'd prefer not to get wet."

Verna got up, too. "I don't suppose the sheriff is really going to arrest Alice Ann, do you? I mean, it's all well and good to question somebody because she seems to have the best motive. But if he's going to arrest her, he has to have *evidence*." She was speaking with confidence now. That's what happened in all the police stories she read. Suspicion was one thing, evidence was quite another. "A can of bug poison, for instance, with Alice Ann's fingerprints on it. That would be evidence."

"But what if she's used the poison just to kill bugs?" Liz asked. "Her fingerprints could be on the can, but it wouldn't prove that she used it in a cake." She shook her head. "Buddy Norris is a good lawman, but he doesn't have a lot of experience with things like this. I hope he wouldn't arrest Alice Ann without some really *good* evidence."

"Well, then," Verna said, "how would you describe 'good' evidence?"

"I don't know," Liz said distractedly. "Fingerprints on the wrapping paper, maybe?"

"There you go." Verna nodded, agreeing. "If Buddy has found Alice Ann's fingerprints on the wrapping paper, that would just about sew up the case." She paused, frowning. "On another subject, you mentioned Violet Sims and Cupcake a few minutes ago. Have you heard—"

"Yes," Liz said. "But I don't have time to talk about it now. Call me later. Okay?"

"I will," Verna said. "Where are you off to?"

"The bakery," Liz replied. "I need to tell Mildred that I suggested to Zelda Clemens that she might be the right person to help Earlynne in the kitchen. Zelda bakes bread."

"Zelda Clemens?" Verna frowned. "Any relation to George Clemens?"

"His daughter," Liz said. "She's been working in Chicago, but she lost her job, so she's come back to Darling."

"That's too bad," Verna said. "But Earlynne could sure use the help. The last loaf I bought was . . . well, it was a disaster, that's all I can say. I hope Zelda works out!"

"So do I," Liz said. "So do I."

# CHAPTER NINETEEN

# MILDRED GIVES LEONA RUTH THE OLD HEAVE-HO

THE BELL IN THE COURTHOUSE TOWER ACROSS THE STREET HAD just finished chiming ten when Mildred Kilgore stepped back and surveyed the glass shelves in the bakery display case.

The early morning customers had come and gone, and there were some gaps to fill among Earlynne's display of delicious pastries: apple strudel, beignets, croissants, eclairs, and macaroons sandwiched around buttercream frosting. It had been a good morning. Their advertising on WDAR was really paying off.

But the centerpiece of this morning's baking had not been Earlynne's sweet treats. No, it had been the entirely unexpected—and hugely welcome—contribution of the woman they had hired the afternoon before. Mildred's glance lingered on the shapely loaves of bread, almost like manna from heaven, that Zelda had produced before their very eyes and in The Flour Shop's very own kitchen. The loaves looked and tasted stunning.

And to think that this treasure of treasures—her name was Zelda Clemens—was living right here in Darling! What's more, she was eager to go to work for them. Just as importantly, she was willing to work at a salary they could afford.

The painful truth was that, when it came to bread, the

bakery had gotten off to a very rough start. They had been only hours away from their grand opening when Earlynne confessed that, as a baker, she was a fraud. She adored baking cakes and French pastries, but she couldn't produce a halfway decent loaf of bread to save her life—and owning a bakery meant baking a dozen or more *perfect* loaves every day. Their enterprise seemed doomed before they even opened the front door.

But Aunt Hetty Little had stepped in, taken command, and organized the Dahlias on a rescue mission. Her firm tutorial help had gotten Earlynne to the point where she could produce a decent loaf—most of the time. If she paid the right attention and wasn't too distracted.

But they had to face it. Bread was not Earlynne's cup of tea. Or Mildred's, either. And they couldn't keep asking Aunt Hetty to come to their rescue.

And then Zelda had appeared yesterday afternoon, a miracle straight from heaven's pearly gates, referred to them (she said) by Liz Lacy. Earlynne had equipped her with an apron and a hair net and had shown her where the flour and yeast and other ingredients and tools were kept. The woman clearly knew her way around a kitchen. Within the hour, as if by some sort of culinary magic, six amazingly symmetrical loaves were rising on the warming shelf. When they were baked a few hours later, the fragrance was utterly divine. Mildred and Earlynne had eaten half a loaf between them, the warm slices drenched with butter. They pronounced it the very best bread they had ever eaten and Zelda a godsend.

And Zelda herself? At this very moment, the miraculous creature was in the kitchen, sleeves rolled up and wearing a big white apron and hairnet. She had come in early that morning to produce another dozen loaves and was now working on what she called "pocket pies": small, savory pies you could hold in your hand, filled with beef or chicken and vegetables—carrots, celery, onions, and potatoes.

Mildred took a satisfying whiff of the remarkable smells wafting from the kitchen. Zelda's pocket pies would be the perfect hot lunch for everybody who worked on the square, and with WDAR, they could get the word out in a hurry. She grinned. The bakery would soon be able to give their friends at the Diner a run for their money.

At that moment, the door opened and Liz Lacy came in. "Oh, Liz!" Mildred exclaimed, and bounced around the corner to envelop Liz in a big hug. "Earlynne and I can't thank you enough!"

"For what?" Liz asked in surprise.

"Why, for sending us Zelda!" Mildred cried. "She's an angel!"

"You like her? You can use her? That's what I came to tell you—that I'd suggested to her that she stop in and introduce herself."

"Do we like her? We *love* her!" Mildred swept out her arm in an expansive gesture. "Her bread is absolutely exquisite. Just look at those beautiful loaves!"

"Oh, my," Liz said, bending over to look. "They *are* lovely, aren't they? I wonder where she learned to bake like that."

"She told us that when she was living in Chicago, she worked at Roeser's Bakery in Humboldt Park. They're famous for their bread, and she was one of their regular bakers. But bread isn't all she knows. She's making pocket pies this morning, and she's promised to show Earlynne how to make Roeser's famous butter loaf. She says it's Danish pastry, baked in a bread mold and topped with sweet-roll icing and streusel." Mildred rolled her eyes. "All I can say is that she is an absolute miracle, Liz. So if you came in to buy something, you can leave your money in your purse. It's on the house this morning, for sending us Zelda."

Liz looked pleased. "Well, in that case," she said, "I'll take two croissants and a loaf of Zelda's bread. Thank you so much!" She looked toward the kitchen. "Is she there now? I'd like to say hello to her."

"She sure is." Mildred raised her voice. "Zelda! A friend of yours is out here. Come and say hi to Liz Lacy."

"Just a minute," came a voice from the kitchen. "I'll be with you when I wash the flour off my hands."

"Oh, I don't mean to interrupt her work," Liz said.

"I'm sure we can spare her for a few minutes," Mildred said with a twinkle. She was putting Liz's croissants and bread into a white paper bag when the front door flew open and a woman barged in, furling her blue umbrella.

"It's raining out there!" she announced. She shook her umbrella, spattering raindrops across the floor. "Thought I'd pop in out of the wet and let you know what I've just heard. It's about Violet Sims and Cupcake." She turned, noticing Liz. "Well, good morning, Elizabeth. You doin' well, dear?"

"I'm fine, Leona Ruth," Liz said. "And you?"

Leona Ruth Adcock was wearing a bright green print dress that didn't do a thing for her sallow complexion and a singularly unattractive green felt cloche that fitted her head like a skull-cap. Shoestring-thin and all angles and elbows, Leona Ruth had brown hair, sharp features, and quick, shiny button eyes that never missed a trick, especially when she thought somebody was dealing from the bottom of the deck. In fact, Leona Ruth was happiest when she could find fault with somebody or criticize what they were doing. She liked nothing better than to be the bearer of bad news—not just bad, but scandalous. And the more scandalous the better.

Mildred sighed. As a businesswoman, she welcomed every Darling customer into the shop and was always as nice as could be. But as she had told Earlynne a few days ago, if there was anybody in Darling she disliked, it was Leona Ruth. The woman lived to gossip, which might not be so terribly bad if you could believe everything she said. And if you weren't a major character—a victim or a villain—in one of her stories. If you were, heaven help you, for her plots tended to be even more twisted than one of Earlynne's double pretzels. It was widely known that if she brought you a juicy bit of information that you might want to know or pass on to somebody else, you couldn't count on its being even halfway true. You might find yourself spreading one of Leona Ruth's infamous fictions.

"I'm doin' good, thank you." Leona Ruth sniffed. "My oh my, but something does smell tasty! What are you and Earlynne baking back there, Mildred?"

"Pocket pies," Mildred replied. "Zelda Clemens has just come to work for us and she—"

But Leona Ruth had turned to Liz and launched into an entirely new subject. "Elizabeth, I'm glad to see you. I've been at the Savings and Trust, where I heard some terrible news. I'm sure you'll want to know, since you're the president of the Dahlias, and this involves one of your members."

There was a spiteful glint in Leona Ruth's eyes. Once upon a time, Mildred knew, Leona Ruth had been a Dahlia. But she'd had a poisonous falling out with the club's founder and then-president, Mrs. Dahlia Blackstone, and had quit in a huff. Since then, she seized every opportunity to disparage the club.

"One of our members?" Liz asked warily. "What's the story?" Her frown told Mildred that Liz was as distrustful of Leona Ruth as she was.

Leona Ruth turned down her mouth. "I really hate to be the one to tell you, Elizabeth, but you'll hear it pretty soon anyway. It would probably be better if it didn't catch you unaware. It's one of the very worst things that has ever happened in Darling, at least that I can remember. And my memory goes back four whole decades."

Which made Mildred smile, since she knew for a fact that Leona Ruth was sixty-two years old. She had surely started remembering things by the time she was twenty-two.

Liz squared her shoulders. "You said it involved one of our members? Who?"

"Alice Ann Walker." Leona Ruth's eyes glittered. She leaned forward and lowered her voice almost to a conspiratorial whisper. "She's been arrested. For the murder of Emma Jane Randall."

Liz stiffened. "Murder?"

"Alice Ann?" Mildred gasped. "I don't believe it!"

"It's true," Leona Ruth said primly. "People are saying that she put some sort of bug killer in a cake. Whatever it was, it was deadly."

"Who told you this?" Liz asked in a steely tone.

"I was at the Savings and Loan a few minutes ago and the tellers were whispering about it. The sheriff came and took her away for questioning, and an hour later, she telephoned Mr. Duffy to tell him she wouldn't be back at work today. She's in jail. She's trying to hire a lawyer to help her get out. But you know the Walkers." Now Leona Ruth sounded almost triumphant. "They don't have one penny to rub against another."

"In *jail*? Oh, no! No, no, *no!*"

All three of them—Mildred, Liz, and Leona Ruth—turned to see a tall, brown-haired woman in a white apron standing in the kitchen doorway.

"Zelda?" Mildred asked. "What—"

"Oh, please!" she cried. "Tell me it's not true! I can't believe . . . He never should have . . . ." She broke into a wailing crescendo. "This wasn't supposed to happen!"

At once, Mildred was galvanized. Whatever was going on here was no business of Leona Ruth's. As it was, the woman had seen and heard enough to cause trouble. Give her any more mud, and she'd fling it all over town. In a flash, she had Leona Ruth by the elbow and was quick-stepping her to the door.

"We're closed," she said brusquely, giving Leona Ruth a little push to get her over the threshold. "Come back later."

On the sidewalk, Leona Ruth fumbled with her umbrella. "*Closed!*" she shrilled. "But I was going to buy a loaf of bread. And I haven't told you what I've been hearing about Violet Sims and—"

"Get it at Hancock's," Mildred growled. "Nine cents a loaf." She slammed the door in Leona Ruth's face, locked it, and flipped the OPEN sign to CLOSED. She dusted her hands, feeling that it was about time somebody finally gave Leona Ruth the old heave-ho. She turned to see that Liz had moved swiftly to Zelda and put her arms around the sobbing woman, while Earlynne looked on, open-mouthed.

"There, there," Liz was saying softly. "Let's go into the kitchen and sit down. We'll have a cup of hot tea and you can tell us all about it."

Forty-five minutes later, Liz and Zelda, huddled together under Earlynne's umbrella, were making their way to the sheriff's office.

# CHAPTER TWENTY

# MR. MOSELEY PHONES IN

THE COURTHOUSE CLOCK HAD ALREADY CHIMED ONE BY THE time Lizzy left the sheriff's office. It was still raining, the streets were puddled with silver, and the wind tried hard to jerk the umbrella out of her hand.

The last few hours had been intense, to say the least. At the bakery, Lizzy had been amazed by Zelda's confession and had listened sympathetically as the story spilled out. It had been difficult to convince the woman that she needed to talk to the sheriff, though, and Zelda refused to go unless Liz went with her. When they finally got to the sheriff's office, Lizzy thought she'd leave Zelda there and get on with her morning.

But Buddy Norris had asked only a few preliminary questions and then dispatched Deputy Springer to the Clemens house to pick up Zelda's father for questioning. He insisted that Liz stay for both interviews as a representative of the county attorney. So for the next several hours, she sat beside the sheriff and took notes during the two separate interviews. She promised the sheriff that she would review them with Mr. Moseley as soon as he called in.

Now, back in the law office at last, Lizzy hung up her pink sweater, collapsed in the chair at her desk, and unwrapped the baloney-and-lettuce sandwich she had brought from home. When she'd eaten, she sat there for a long time, looking out the window at the falling rain and thinking about everything that had happened. She might have sat there for the rest of the day if the telephone on her desk hadn't startled her with a brisk ring. It was Mr. Moseley, calling from Mobile.

"Busy morning?" he asked. "I phoned a couple of times earlier, but you were out." He didn't sound annoyed, just curious. He added, "When I called the Exchange to see if anybody knew where you were, Violet said she'd heard that you were at the sheriff's office. Somebody told her that you had just nabbed Mrs. Randall's killers—two of them." He chuckled lightly. "Is it true?"

"You wouldn't believe," Lizzy said, thinking that it was impossible to do a single thing in Darling without everybody knowing *something* about it—and not the right thing, either.

"Try me." Mr. Moseley said. "I'm all ears, Liz."

It took several minutes, with Mr. Moseley interrupting every few sentences with a question or a muttered *Did I hear that right?* or *I'll be damned* or just a low, incredulous whistle. And Lizzy forgetting important details, like Violet's discovery of where the anonymous phone call had come from and what Edna Fay had related about the nicotine being in liquid form—but of course omitting any mention of Moira Skelton. While Edna Fay hadn't sworn her to secrecy, their conversation had clearly been confidential.

Anyway, what Bent Moseley did with his evenings and weekends in Montgomery had nothing to do with her, did it? Of course not! If he wanted to date Moira Skelton—if he wanted to propose to her or marry her, or anybody else, for that matter—he was perfectly free to do that. He was an adult, and totally in charge of his life. *She* didn't care, although what Edna Fay had said about "dangerous liaisons" was perhaps a little worrisome. It connected with a few things she had overheard in various phone conversations but didn't like to think about. And she didn't like to think that Bent Moseley might need rescuing. That wasn't in her job description.

"Tell you what," Mr. Moseley said when she finally got to the end of her story. "To be sure I'm not missing something, let's do it again. Okay? This time, take it from the top, in chronological order. Start with the Clemenses, father and daughter, and tell me what they say they did—or what they thought they were doing."

So Lizzy pulled out her notes of the interviews in the sheriff's office, took a deep breath, and reconstructed the story, drawing on Zelda Clemens' tearful tale at the bakery and her father's morose confession.

It began a week or so before Emma Jane Randall's death, when Harold Parsons told George that he had been left out of his sister's latest will. The old man was furious. That house in Birmingham had belonged to his family. He'd been betrayed. He'd been cheated out of something that should be his.

"So Mr. Clemens lied when he told me yesterday that he was going to inherit under the first will," Lizzy added. "He already knew that his sister had made a new will and that he was no longer the beneficiary."

Mr. Parsons made it clear that there wasn't much that could be done about the will, so George decided to cause some trouble for the new beneficiary, Alice Ann. He would send Emma Jane a gift of food—a cake or cookies, maybe a pie—that would make all the Magnolia ladies sick. Not terribly sick, of course. Just sick enough to be miserable for a few hours. The gift would appear to come from Alice Ann, so Emma Jane and the others would blame *her*. Emma Jane (who was paranoid and quick to jump to conclusions) might decide that Alice Ann was trying to poison her. She might even be so angry that she would go straight to Harold Parsons' office and tell him to tear up the new will, leaving the previous one in force, with her brother as the beneficiary.

George first thought of telling Zelda what he had in mind and enlisting her help, but he decided that was too dangerous. She didn't get on with Emma Jane (very few people did), but she might think he was going too far. She might even try to warn her aunt. Anyway, he knew he could carry it off without telling Zelda what he was up to.

So George suggested that—to mend fences with his sister— Zelda should bake Emma Jane's favorite chocolate-and-chicory cake. Zelda thought that this was a splendid fence-mending idea. She even made a special trip to Hancock's for a can of Luzianne coffee and chicory powder for the cake.

Back in the kitchen, she began to mix the batter. Her father watched for his chance, and when she had her back turned at the sink, he poured what he said vaguely were a "couple of healthy glugs" of Black Leaf Forty—a clear, nearly odorless, slightly viscous liquid—into the thick, dark, chocolate-chicory batter. Zelda finished making the cake, put it into the oven, and when it had baked and cooled, she frosted it. She had no idea that her father had tampered with it. Not at that time, anyway.

When the cake was finished, Mr. Clemens put it into a box, along with a carefully printed card saying that it was a gift from Alice Ann. He wrapped the box in brown paper and drove over to the post office in Monroeville to mail it. All of this was con-firmed by the fingerprints on the card, on the box, and on the wrapping paper—George Clemens' fingerprints. There were none of Zelda's prints.

The cake arrived at Magnolia Manor and everything seemed to go according to George's plan—except that Emma Jane decided not to share Alice Ann's beautiful cake with anybody.

Chocolate was her favorite. For once, she said, she would have all the chocolate cake she could eat.

And she did. She ate the whole thing herself, down to the very last slice. And then she died.

And George Clemens? When he learned from Bessie on Sunday night that Emma Jane had died—of a stroke, according to Doc Roberts' first assessment—he couldn't understand it. He wasn't especially fond of his sister, and he couldn't pretend that her death was a great tragedy. But his trickery had backfired. Emma Jane was dead. There hadn't been time for her to get mad at Alice Ann and tell Harold Parsons to tear up the second will. She had just . . . died. And the second will was still in force.

But the doctor said that Emma Jane had died of natural causes. There was apparently nothing to tie her death to the nicotine-laced cake. Which meant that Alice Ann, the legal beneficiary under the second will, was now home free, with a big potful of money and property. She had done nothing to deserve what George thought was rightfully his, but she was going to walk away with it—unless he could think of some way to stop her.

And he could, of course. On Monday morning, he picked up his telephone, disguised his voice, and made an anonymous phone call to the sheriff, reporting that the cake had been loaded with nicotine poison and implicating Alice Ann as Emma Jane's killer. That call was crucial. If George hadn't raised the sheriff's suspicion and prompted him to discuss the situation with Doc Roberts in time for a proper autopsy, Emma Jane's death certificate would have listed stroke as the cause of death. The call was key to the success of George's plan.

But it was the call that tripped him up. The girls on the switchboard at the Exchange—Violet and Opal—had finally figured it out. Opal told the sheriff that the call had come in on one of just three telephone lines on her board. And Violet had deduced which of those three phones belonged to the anonymous caller. She had noticed that the phones were all located on Jefferson Davis Street. One of the numbers belonged to Liz Lacy. The second belonged to Liz's mother, across the street. The third was George Clemens' phone, next door to Lizzy's mother. It likely wasn't Liz or her mother who called. Which left Mr. Clemens.

Confronted with this information, George first tried to bluster, then to blame his daughter. "Wasn't me that called. Could've been Zelda."

No, it wasn't Zelda. In fact, Zelda had told them that she had overheard her father making the call. She was horrified.

"I confronted him," she said, and she kept at him until he told her the whole story. "At first, I couldn't believe that he had done such an awful thing—poisoning the cake I was baking for Aunt Emma Jane and pinning the blame on poor Alice Ann. And then I thought about all the awful things he had done when I was young. And I believed it."

"The awful things?" Mr. Moseley asked, when Liz had reported this. "Do you know what she's talking about?"

Lizzy sighed. "That goes back a long way. The day before Zelda left home to go to Chicago, I heard Mrs. Clemens telling my mother that she had just found out that her husband had been . . . molesting their daughter, over a period of several years."

"Damn," Mr. Moseley said softly. "Damn."

Lizzy took a breath. "I was nine or ten—too young to understand what they were talking about. Or maybe I understood it and couldn't bear the thought of it. I pushed it so far out of my mind that I forgot all about it. But when I saw the way he treated her yesterday, and the way she acted around him, I remembered. I was stunned. I'm sure she wouldn't have come back to live with him unless she was desperate. She must have had no other choice."

"The sins of the fathers," Mr. Moseley muttered grimly.

"Yes," Lizzy said. *The sins of the fathers.*

There was a silence. At last, Mr. Moseley said, "What charges is Buddy considering?"

"He wants to talk to you about that," Lizzy replied. "Manslaughter, perhaps. For Mr. Clemens."

"I would agree with that," Mr. Moseley said slowly. "Give him the benefit of the doubt and accept his statement that he didn't mean to kill her. Get him to plead to manslaughter in return for avoiding trial on a murder charge." He paused. "What about the daughter—Zelda?"

"Buddy doesn't think she should be charged, at least not now. She says she didn't know anything about the nicotine in the cake until she heard her father talking to the sheriff yesterday morning. Her prints aren't on the wrapping paper or the box, or on the can of Black Leaf Forty that Deputy Springer found on the Clemenses' back porch. And when she heard Leona Ruth blurt out that Alice Ann had been arrested—which wasn't true, by the way—she knew she had to tell the whole story."

"Does Leona Ruth Adcock ever say a true thing?" Mr. Moseley remarked rhetorically.

"Actually," Lizzy said, "her untrue story about Alice Ann compelled Zelda to tell us the *true* story. If Zelda hadn't spoken up, we might never have known what George Clemens did. And the sheriff might *really* have arrested Alice Ann. Deputy Springer found that same brand of nicotine poison at her place—and some chicory, too, with her prints all over both. Buddy thought it was almost enough for an arrest—especially since Alice Ann told him she didn't know anything about nicotine poison. She said she wouldn't even know what to ask for if she had to buy it." Which might be true, Lizzy thought. Arnold might have bought it and she used it without realizing what it was.

But maybe that wasn't the only reason Zelda spoke up. Had she also been motivated by what her father had done to her when she was a girl? Was it her way of getting even? And what would she do now? Once the trial was over—if there was one—would she stay in Darling and work at the bakery? Or—

"Tell us the true story?" Mr. Moseley repeated. "Who's us?"

"Mildred and Earlynne and me. At the bakery. After Leona Ruth was gone, Zelda told us everything."

"Ah," Mr. Moseley said dryly. "Mildred and Earlynne. The usual suspects. Have they learned to bake bread yet?"

Lizzy tried not to laugh. "Actually, they've hired a professional baker—if she stays out of jail."

"I don't think I want the details," Mr. Moseley said. "Anything else going on that I need to know about? Has Parrish's pig gotten out again?"

"A couple of things." Lizzy took a breath and consulted her notebook again. "Charlie Dickens caught the tax stamp forger."

Lizzy repeated the story that Buddy had told her of Charlie's all-night stakeout with Hobart Mooney and his early morning talk with Osgood Fairchild, whose real name, it turned out, was Daryl Goodwin. Buddy thought he could talk Mooney out of arresting Daryl, which would make Charlie happy. Daryl knew how to handle that bad-tempered old Babcock. Charlie didn't want to lose him.

"Tax stamps, forgery, the syndicate, and an all-night surveillance?" Mr. Moseley asked, sounding amused. "I thought small-town life was supposed to be boring. But tell me—what's happening with Mickey LeDoux and Baby Mann? Have they had their showdown? Are there any survivors?"

"I was coming to that," Lizzy said. "Nothing's happened yet, probably because Baby's been hiding out and nobody dares to tell Mickey where he is because Mickey is vowing to shoot him."

"The Hatfields and McCoys," Mr. Moseley muttered.

Lizzy cleared her throat. "Twyla Sue Mann thinks you ought to intervene." She related the conversation in the Mercantile.

"But what about Purley's father?" Mr. Moseley asked. "Or Mickey's brother? It's their lookout, not mine. They ought to make those boys sit down and work it out."

Lizzy chuckled. "That's what I said, too, but Twyla Sue said that when the word comes from family, it goes in one ear and out the other. You, apparently, are the law here in Darling. When you say something, both of those boys have to listen."

"We'll see about that," Mr. Moseley said. "What else?"

"Nothing you can do anything about." Lizzy was thinking of Violet and Cupcake and the Shirley Temple look-alike contest.

"That's a relief," Mr. Mosely said. "I have a dinner engagement tonight and a hearing here in the morning. I'm expecting to be back in Darling about five-thirty or six tomorrow." He paused and his voice changed. "What would you say to dinner at the Old Alabama, Liz? We can enjoy a nice, leisurely evening and you can bring me up to date on everything."

Lizzy thought about what Edna Fay had said and found herself frowning. She had no intention of trying to rescue Bent Moseley from Moira Skelton or from anyone else. And while she still had that adolescent yearning feeling about him—and doubted now that it would ever go away—she didn't like the idea that she was one of those small-town, down-home girls who held the fort and did whatever had to be done. The kind of girl who was expected to be available for an evening's dinner and maybe a kiss or two at the door and . . .

And then, nothing, while Bent Moseley did whatever he did in Montgomery and Mobile, imagining that his assistant would be happy to be treated to a white-tablecloth dinner and a grown-up conversation with a—

She broke off the thought. Would she *always* feel this way about Bent Moseley? Torn between her longtime attraction—love, if that's what you wanted to call it—and the meager reality of what he was willing to offer?

But he was waiting. And it was just a date, not the beginning of something new and different. Or the end of it, either.

"Sounds like fun," she said lightly. "And who knows? Maybe I can report to you that everything has been resolved. That Hobart Mooney has left town and Daryl Goodwin is still here, and that Mickey and Baby have kissed and made up."

"Kissed and made up?" Mr. Moseley laughed. "Now, that would take some heavy-duty magic. See what you can arrange."

# CHAPTER TWENTY-ONE

# BURYING THE HATCHET

AT THE DINER DOWN THE BLOCK, VIOLET HAD LEFT TESSIE Mason on the Exchange and was keeping an eye on the counter while Myra May took the previous week's deposit to the bank and ran a couple of errands. The lunch crowd had left and the dishes were done. Euphoria had taken Cupcake out to the garden to pick a bucket of green beans to go with the fried catfish and hush puppies on the supper menu. And Raylene was running the sewing machine upstairs, putting the finishing touches on the red overalls and yellow shirt she was making for Little Cupcake, the former Shirley Temple doll.

The coffee urn was empty, so Violet filled the basket with ground coffee from the big red tin of Old Judge (*Old Judge settles the question*) and poured water into the reservoir. She had just finished that chore when a man opened the front screen door and came in, looking forty pounds lighter and ten years older than the last time Violet had seen him. He was wearing stained blue twill trousers and a wrinkled blue work shirt with the sleeves rolled up over the dirty sleeves of his long johns. A gun belt was slung low across his hips and out of the holster jutted the handle of a gun.

"Afternoon, Mickey," Violet said. To give herself something

to do, she picked up a cloth and swiped it across the counter. "I heard you were back in town."

"Yeah, seems everybody's heard." His voice was raspy and low, as if his throat hurt. Violet remembered him as smiling and cheerful, but this man's eyes were dull and his expression was wooden.

He sat down on a stool—the same one he'd occupied before he was hauled off to Wetumpka for moonshining—and folded his arms on the counter. She sniffed. It smelled like he hadn't had a bath since he got back.

"Got any of that chocolate pie left?" As he spoke, she saw that he had a broken tooth. "I'll have a cup of java, too."

"The coffee's brewing," Violet said. "It'll be a few minutes. But yes, I saw a chocolate pie in the kitchen." Mickey LeDoux had always had a sweet tooth, especially where Euphoria's chocolate pie was concerned. "How about two pieces, in honor of your homecoming? One on the house." Maybe some chocolate would mellow his mood.

His mouth twisted. "Some homecoming," he said. "Baby Mann been in yet? We got us a date."

"A date? Here? Today?" Violet smiled uncertainly. It was no secret that Mickey had a massive grudge against Baby. She could only hope there wasn't going to be any fighting in the Diner. Especially not *gun* fighting.

"Yeah. Here. Today." His face was grim. "You got a problem with that, sweetheart?"

Violet's mouth was dry and she pressed her lips together, wishing that Myra May were here. She would know how to handle this. Baby usually minded what Myra May told him, but she'd probably have to throw Mickey out before anything got broken. Or anybody got shot.

His eyes were slits. "You got a problem, Violet?"

"Well," she said slowly, "I guess maybe it depends on why

you're getting together. I mean, we don't want any trouble here. We—"

His face became even grimmer and she swallowed the rest of the sentence. "You're hungry. I better get your pie."

"Yeah," he growled. "Get my pie."

She went into the kitchen, closed the door, and leaned weakly against it, shutting her eyes and gulping a couple of ragged breaths. Whatever was going to happen when Baby showed up, it wouldn't be good. He could die in a pool of blood on the floor of the Diner. And this time, Mickey wouldn't get off with a prison sentence. For shooting a man in cold blood, he'd get a one-way ticket to Yellow Mama, the electric chair at Kilby Prison.

But what could she do? She didn't have a gun and if she did, she wasn't nearly brave enough to shoot it. She'd probably miss, and then, judging from the look on Mickey's face, he would shoot her before he turned his gun on Baby. Anybody going to Yellow Mama might as well take two with him instead of just one.

Well, if she couldn't stop him, maybe she could slow him down. Hands trembling, she took a chocolate pie off the shelf and cut it into four pieces. She put two of them—half the pie—on a dinner plate. As she remembered it, Mickey really did like chocolate. He surely wouldn't want to start shooting until he'd finished both pieces *and* his coffee, which would take a while.

And then, just as she was putting Mickey's pie and a fork in front of him, the front door banged open and Baby Mann tromped in.

Violet's heart stopped and her blood seemed to run cold. Baby might have a cherubic face and fine, silvery hair and a voice that made people think of angels. But he was a big man, six feet plus and two hundred pounds, with shoulders like an ox and arms like tree trunks. In one of his big hands, he held his leather-bound Bible. In the other, he was carrying a wicked-looking long-handled, double-bladed axe. His tread was so heavy that Violet could almost feel the floor shake under her feet.

Violet's eyes widened. Baby was holding himself straight, not hunched over the way he usually was. He seemed to have grown at least a foot since she had seen him that morning, pulling weeds in Myra May's garden.

And that axe? It looked lethal. One swing could split Mickey's head like a ripe pumpkin. But against a gun? Here, in the *Diner*? If they were going to fight, why couldn't they do it outside?

Mickey swiveled on his stool to face him. "Hey, Baby boy," he growled. "What you doin' with that axe? Cuttin' some kindlin' for your mama?"

Baby's usually bright face was uncharacteristically dark. "Fixin' to do me a little splittin'," he said. He laid his Bible on the counter, leaned the axe against the base of the counter, and took a stool, leaving two empties between himself and Mickey—but still close enough to whack him with that axe.

In a voice that sounded nothing like angels, he added, "And you're gonna stop calling me Baby. My name is Purley. You got that, Mickey? My name is *Purley*." He slammed his fist on the counter and Mickey's plate rattled. He looked at Violet and lowered his voice.

"Reckon you could fix me up with some of Euphoria's lemon meringue pie, Violet? It's my favorite. And I'll have a cup of coffee, too. Please."

"Sure thing, Ba—er, Purley."

Her heart in her mouth, Violet retreated to the kitchen again. If she had to bet on that pair out there, she'd bet on the one with the gun. But Purley had the muscles of a lumberjack. In fact, hadn't he won the lumberjack competition at the Cypress County fair last year? In axe throwing? She shuddered, remembering the ominous *thunk* of an axe thrown into a sawed-off stump—which was what it would sound like if Purley threw that thing at Mickey.

Her hands trembling, she was cutting Purley's pie when from outside the kitchen came the sudden sound of loud, angry voices, first Mickey's, then Purley's.

"Damn it, Ryder's *dead*, Baby. If you'd kept your damned mouth shut, them revenuers woulda never found us. What'd you do it for? You're a—"

"Don't you go blamin' me, Mickey." Purley's voice was unaccustomedly forceful. "You're the dad-blasted' bootlegger, you know. You set Ryder up, lettin' him go to work out there at your still. You deserved to go to jail! You oughtta be locked up still, instead of—"

"—stinkin' stoolie. You got that? You're nothing but a confounded, barefaced *stoolie*. In prison, the cons know what to do with the likes of you. They'd cut out your eyes and then—"

"—comin' back to Darling with your tail between your legs like the cur you are, but you can't—"

"—rip out your tongue and then slice off your—"

The exchange disappeared in a crescendo of snarls, like two vicious mongrels facing off in a dog-fighting pit, eyes red, teeth bared, rage flaming. There was no mistaking it. They were ready—eager, even—to fight to the death.

Violet stood stock still, trying to think what to do. Could she sneak out of the kitchen and into the Exchange without being seen? If she could, she could tell Tessie to call the sheriff. But Buddy couldn't get to the Diner in time to keep them from killing each other. And if he got there any sooner, they'd probably kill him, too.

Helplessly, Violet thrust her hands into the pockets of her

blue skirt, and her fingers touched the mojo bag the Voodoo Lily had given her. As if by magic, a calmness settled upon her like a soft shawl and she heard Euphoria's voice.

*Lil didn't give it to you for no medicine, girl. She give it to you for a diff'rent kind of healin'. Inflammation ain't just in your joints, you know. There's all kinds of heat.*

She pulled out her mojo bag, took out the vial of bammygilly oil, and tucked it, loose, into her pocket. Then she put two very large pieces of lemon meringue pie on a dinner plate, added a fork, and carried it out to Purley.

Red-faced and sweating, the two men abruptly stopped hurling abuses when Violet came through the kitchen door. She put the pie in front of Purley.

"Coffee's ready, boys," she said sweetly. "I'll get it for you."

She turned her back, pulled down two coffee mugs, and set them on the shelf in front of her. She filled both cups, then— her body blocking the two men's view—put a drop of oil into each mug.

"Hot and strong, just the way you like it," she said as she put the mugs in front of the men, hoping they wouldn't notice the faint shimmer of oil on the surface.

They didn't. They were too busy glaring at one another.

Mickey had finished one piece of chocolate pie and was half-way through the other. He put down his fork, picked up his cup, and took a quick gulp.

"Well, I can tell you one thing, Baby. You and me are going to settle this, once and for all. I got my gun and you got your axe and we're gonna take care of bidness. To-*day*." He wiped his mouth with the back of his hand. "But we ain't gonna settle it here. We're goin' somewhere we can have it out without doin' damage to other folks. You got that, *Purley*?" The last word dripped with ridicule.

"I got it. And I got just the place, too," Purley said around a big bite. He lifted his mug and washed down the pie with a mouthful of coffee. "You know that field on the other side of the Jericho Road, out past the graveyard? I'll bring my cousin Halston. He'll make sure there's no . . . there's no . . ."

His voice trailed away as if he had lost his train of thought. He took a breath and tried again. "You bring your . . ."

"I'll bring my friend, Jim Ben," Mickey said. "He'll see you don't pull any funny . . ."

He tilted his head, closed his eyes, and blinked them open again. "Funny tricks," he said. Then he said it again, this time with a chuckle. "Funny tricks. He'll see there ain't no funny tricks."

"That's right," Purley said. "No funny tricks." He chortled. "No dealin' off the bottom of the deck, like old Rainy always does. You ever been in a game with him, Mick? Talk about *funny* tricks!"

"Yeah." Mickey grinned widely. "And no stackin' the deck." His chuckle became a loud laugh. "No ratholin' the chips, neither. You got that? Chips on the table, where ever'body can see 'em."

Purley threw back his head, laughing raucously. "Say, how about this one? Charlie Dickens told it to me the other day. How come gamblin' ain't allowed in Africa?"

"I don't know!" Mickey said. "How come gamblin' ain't allowed in Africa?"

Purley was laughing so hard he was about to choke. "It's 'cause of all the cheetahs." He looked up at Violet. "Get it, Vi'let? 'Cause of all the *cheet-ahs*. That's why you can't . . ."

"I got it. Too many cheetahs!" Mickey was doubled over, gasping for breath. In a moment, the two men were holding one another, roaring with laughter and trading backslaps.

Violet watched them, bemused. If she hadn't known better, she would have thought they were both drunk as skunks.

"Nice to see you boys being buddies again," she said.

"Again?" Mickey roared. "*Again?* We're always buddies, ain't we, Purley?"

"Hunnerpercent," Purley said. "Say, Mick, you ain't been to my house since you got outa jail. Why don't you come tonight?"

"Best offer I've had all week," Mickey said. "Sure, I'll come. It'll be good to see Aunt Twyla Sue and Uncle Archie. And now that I think of it, this old feud has been goin' on long enough. 'Bout time the families buried the hatchet."

*Buried the hatchet.* Violet half-smiled to herself, thinking of Big Lil. *Reconciliation.* Maybe the bammygilly oil was only a quick fix and would wear off tomorrow or the next day. But maybe by that time, they'd come to their senses.

"Tell you what," she said. "Purley, there's a nice big buttermilk pie back there in the kitchen. You know how your daddy likes Euphoria's buttermilk pies. Why don't you take it home with you? Mickey, you could go along with him to make sure he doesn't eat it all before he gets home." She paused. "And I bet Twyla Sue and Archie would be glad to invite you to supper."

"Sure!" Purley exclaimed. "Tuesday night is pork chops smothered with onions." He got off the stool and dug in his pocket. "Violet, how much do I owe you? Mr. Dickens just paid me and—"

Mickey put his hand on Purley's arm, pushing him back down on the stool. "Keep your money in your pocket, son. I'm buying." As Purley thanked him, he picked up his mug and drained it. "Violet, I sure missed your coffee when I was in the lockup. Tastes better even than I remember it. And that chocolate pie—" He shook his head. "You tell Euphoria to bake me another one. I'll be back tomorrow for more."

Purley stood and put an arm around Mickey's shoulders. "Come on, Mick. The good Lord has saved me from the Demon Drink, but I know my daddy has a bottle or two of your white lightnin' stashed away, from back when you were still 'shinin'. He'd be right pleased for you to join him."

"Sounds good." Mickey tossed two dollars on the counter. "Here's for Purley's lemon pie and coffee, sweetheart. And mine, and that buttermilk pie."

"I'll get it for you," Violet said, and headed for the kitchen. She was thinking that whatever was wrong with this cantankerous old world could likely be cured with a couple of barrels of the Voodoo Lily's bammygilly oil, doled out one drop at a time.

⊛

BUT HARMONY DID NOT REIGN EVERYWHERE. AT BEDTIME, Cupcake buried her head under her pillow and flatly refused the rag curlers.

Violet was tempted to try a drop of Lil's oil in a cup of cocoa but felt it might be dangerous to experiment on a child. Pretending nonchalance, she shrugged her shoulders.

"Suit yourself, sweetie. But all the other girls in the Shirley Temple look-alike contest on Friday night will have curly hair. You won't look a thing like Shirley."

Cupcake jerked her head out from under her pillow "I don't *want* to look like Shirley!" She held up her doll, now dressed in the red bib overalls and yellow blouse that Raylene had made. The doll's shoes were red, too, like the shoes that Liz Lacy had bought her. Cupcake had painted them with Violet's red nail polish.

"See?" she cried. "Shirley looks just like *me!*"

Violet tried again. "But you're going to wear Shirley's pretty blue dress when you sing 'On the Good Ship Lollipop.'" She went to the closet and pulled out the blue plaid dress with the big white collar and dark blue tie. "It's just like the one Shirley wears when she sings in—"

"I'm not singing. I'm not dancing, neither." Cupcake lay back against the pillow, folding her small arms around her doll. "I'm not going to Nashville."

"But if we don't go to Nashville, we won't be able to go to Hollywood," Violet said, trying to be reasonable. "And if we don't go to Hollywood, you won't be able to—"

"I don't want to go to Hollowood! I want to stay in Darling with Mama Myra and Gramma Ray and Euphoria and all my other friends." Cupcake fixed her earnest gaze on Violet. "I *want* you to stay in Darling, too, Mama Violet. Please."

*Hollowood.*

The image of Lil with her forehead pressed against Shirley Temple's forehead came into Violet's mind, and she stopped, frozen. What if Lil had used her voodoo magic to make Cupcake want a doll that looked like her? And what if this made Cupcake want to stop being like Shirley? Could Lil actually do that? And what did it *mean*?

There was a lot more here than Violet understood. She swallowed hard and tried to think what to say. But in the end, she settled for "We'll talk about it in the morning, pumpkin." She kissed the little girl goodnight and turned out the light.

A few hours later, after Myra May was asleep and the flat was silent, Violet climbed quietly out of bed, pulled on a pair of Myra May's trousers under her pajama top, and retrieved the doll—transformed now, no longer Shirley—from Cupcake's sleeping grasp. She gathered up a spool of red thread and the pink candles she had brought from Lil's, and took them downstairs, bypassing the Exchange, where a thin wedge of light shone under the door and Lenore Looper's low voice asked, "What number are you calling?"

That afternoon, Violet had walked down the block to the ash tree beside Mrs. Perkins' daylily bed and cut a supple ash switch about two feet long. Now she added it to her other things and carried them all outside, into the little garden. The weather was warm and the southern night air was heavy with the scent of honeysuckle, mixed with the rich fragrance of jasmine tobacco blooms and the heavier scent of moonflowers. The moon wasn't up yet and the stars were scattered in patterns and swirls of diamond-bright glimmers against the velvety darkness of the sky. In the distance, an owl called out a melancholy *who-looks-for-you*. As if that were a signal, the clock in the courthouse tower began to chime the magical hour of twelve.

Violet bent the pliable ash switch into a circle and bound the ends together with the red thread, looping and tying it firmly. She laid the ash circle on the ground in front of her and laid the doll on it, with the candles at the doll's head and feet and outstretched arms. For good measure, she took her mojo bag out of her pocket, opened it, and spilled its objects into the circle. When she saw the little glass vial of bammygilly oil, she opened it and—on an impulse—placed a drop of oil on each candle as she lit it.

And then, in the flickering light of the candles, she gazed at her handiwork. But the doll she was looking at was not the Shirley Temple doll she had taken to Lil, nor was it the doll Lil had cast a spell over—if that's what she had done. Gone was the flirty red-polka-dotted dress and its red silk sash. Gone were the golden banana curls and the big red bow.

And gone was Shirley Temple. The doll was now a Cupcake doll, with Cupcake's straight hair, red bib overalls, yellow shirt, and red shoes.

And as Violet looked down at the doll and at the ash circle and the four pink candles, she began to see what she hadn't seen before, and as she saw, she began to understand, even though there were still questions.

Had Lil cast a spell over the doll? Had the doll cast a spell over Cupcake—or revoked the spell the Shirley Temple doll had cast? Lil's magic had reached out to Baby and Mickey. How much farther could it reach?

Then, whispering it to herself, she repeated the spell Lil had given her. "Safe we go, safe we come back, and may we get what we need." She couldn't remember exactly how many times she was supposed to say it, but that probably didn't matter. If it was going to work, it was going to work.

So she repeated the spell, in a kind of sing-songy way, watching the candles flicker in the soft midnight breeze. She thought about going and about coming back, and getting what she needed—and about Florida and her sister Pansy and their brief career as dancers. She thought about Shirley Temple and Hollywood and all that had happened right here at home. About Big Lil and Baby Mann and Mickey LeDoux. About Cupcake and Myra May and Raylene and Euphoria. And about the Dahlias and the rest of her many friends, all here in Darling.

And after a while, she fell asleep. If she dreamed (and most likely she did), she didn't remember it. She woke up with a start when the clock struck one, and the owl called again, more sharply this time, as though it really wanted an answer: *Who-looks-out-for-you? Who? Who? Who?*

And suddenly, the whole thing seemed very simple and quite clear and she knew what she had to do. The candles had burned out, and she carefully gathered them up and the doll and the ash circle and her mojo things and went upstairs. The doll was restored to Cupcake's sleeping embrace and Violet went to bed, where she lay for a long time in the dark, listening to the reassuring rhythm of Myra May's soft breath.

In the morning, she would tell her what had happened, and what she had learned.

If Cupcake wanted to be herself, that was the best self to be. She could sing and dance to please her friends—not to step into Shirley Temple's shoes.

There would be no Nashville. And no Hollowood.

Darling was where she and Cupcake belonged, and where she wanted—truly *wanted*—to be.

# THE GARDEN GATE
# BY ELIZABETH LACY

### The Dahlias' Magic Garden

I think everybody would agree that, right about now, we could use a little magic in our lives. As Reverend Kenny said in his sermon last Sunday, the Great Depression has gone on so long that we feel as if we've been living through the ten plagues of Egypt. Some of us might be looking for ways to bring a little enchantment into our lives.

That's why the Dahlias decided to create a magic garden in the big yard behind our clubhouse. We may not be able to change the world, as Aunt Hetty Little says, but we can change our corner of it. Aunt Hetty offered her expertise by giving us a tutorial in the "old ways" of using plants. Ophelia Snow collected pass-along plants and seeds from members and friends, and Verna Tidwell led the group of volunteers who dug and planted the bed and are keeping it neat. It's been a team project all around.

This intriguing little corner garden has taught us that you don't need to be a green witch or a conjure queen to practice a little magic. Here are a dozen plants you can begin with.

BASIL (*Ocimum basilicum*)
A delightful culinary herb, basil plays an important role in

many magical traditions. It is used to invoke love, prosperity, protection, peace, purification, and success. Plant basil near the doorway of your home to keep out the negative energies and welcome all that's positive. Easy to grow in many garden settings—and an indispensable herb with fresh tomatoes, seafood, and sauces.

BAY (*Laurus nobilis*)
The Greeks and Romans crowned their victors with bay, so it has become associated with reward and success. The Dahlias have planted a small bay tree at the back of the bed—in a pot, so it can come indoors for the coldest months. You probably know that bay is wonderful in stews, soups, tomato sauces, and with beef and lamb. But you might not be aware of its traditional magical properties. Aunt Hetty suggests writing a wished-for outcome on a bay leaf and tucking it under your pillow—a dream may offer some guidance for achieving your goal. When you do, celebrate by burning the leaf on which you've written your wish.

DILL (*Anethum graveolens*)
Dill is easy to grow, lovely in the garden, and a favorite host plant of swallowtail butterflies (which, all by itself, makes it magical). In the kitchen, the fresh or dried leaves star in seafood, soups, salads, and sauces, while the seed flavors pickles. Thought to be ruled by the planet Mercury (all those divided leaves!), dill has enjoyed a magical reputation. In Europe, it was hung over babies' cradles to ward off witches and protect the little one. In the Middle East, it was part of a love potion. In voodoo, it is used to repel jealousy, attract good luck and money, and inspire love.

GINGER (*Zingiber officinale*)
The Dahlias are growing a pot of ginger root and regularly harvest a tuber or two (called "hands") to use in the kitchen. Freshly grated, ginger flavors cakes, cookies, breads, and fruits, as well as seafood, sauces, and beverages. (You'll find Aunt Hetty's ginger ale recipe at the end of this article.) Medicinally, ginger is used to fight colds, calm the stomach, and suppress nausea. In voodoo, ginger is considered an excellent addition to rituals and spells because it boosts the energy involved. It is used to kindle love, stimulate finances, and enhance the potential for success.

LAVENDER (*Lavandula sp.*)
In northern gardens, varieties like Hidcote and Munstead lavender do well; in our southern gardens, we usually grow Spanish lavender (*Lavandula stoechas*). All lavenders prefer excellent drainage and turn sulky when their feet are wet. You may have used lavender as a bath herb or in toilet water and soaps or in your linen closet (lavender-scented sheets make for tranquil nights). It is also used as a flavoring for cookies and breads. In magical traditions, it is believed to attract romance, banish harmful energies, and harmonize opposites. Its association with washing accounts for its use in cleansing spells.

MINT (*Mentha spp.*)
The Dahlias have many mints—spearmint, peppermint, and flavored mints (apple, pineapple, orange, and chocolate). It's a good thing that mint has many uses, for it is a confident, self-assertive plant that will crowd into places in your garden you might not want it to grow. In recipes, mint is welcome in sweets, traditional with lamb, and delicious in drinks—mint

juleps are high on the list, of course. Medicinally, a hot or cold mint tea helps ease headaches, stimulates the appetite, and aids digestion. Magically, its goal of spreading and reproducing itself far and wide has associated it with the idea of increase. It is used in spells to increase money, success, prosperity, fertility, love, and joy.

### MORNING GLORY (*Ipomoea sp.*)

Morning glories are a gorgeous addition to any garden. The delicate blossoms fade in a few hours, but the vine itself is strong and tenacious and as twisty as a snake. It reaches high and cleverly interlaces itself into any support. These qualities make it important in voodoo magic, where it is associated with the mythic figure of John the Conqueror, an African prince who was sold as a slave. But John's strong, tenacious spirit was never broken. He survives in folklore as a trickster who reaches high, is strong and determined, and always outmaneuvers those who would like to use and manipulate him. In voodoo magic, the root of one species of morning glory, *Ipomoea jalapa*, is used in spells that strengthen, empower achievement and high-reaching, protect, support endurance and craftiness, and increase good luck.

### PATCHOULI (*Pogostemon cablin*)

This heavily fragrant plant grows to three feet tall and produces an abundance of purplish-white flowers. The plant is primarily known for a deep, earthy scent that is prized in soaps, oils, incense, and potpourri. In the magic traditions of India and the Far East, it is associated with love, passion, wealth, and prosperity. In voodoo, the dried, powdered leaves, the fragrant oil, and incense made with patchouli are used in spells involving money, fertility, and romance.

ROSEMARY (*Rosmarinus officinalis*)
A favorite in the kitchen and in the medicine cabinet, rosemary has long been thought to boost the memory. ("There's rosemary, that's for remembrance," Ophelia says in Shakespeare's *Hamlet*.) In Egyptian magical practice, it was sacred to the memory and used as a preservative in embalming. In European folk magic, rosemary was used as a protector and in cleansing, was often planted beside the door to keep evil spirits out, and was burned as a purifying incense. In voodoo, conjure queens and root doctors often use it as a wash, to purify a person or a place. It is also associated with love and fidelity and with wisdom, health, and healing.

SAGE (*Salvia spp.*)
Miss Rogers loves to quote a Latin proverb that she says dates back to the medieval period: *Cur moriatur homo cui salvia crescit in horto?* "Why should anyone die when sage is growing in the garden?" Sage is a staple in the kitchen, where sausages require sage and it wouldn't be Thanksgiving without sage in the turkey dressing. For centuries, sage has been used as a "heal-all" herb, treating a long list of ailments. It is also one of the most common herbs in magical traditions, where it is used to protect, purify, and ensure a long and healthy life.

VOODOO LILY (*Amorphophallus sp.*)
This plant goes by a variety of folk names: snake lily, stink lily, black dragon, dragonwort, dragon tongue, and—our favorite—voodoo lily. The magic in this plant is hidden in its unique habit of growth. In the spring, it flowers from a spherical tuber, with an enormous blossom that might remind you of the more familiar canna lily: a flower spike (the spadix) as

large as or larger than a fat cattail, pushing up out of an elaborate envelope (or spathe) of colored leaves. The spadix smells like ripe carrion, attracting pollinating flies. The spathe of the voodoo lily in the Dahlias' garden is a rich purple, varying from magenta to near black. In its native Africa, the voodoo lily is said to be the queen of the underworld. It is also said that if the bloom stalk is broken, a death will occur soon. Beware.

YARROW (*Achillea millefolium*)
Yarrow is a common garden herb grown for its attractive silvery foliage and its many medicinal uses. The most important of these is as a wound dressing, as its ancient folk names—soldier's wound wort and knight's milfoil—testify. Because of the association with war, yarrow has been used magically to restore courage and strength and in incantations to protect from evil. In the Far East, yarrow is used in divination. In Eastern Europe, yarrow was thought to have its dark side, too. It belonged to the Evil One and was called devil's nettle and devil's plaything, a reference to the use of the dried stalks in gambling. Conjure queens have used it in spells involving exorcism and protection and to promote inner strength, psychic powers, and courage.

Many thanks to Aunt Hetty Little, who loaned me her copy of *A Modern Herbal*, by Maud Grieve (1929); and to Miss Dorothy Rogers, for locating "Hoodoo in America," by Zora Neale Hurston, published in *The Journal of American Folk-Lore*, vol. 44, October–December 1931.

### Aunt Hetty Little's Homemade Real Ginger Ale

1 1/2 cups chopped peeled ginger (about 8 ounces fresh
    ginger)
2 cups water
3/4 cup sugar
Pinch salt
About 1 quart club soda
Fresh mint for garnish

To make the ginger syrup: In a small saucepan, partially covered, simmer chopped ginger in water for 45 minutes. Remove from heat, cover, and let steep for 30 minutes. Strain through a sieve into a bowl, pressing ginger to remove all liquid. (Discard ginger.) Return liquid to saucepan. Add sugar and a pinch of salt and heat over medium heat, stirring, until sugar has dissolved. Chill. To make a drink: Stir ginger syrup into club soda: start with 1/4 cup syrup to 3/4 cup club soda, adjust to taste. Serve over ice, with a sprig of fresh mint.

# AUTHOR'S NOTE

✹ One of the quite remarkable energies countering the lethargy of the Great Depression was the burgeoning growth of small-town local radio stations in rural areas across the country. Since the 1920s, people were getting used to the major networks' broadcasting mix of music, drama, and news. But the new local stations were beginning to showcase local talent. I've never forgotten the thrill of a St. Patrick's Day in the late 1940s, when I went with my third-grade schoolmates to sing Irish folk songs on WDAN, in Danville, Illinois. And there were the real-life on-air homemakers who appeared on KMA, in Shenandoah, Iowa, like Edythe Stirlen and Leanna Driftmier—women who helped other women learn new ways of using what they had (which probably wasn't very much) and get through lonely days when there might not be a lot to look forward to.

In this novel, radio moves into Darling as WDAR. I was helped in imagining *The Flour Hour* by Evelyn Birkby's book *Neighboring on the Air: Cooking with the KMA Radio Homemakers* and *American Radio Then & Now: Stories of Local Radio from the Golden Age* by Robin Miller. I also learned something of the technical end of radio broadcasting from the many intriguing posts on this site: **earlyradiohistory.us**.

Another important strand of this story (carried over from

*The Darling Dahlias and the Poinsettia Puzzle*) is the 1930s Shirley Temple phenomenon and Violet's desire to take Cupcake to Hollywood so she can star in a movie. Violet wasn't the only starstruck mother of a talented child. In *The Little Girl Who Fought the Great Depression: Shirley Temple and 1930s America*, John F. Kasson reports that all across America, thousands of hopeful "studio moms" dreamed of hitching their daughters' wagons to Shirley Temple's star. In a 1934 issue of *Modern Screen*, one writer observed that Shirley was a "potential threat to the happiness of families all across America." Mothers bowled over by Shirley's eye-popping contract-plus-bonuses ($1,250 a week plus bonuses up to $35,000 per film) would grab their little girls, abandon home, hearth, and husband, and catch the next train to Hollywood.

But if all they wanted was a look at Shirley, her fans didn't have to go any farther than downtown. In the nine years between 1931 and 1930, the little girl appeared in twenty-nine movies, nineteen of them full-length features. And it wasn't just those movies, either. Shirley's "adorable little face" could be seen on the cover of every movie magazine, in newspaper and magazine photos, on billboards. More lucrative yet was the Shirley Temple merchandise that filled the stores: clothes, dolls, toys, songbooks, paper dolls, coloring books, soap, toilet articles, and more. The look-alike dolls were often tied to Shirley's big-screen features: "Every Shirley Temple film is a Shirley Temple Doll promotion," crowed Ideal Novelty and Toy Company, which owned the patents.

And there were the Shirley Temple look-alike contests. From 1934 through the end of the decade, Twentieth Century-Fox—with local movie theaters, newspapers, department stores, and other retailers—staged dozens of contests. These offered a variety of prizes, from photography sessions to Pekinese puppies to passes to Shirley's movies. The contest in Nashville really happened. "Shirley Temple is taking the town!" crowed the *Nashville Banner* of December 13, 1934. There were forty-seven entrants wearing Shirley-style dresses and Shirley-style banana curls lined up to compete for the first prize of a large Shirley Temple doll. (Violet's hoped-for trip to Hollywood is fictional.)

Was this imitation all bad? Not by any means. Shirley's charm, cheeriness, and courage enchanted both children and adults. FDR really did say, "As long as our country has Shirley, we will be all right." By imitating her brimming optimism, people could momentarily forget their troubles. Shirley's film stories repeatedly showed her healing broken bodies, broken families, and broken hearts. She spoke to audiences everywhere—and especially to those hit hardest by the miseries of the Depression. Shirley Temple gave them the power of hope.

And yet, a mark of maturity is the ability to be yourself, not a copy of someone else, however pretty or happy or sweet. I must confess to being personally very glad that Cupcake is able to step out of the Shirley Temple mode and into an independent expression of who she is and what she wants. If that required a magical boost from a little bit of Big Lil's voodoo, well, that's perfectly okay with me (as long as it doesn't involve sticking pins in Shirley).

And speaking of voodoo . . .

In the early 1980s, I lived in New Orleans. There, on a warm spring night under a full moon, I met a conjure queen. She lived in a picturesque little house with a curtained consulting room in the front and a garden in the back. An Afro-Haitian American, she was impressively costumed and spoke with a Haitian Creole accent flavored with French and as smoothly mellow as the best chicory coffee and beignets you'll find in the French Quarter. In her garden, she grew—and understood—most of the plants she conjured with, speaking of them as though they were animated spirits. This fascinated me, for the way she used plants in her spells and incantations corresponded in interesting ways with the medieval European astrological herbalism I had been studying for years.

Later, back at Newcomb College, where I was working, I discussed my encounter with a colleague. She suggested that I do some serious research on New Orleans voodoo queen Marie Laveau and recommended the section called "Conjure County" in Carl Carmer's 1934 book, *Stars Fell on Alabama*. She also gave me a copy of a then-hard-to-find research study compiled by Zora Neale Hurston and published in *The Journal of American Folk-Lore* some fifty years previously. (To date, the best book on Laveau is Martha Ward's 2004 study, *Voodoo Queen: The Spirited Lives of Marie Laveau*.)

This was the beginning of my interest in what Whites call voodoo and Blacks call hoodoo, conjure, and root-doctoring—"roots" standing for all the parts of a plant: flowers, leaves, stem, and roots. These plants, the magical uses of which are shared by spiritual traditions around the globe, remain an important part of my garden-life, and I am still learning new and fascinating things about the traditional practice of sympathetic magic. The Voodoo Lily herself, as well as the plants in the Dahlias' magic garden (described in Liz's current Garden Gate column) all grow out of that continuing interest. Looking ahead, I'm hoping that Zora Hurston will agree to drop in on a later Dahlias adventure. I'd like to meet her. And I think she would be very interested in meeting Big Lil.

A word about words. To write about the people of the rural South in the 1930s requires the use of terms that may be offensive to some readers—especially "colored," "colored folk," and "Negro" when they are used to refer to African Americans. Thank you for understanding that I mean no offense.

A word of thanks to Elsie and Steve Rippel for sending the voodoo lily bulb. I can't wait for it to bloom!

And a last word about the recipes associated with this book. I've put them where you'll find it easy to print them out (and find them again when you've returned the book to the library): **susanalbert.com/the-darling-dahlias-and-the-voodoo-lily**.

Enjoy!

Susan Wittig Albert

# ABOUT SUSAN WITTIG ALBERT

Growing up on a farm on the Illinois prairie, Susan learned that books could take her anywhere, and reading and writing became passions that have accompanied her throughout her life. She earned an undergraduate degree in English from the University of Illinois at Urbana and a PhD in medieval studies from the University of California at Berkeley. After fifteen years of faculty and administrative appointments at the University of Texas, Tulane University, and Texas State University, she left her academic career to write full time.

Now, there are over four million copies of Susan's books in print. Her best-selling mystery fiction includes the Darling Dahlias Depression-era mysteries, the China Bayles Herbal Mysteries, the Cottage Tales of Beatrix Potter, and (under the pseudonym of Robin Paige) a series of Victorian-Edwardian mysteries with her husband, Bill Albert.

Susan's historical fiction includes *The General's Women*, a novel about the World War II romantic triangle of Dwight Eisenhower, his wife Mamie, and his driver and secretary Kay Summersby; *Loving Eleanor*, a fictional account of the friendship of Lorena Hickok and Eleanor Roosevelt; and *A Wilder Rose*, the story of Rose Wilder Lane and the writing of the Little House books. She is also the author of two memoirs: *An Extraordinary Year of Ordinary Days* and *Together, Alone: A Memoir of Marriage and Place*. Other nonfiction titles include *What Wildness Is This: Women Write about the Southwest* (winner of the 2009 Willa Award for Creative Nonfiction); *Writing from Life: Telling the Soul's Story*; and *Work of Her Own: A Woman's Guide to Success off the Career Track*.

Susan is an active participant in the literary community. She is the founder of the Story Circle Network, a nonprofit organization for women writers, and a member of Sisters in Crime, Women Writing the West, Mystery Writers of America, and the Texas Institute of Letters. She and her husband Bill live on thirty-one acres in the Texas Hill Country, where she gardens, tends chickens and geese, and indulges her passions for needlework and (of course) reading.

BOOKS BY SUSAN WITTIG ALBERT

SERIES MYSTERIES
The Crystal Cave Novella Trilogy
The *Pecan Springs Enterprise* Novella Trilogy
The Darling Dahlias Mysteries
The China Bayles Mysteries
The Cottage Tales of Beatrix Potter
The Robin Paige Victorian-Edwardian Mysteries
(with Bill Albert, writing as Robin Paige)

HISTORICAL FICTION
*Loving Eleanor*
*A Wilder Rose*
*The General's Women*

MEMOIR
*An Extraordinary Year of Ordinary Days*
*Together, Alone: A Memoir of Marriage and Place*

NONFICTION
*Writing from Life: Telling the Soul's Story*
*Work of Her Own*

EDITIONS
*What Wildness Is This: Women Write about the Southwest*

Made in the USA
Monee, IL
04 December 2020

50845789R00155